Neither of them spoke for a moment.

"I feel so close to you right now," Taki whispered. "Do you feel it, too?"

Reese sucked in a quick breath, then released it. "Yes."

And it was true. He did feel somehow connected to Taki. What had happened to his common sense? His usual levelheadedness must have fled at the same time as his sense of balance. And that had all occurred when he'd met her.

She raised her hand to his cheek, stroking his face as if caressing a precious keepsake. "I know I met you for a reason," she said, her voice full of wonder.

"Taki, I..." He cupped her neck with both hands and pulled her toward him, never wanting to let her go.

Dear Reader,

This story began one evening when I saw a totally hot guy in the parking lot after yoga at the gym where I practiced at the time. His car and several others (not mine, fortunately) had been broken into, and he definitely was not happy. My mind played the what-if game—and Reese, dedicated workaholic, spiced with the personalities of a few attorneys I'd worked with over the years, was born.

Taki was inspired by one of my early yoga teachers, a lovely woman who always lived by yogic principles. She never worried about tomorrow or the past, didn't react to anything negative, always remaining serene and positive no matter what occurred. We'd all be a lot healthier if we could behave like her.

Have you ever tried to stay totally in the present moment? It's not easy. Once, while hiking through a magnificent old-growth forest, surrounded by incredible natural beauty, I realized even then my mind wandered someplace else. Why? What better place was there for me to be at that moment?

Life is a beautiful journey for us all to cherish. *The South Beach Search* is the story of Taki and Reese, how they fall in love and change each other. I hope you enjoy their journey!

Sharon Hartley

SHARON HARTLEY

—

The South Beach Search

H HARLEQUIN® SUPER ROMANCE®

Recycling programs
for this product may
not exist in your area.

ISBN-13: 978-0-373-60882-9

The South Beach Search

Copyright © 2014 by Sharon S. Hartley

Printed in U.S.A.

ABOUT THE AUTHOR

Sharon Hartley has been practicing yoga for over thirty years and became a teacher in order to share her love of this ancient practice. Sharon believes yoga can be healing—just like a great story, and she loves writing stories as much as teaching yoga. Both can nourish our souls and teach us things about ourselves. She lives near South Beach with her husband, a Jack Russell terrorist and too many orchids. Sharon loves to hear from readers! Please visit her website at sharonshartley.com.

Books by Sharon Hartley

HARLEQUIN SUPERROMANCE

1876—TO TRUST A COP

Don't miss any of our special offers. Write to us at the following address for information on our newest releases.

Harlequin Reader Service
U.S.: 3010 Walden Ave., P.O. Box 1325, Buffalo, NY 14269
Canadian: P.O. Box 609, Fort Erie, Ont. L2A 5X3

For Max, my soul mate.
Without him, I'd be forever searching for my other half.

CHAPTER ONE

HER BACK FLAT on the floor, Taki pushed into the yoga mat with both feet and lifted her hips toward the ceiling.

"Picture your spine as if it were a string of pearls," she told her class as she demonstrated bridge pose. "Raise each vertebra one at a time and edge your shoulders closer together."

Taki released the pose and stood to observe her students, making certain they didn't hurt themselves. Placing a block between one student's legs, she said, "Remember to keep your knees close together."

A chorus of groans answered her reminder.

"But only go to your personal edge," she instructed. "When you feel resistance, back off. In yoga, we never want to cause any pain."

Benny, one of her regulars, laughed and moaned at the same time. Taki glanced his way and hurried to adjust him. Poor skinny Benny. He tried so hard, but, at seventy, had little flexibility and she always worried he'd push too hard.

"Now make yourselves as comfortable as possible," she said. "Our final pose is the most important one we do, where we give ourselves the gift of a few minutes of total relaxation."

"Time for our reward," Benny said with a deep sigh.

As her students covered themselves with towels or blankets for warmth, she dimmed the lights. They would all sleep better tonight after she helped them progressively relax each part of their bodies. In a few minutes Benny would likely start snoring.

"Close your eyes," she said, making her voice gentle, "and allow your attention to focus on your breath." Taki smiled, loving this part of the class where she helped her students achieve at least ten minutes of stress-free existence. Something everyone badly needed in this fast-paced world.

"Imagine yourself in a field full of yellow daisies. Beautiful fragrant flowers stretch as far as the eye can—"

The door slammed open, hitting the wall like a gunshot. "Taki!" an excited female voice shouted.

"Shhhh." Taki glared at Debbie, one of SoBe Spa's energetic aerobics instructors. Deb knew better than to interrupt the end of her yoga class.

"I'm so sorry, but there's an emergency," Debbie said. "I need to speak with you right away." She brightened the overhead light, making Taki wince in surprise.

A sense of dread replaced her peaceful mood as she approached the door. "What's going on?" she whispered. The class began murmuring.

"The police want to speak to you," Debbie whispered back. "Get your purse. Someone broke into your Jeep. You'll need your registration."

Immediately thinking about the package behind the driver's seat, Taki told the class to remain in relaxation as long as they chose and redimmed the lights. She grabbed her cloth bag and draped it over her neck and shoulder, then followed Debbie.

"What happened?" she asked.

"Nobody knows," Debbie replied as she pushed open the glass doors to the spa.

Taki shivered as she stepped into the crisp February air and wished she'd grabbed her sweatshirt before rushing out into the dark night. Still worried about the package, she hurried toward the bright lights illuminating a paved lot jammed with cars.

"I thought our parking area had security," Taki said.

Debbie nodded, her ponytail swinging with the motion. "So did Reese Beauchamps. Whoever robbed you also broke into his brand-new Jag."

"Oh, no," Taki murmured. She'd never spoken to Reese, but knew him by sight as he was popular with most of the female staff.

"He's not happy," Debbie said, "and is even sexier when he's mad."

Taki continued toward where Reese stood tall and confident with his arms folded across his chest, speaking to a uniformed police officer. His dark hair was damp, either from his workout or a shower, and the way he'd combed it back accentuated the strong, high cheekbones of his handsome face.

She couldn't understand his words but sensed irritation in the jab of his index finger. Oh, right. Wasn't he some sort of big-shot lawyer? He definitely needed one of her relaxation sessions.

Then she spotted her Jeep, and her breath caught with a painful lurch. Her heart hammered inside her chest.

The canvas top had been cut twice with long, jagged slashes.

She took a deep breath and released it slowly to calm herself. The package had to be there. The bowl had no value to anyone except her.

"My briefcase contained my cell phone and other valuable papers," Reese told the cop as she approached. "It is imperative that I get them back."

"We'll certainly do our best, Mr. Beauchamps." It seemed to Taki that boredom dripped from the policeman's voice. But maybe he was just overworked.

When Reese Beauchamps's angry dark eyes met her stare, a whisper of familiarity brushed over her, an unexpected feeling that she'd met him before. But she hadn't. No one would forget meeting this man.

"I'm Taki," she said, forcing her attention to the policeman. "I own the Jeep." The officer's eyes widened when he faced her.

As the two men openly checked her out, she again wished she'd thrown some sort of cover over her form-fitting yoga pants and halter top.

She reached into her cloth bag for her wallet. "Here's my registration, Officer."

"Taki?" The officer frowned as he studied her

papers. "That's your legal name?" He glanced up. "Just…Taki?"

"Just Taki. And here's my driver's license and proof of that PIP insurance we all have to buy."

She turned to Reese Beauchamps to offer her sympathy, and the buzz of recognition again surged through her.

Disoriented by the strange sensation, she glanced at his car. A temporary tag lay beneath shards of tinted glass from the shattered rear window. The trunk yawned open, its lock obviously forced. Poor guy.

"They stole your briefcase?" she asked.

He nodded. "From the trunk, yeah, with my cell phone inside. You have no idea how—" He ran a hand through his wet hair. "My whole life is in that damn phone."

"Really?" she murmured. *Your whole life?* Refusing to be tethered to some addictive electronic device, she didn't own a cell phone, but understood the rest of the world considered that beyond odd.

"Check to see if there's anything missing from your vehicle," the officer told Taki as he scribbled across a form. "I need to document it in my report."

Somehow certain that the next few moments would impact the rest of her life, she straightened her shoulders and approached the rear of the Jeep with a quick prayer that she'd find a one-foot-square cardboard box with a Tibetan postmark wedged behind the front seat. She peered inside her vehicle.

The box wasn't there.

After a thorough search, she accepted her bowl was gone. Stolen. Her stomach plunged toward her ankles. A year of hard work—and all for nothing. She closed her eyes and leaned against the Jeep's hood. How could she have been so foolish?

But who would want an old metal bowl?

"Are you okay? Do you need to sit down?"

Reese Beauchamps's voice brought Taki back to the present moment. Opening her eyes, she blinked back tears, refusing to cry. She had to accept another painful truth. Obviously she had more work to do.

"I'm okay," she said, although she felt anything but.

"Are you sure? You're not going to faint, are you?"

"Hardly." She attempted a reassuring smile. "It's just that my singing bowl is missing."

"Your singing…bowl?" he asked. "You mean like a fruit bowl?"

She nodded, thinking only an attorney would compare a spiritual object to a bowl of apples.

"Was it an antique?"

"Yes," she said. Better to leave it at that.

"I guess we both learned a painful lesson tonight about valuables in cars." He held out his hand. "I'm Reese Beauchamps."

"I know who you are," Taki said as she grasped his warm hand. When they made contact, an electric sensation shot down her arm, and she felt a tug at her belly. That eerie sense of recognition washed over her again.

Had she known Reese Beauchamps in a previous lifetime? Could be. Or maybe she was just intensely attracted to him. The man was unbelievably good-looking.

"I'm the spa's yoga instructor," she said, still holding on to him, enjoying the sensation. "I know who most of the members are."

"But I've never been to your class."

"You should come," she said, reluctantly releasing his hand. His strong grip was somehow reassuring. "Yoga would help you relax."

Confused by her powerful reaction to him, she stared at a pulse beating steadily at the base of his neck, then raised her gaze to be captured by a pair of intense brown eyes. No wonder Debbie gushed over Reese.

"Hey, too bad, Taki."

She glanced toward the voice. Hector, one of the spa's personal trainers, approached with a purple gym bag slung over his heavily muscled shoulder. The police officer continued working on his forms.

"Reese," Hector said with a nod at the Jag. "Wow. The new wheels. Bad luck, huh, man?"

"No," Reese said. "Stupidity is more like it."

"You lose anything?" Hector asked Taki.

"The bowl," she said simply.

"Bummer." Hector patted a Free Tibet sticker on the Jeep's rusted bumper and shook his head. "Maybe you're right, girl. Maybe you do have a spiritual blot on your soul. Gotta go, but let me know if I can do anything."

With a wave, Hector continued to his red Camaro. Taki cursed herself for telling big-mouth Debbie her theory of why her life was such a wreck. When would she get it that most people didn't understand her unusual slant on the cosmos?

"Listen...Taki, is it?" Reese Beauchamps's husky voice grabbed her attention again. He now stared at her as if she'd materialized before him from another dimension. "I'm confident I know who took my briefcase and why," he said. "I had important notes inside regarding a missing witness."

She raised her chin. "You lost a witness?"

"Not exactly." His dark eyes still searching hers, he shook his head. "Anyway, if we find the stolen property, I'll make sure you get your bowl back."

"Okay, Miss Taki," the officer called out, his voice emphasizing her name. "What's missing? They get your radio?"

Taki and Reese approached the policeman. "The only thing that's gone is a box with an ancient Tibetan bowl," she said.

"An old bowl?" The cop frowned. "Give me a description."

"It's copper and brass, eight inches in diameter. There was also a wooden wand that came with it."

The cop nodded as if *now* he understood. "A magic wand. Okay. So what's the approximate value?"

"Priceless. I had it blessed by a holy man, so there's not another one like it in the world."

The officer raised his gaze and stared at her as if she were an alien invader. "Uh-huh. What'd you pay for it?"

"Nothing. It was a gift. From a Tibetan monk."

"Come on, Miss Taki," the cop insisted. "Give me a figure. What's it worth?"

"My mortal soul," she murmured. "I made a promise to give the bowl, as a symbol of gratitude more than anything, to the Paradise Way Ashram. If I don't…" Taki looked down, but not before she saw the policeman roll his eyes heavenward. Reese Beauchamps said nothing, but she sensed his curiosity.

"What's an…ashram?" the officer asked.

"Like a secluded religious retreat, right?" Reese answered.

She nodded. "Something like that."

"Well, a hundred bucks ought to cover it," the officer said. "I'm done here." He handed Taki her registration and driver's license. "You can get a copy of the police report for your insurance company in a couple of days."

"Thank you, Officer," Reese said. "I'm sure you'll get to work on this right away."

"Too bad I don't have insurance," Taki said when the officer returned to his black-and-white police cruiser.

"You don't have insurance?"

"Just the required liability thing. Theft is too expensive." As the enormity of her loss sank in, she blinked back tears. The bowl was supposed to right so many wrongs.

"If the perpetrator is who I think it is," Reese said, "I'll see what I can do about getting you some restitution."

Thoroughly chilled now, she hugged her elbows,

looking for warmth. "Thanks, but I just want my bowl back."

"And believe me, I want my briefcase." Rattling his keys as if anxious to leave, Reese gave his broken window a disgusted glance. "Well…I'll be in touch."

"Let me know as soon as you hear anything. That bowl is very important to me."

"I can tell. But then, not many bowls are able to sing." He raised his brows. "Does it perform opera or more like rap?"

She narrowed her eyes at the amusement in his voice, wishing people wouldn't make fun of what they didn't understand. But seriously, what did she expect? A man like Reese would never appreciate the peaceful tones created by her bowl, how sooth-ing the sound was to her troubled soul.

"Mostly yodeling," she said, trying to make her voice as earnest as possible.

He shook his head, obviously unsure whether she was serious. Good.

"Don't get your hopes up too high, though," he said as he opened the Jag's door. "I can't make any promises."

After watching Reese drive away, Taki trudged back to the warmth of the spa. No matter how hard she tried to set things right with the universe, her karma always came back to haunt her. She tried to do the right thing, but maybe she was doomed to un-happiness forever.

She'd planned to deliver the bowl to the ashram immediately after her last class. Why, why had she been so foolish to leave it in the Jeep? She should have taken it into the spa and stashed it safely inside her locker. Yeah, she had been worried someone would ask her about it, want to see it, and of course she didn't want to talk about the challenge Guru Navi had given her and how long she'd waited for the package to arrive from Tibet after the blessing. But maybe no one would have noticed.

She was just plain stupid. She deserved everything bad that ever happened to her.

Inside the ladies' locker room, after a long steam bath which she hoped would melt away lingering negativity, Taki tried to think about what to do next. Unfortunately, no amount of steam could halt her depressing thoughts.

No point in visiting the ashram tonight. She could start over with another task, but where would she find the money to go back to Tibet? It had been a miracle she got there last time. With her lack of skills, she wasn't likely to find another steamer captain willing to let her work her way across the Pacific Ocean. Although she had learned how to cook vast amounts of food for the always-hungry crew.

Debbie approached while Taki towel-dried her hair, wishing her brisk movements could push a new idea into her brain. She'd been seasick for three months on the last voyage and really didn't want to go through that again.

"So what's Reese going to do?" Debbie asked.

"He thinks he knows who stole his briefcase," Taki said. She wrapped the towel around her head to secure her hair. "Maybe the same person took my property."

"Did he call in the FBI?"

"The FBI? Why would he do that?" Taki rummaged in her locker to find a comb.

"Because that's what federal prosecutors do when their stuff gets stolen."

Taki looked back. "He's a federal prosecutor?"

"Don't you know anything?" Debbie shook her head. "He's handling the Romero case. His picture is in the *Miami Herald* all the time. He's—"

An accented voice interrupted Debbie. "Taki, what happened with Reese Beauchamps?" Lourdes Garcia, the manager of SoBe Spa, paused by Taki's locker with a worried frown. "Does he blame the spa for the theft? Do we need to notify our attorneys?"

Taki shrugged. "He didn't seem mad at the spa particularly, just the world in general."

"That sounds like him," Lourdes said with a nod. "The man is so intense he gives me a headache."

"Intense, yes. And, man, those deep brown eyes…" Debbie exhaled slowly. "I swear he doesn't miss a thing."

As she combed her damp hair, Taki remembered his penetrating gaze. Yeah, Reese Beauchamps did notice everything around him. And the eyes were the windows to the soul. Reese sure had gorgeous eyes.

"When he works out with free weights," Debbie continued, "I can barely concentrate on what I'm doing. He performs each rep as if his life depended on it."

Lourdes laughed. "He's a perfectionist, all right. Type A for sure. Rumor is he's running for office. With his conviction record, I'll bet he ends up attorney general or a U.S. senator."

"Maybe even president someday," Debbie added dreamily.

Taki shut her locker door with a clang. "I just hope he finds my bowl."

THE NEXT MORNING, Reese arrived at his office in the federal building in downtown Miami at 6:00 a.m., his usual time. Leaving his condo at five-thirty meant no traffic on the roads and an easy commute. Even better was the fact that there were few colleagues around to interrupt him with phone calls or casual chats. He got a lot accomplished before other employees began arriving.

At 10:00 a.m. his secretary buzzed him.

"Agent Rivas is on line one."

"Thank you, Joanne." Reese had alerted Javier Rivas, the lead investigator on the Romero case, within hours of the theft. Hoping Javi had developed leads overnight, Reese grabbed the receiver and leaned back in his black leather swivel chair.

"Give me some good news, Javi."

"Sorry, Reese. I've got nothing for you."

"There's really no sign of Izzo?"

"Not a whisper."

"You checked all his haunts on South Beach?"

"Romero's favorite thug is either dead or in hiding."

Reese turned and looked over the sparkling aqua

water of Biscayne Bay eight stories below. Winning the headline-grabbing Feldman case last year had earned him this office with a view, but he'd vacate the prized space tomorrow to keep Carlos Romero— a domestic terrorist with a violent, if murky, cause— behind bars.

"Izzo must know we're looking for him."

"Probably," Javi said. "The bureau will stay on it, but without something else to go on, it's pretty much a waiting game. He'll poke his head up eventually."

"Probably when he commits another crime."

"Was anything besides your briefcase stolen, something that might end up with a fence?"

"Maybe," Reese said after a pause. "A woman who works at the spa had some sort of Tibetan artifact taken from her vehicle. She insists it's old and rare."

The image of Taki, her long blond hair blowing in the evening breeze, blue eyes tragic with unshed tears, hadn't been far from Reese's thoughts since last night. Neither had strong, slender legs encased in black leggings flowing into a slim waist and perfectly formed breasts straining against her pink halter top.

He remembered with vivid detail the goose bumps that dotted her graceful arms as she'd tried to warm herself in the chilly evening air.

All of this going on in his head scant minutes after discovering that someone had stolen his cell phone, the device that coordinated the details of his way-too-complicated and overscheduled life.

And the photocopy of Claudia Romero's journal in his briefcase, with detailed trial notes on every page.

Javi's hard voice brought Reese back. "Izzo is no antiques dealer. I doubt he would know anything about Tibetan antiquities."

"You're probably right. He could have broken into the spa employee's Jeep to throw us off track. The loss of the bowl upset the woman badly, though."

"Or it could have been pure convenience. This wouldn't be the first time Izzo pinched something he could dispose of easily."

"We need to find him and ask him," Reese said.

"Man, talk about bad luck. First your witness disappears and now your briefcase. Do you think Romero was fishing? Searching your vehicle in hopes of finding a lead to his ex-wife's location?"

"Maybe. They want to find her as badly as I do."

"Probably more," Javi said. "I'll send agents to major fences and Miami pawnshops and see if they come up with the missing bowl. I need a description. A photo would be better."

"I'll call the spa."

Several hours later, Reese nodded at his secretary, confident his instructions would be carried out as ordered. Joanne was the best assistant he'd ever had.

"And those grand jury subpoenas need to be served today," he ended.

Joanne nodded as she rose. "Yes, sir. Oh, I'm sorry, but I can't find a number for this Taki person. There's nothing listed, and the number she put down on the police report is for SoBe Spa."

"Did you try the spa?"

"Yes, but she only teaches on Monday and Thursday nights, and the manager—" Joanne consulted her spiral-bound notebook "—Lourdes Garcia, wouldn't give me Taki's home number."

"Did you tell her the U.S. Attorney's Office needed to contact their employee?"

"Of course, but that didn't make a difference. They have a strict policy not to give out the instructors' numbers to anyone."

"Get Ms. Garcia on the phone."

Irritation gnawed at Reese when Joanne alerted him she'd reached Ms. Garcia. He wasn't used to a road-block over something as simple as a phone number.

"But, Reese, you surely understand our policy not to give out the instructors' addresses or phone numbers," Lourdes told him when he'd explained the reason for his request. "I might normally make an exception considering the circumstances, but Taki insists on her privacy. She's one of the most popular members of our staff."

"If I give you my office and cell number, will you call her and leave a message?"

"Certainly. She rarely checks voice mail, though— something about negative energy—so it might take a while to reach her. If I don't hear from her, I'll make sure she gets your message on Thursday."

"It's important, Ms. Garcia."

He heard her release a long breath. "Everything is important to you, Reese."

INSIDE THE ELEVATOR at his condo, Reese dropped his new briefcase and pushed the button for the twentieth floor. As the car lurched upward, he glared down at the stiff black leather, thinking the miserable bag was much heavier than the one stolen. And he'd liked his old case, a gift from his mother. It'd been well-made, and he'd used it since law school.

Reese was glad to be home. His condo was decorated by a woman he'd once dated. He often wondered if the antiseptic white-on-white living room reflected what she thought of his personality. He'd found her a bit boring, too, though, and their romance had been brief. He didn't have time to date.

After depositing the attaché by a cream-colored sofa, Reese opened his vertical blinds, the sound a quiet whoosh. Five miles in the distance, the lights of South Beach glittered across Biscayne Bay. He searched for the blue zigzag neon strip that identified SoBe Spa. Was Taki conducting one of her classes? No, not until Thursday, according to the manager.

He turned away from the stunning view. He had two hundred pages of trial transcript to review and could never get any serious reading done at the office with all the interruptions. He'd pop the take-out pasta from Risotto's into the microwave, sip one glass of Napa Valley Cabernet, then work until his eyes gave out.

Three delicious bites into garlic-laced linguini, his cell phone rang.

"Reese Beauchamps," he said, his attention still focused on page twenty of the Romero versus Romero divorce transcript.

"Hi, Reese Beauchamps," a soft feminine voice

replied. "This is Taki. I got an urgent message to call you."

Reese placed his fork across his plate and sat back. He glanced at the caller ID display. Private.

"Have you found my bowl?" she asked, her voice anxious.

"Sorry, not yet. I need more of a description."

She released a sigh. "Would you like a photograph?"

"If you have one, that'd be great."

"Oh, I've got lots of photos of my bowl, but I'd much rather have the real thing."

"Because your mortal soul is in danger without it, right?"

He waited through a long pause before she answered. Why wasn't her phone number available? Well, Lourdes Garcia said she valued her privacy. Nothing wrong with that unless you had something to hide.

"My soul was in danger before I got the bowl. The bowl was supposed to correct that problem."

"A bowl can rescue your soul?" Reese suppressed a laugh. "How is it going to do that?"

"By repaying a karmic debt."

Amused by Taki's serious tone as she babbled her New Age nonsense, Reese tried to recall what the personal trainer had said to her in the spa's parking lot. Something about a blot on her soul?

The woman might be easy to look at, but she was as nutty as psychics who predicted the future over the phone. *Karmic debt? How would she know when the debt is repaid?*

"Never mind. Where is your office?" she asked, now businesslike.

"In the federal building, the U.S. Attorney's Office."

"You're not the United States attorney, are you?"

"Only one of many assistants," Reese answered, thinking she didn't sound at all impressed.

"I'll drop off a picture tomorrow."

"Thanks. That'll help."

"What will you do with it?" she asked.

"The FBI will show the photo to fences and pawnshops and hope for a hit."

"Oh. Pawnshops." After a moment she said, "Listen, thanks for trying to find my bowl. Lourdes says you're a busy man."

"You're welcome," Reese said, deciding it best not to tell her he hoped the bowl led him to Izzo, Romero's top hit man. One way or another, he'd make sure this goofball got her bowl back.

He listened to the dial tone after she hung up, strangely dissatisfied at the prospect of spending the next three hours reading the messy details of the divorce between Claudia and Carlos Romero.

AFTER DISCONNECTING WITH Reese, Taki lay on her bed and gazed at the multitude of angels suspended from the white ceiling overhead. Surrounded by soft light from flickering candles, the colorful winged ceramic and papier-mâché creations looked as if they were flying as they swayed on thin filament wires.

As friends added to her collection, Taki hung her glorious angels one at a time, hoping the hovering guardians would protect her from the negative thoughts in the world.

She really needed the angels' protection tonight. Why did she feel this odd, wild connection to Reese Beauchamps? Goose bumps popped up along her arms as she pictured his handsome face, his soulful dark eyes when she'd met him last night.

And why did the sound of his deep voice excite her in an unsettling physical way? It made no sense to be attracted to an intense, detail-focused lawyer. One who made fun of her bowl and the whole concept of karma.

Disturbed by her thoughts, Taki brought her fingers to her temples and applied gentle pressure. Hadn't Guru Navi warned her about judging others? Reese was just upset, as she was, about the loss of important property. Guilt, her constant companion since childhood, weighed upon her, almost pressing her into the mattress.

There had to be some reason he stirred such strong emotions. Maybe her suspicion that she'd known him in another lifetime was the answer. She closed her eyes, deciding he'd likely made her life miserable for centuries. No doubt the man had a lot to answer for.

A light, cool wind rustled through the open window, tinkling her mobiles and sending the angels into flight. Her home had no heat, but she didn't need any.

Where she grew up, this temperature was considered balmy. To her, South Florida's weather seemed heavenly tonight.

She inhaled deeply, taking in clean air, then stretched her arms high overhead, enjoying the breeze as it brushed across her overheated skin, her thoughts circling back to Reese. Since last night, she hadn't been able to stop thinking about him. It was possible his obvious position and power reminded her of what she'd gladly left behind, what she continued to run from.

She turned on her stomach and lifted her shoulders, stretching along the front of her body. She needed to clear her mind. She refused to think about greed and selfishness, the things her father's endless parade of lawyers knew best.

The bowl's disappearance was already beginning to affect her. She needed to find it as soon as possible. She'd do a short practice and meditate until tranquil.

Tomorrow she'd look for her bowl by visiting pawnshops herself.

CHAPTER TWO

Office of the United States Attorney for the Southern District of Florida.

TAKI GLARED AT the gold leaf letters adorning the heavy wooden door to Reese Beauchamps's office. Of course she wasn't actually experiencing déjà vu. She *had* already been here once today, at 9:00 a.m., when she'd left two photographs of her missing Tibetan bowl with a receptionist before setting off to the pawnshops.

She pushed open the door. What an adventure that had turned out to be.

At the sixth musty, crowded, depressing store she visited, she found a man who thought maybe someone had possibly come in with something that looked like her bowl yesterday. A bit vague, sure, but she'd been thrilled and pressed him for more info. But he put her off, telling her to come back later and talk to his boss.

"I'd like to see Reese Beauchamps," Taki told the same pale, pregnant receptionist from this morning, having decided it best to relay the information directly to Reese. While she normally avoided lawyers like flu germs, she hoped his authority might encourage the pawnshop owner to talk.

"Do you have an appointment?" the woman asked. She placed her hand on her swollen belly and winced as if in discomfort.

"No. But I have valuable information I'm sure Reese will want. Please let him know I'm here."

The receptionist lifted arched eyebrows at the use of his first name. "Your name again, please?"

"Taki."

"Taki…?"

"Just Taki. How far along are you?" she asked.

The woman rubbed her abdomen and sighed. "Six months, but I have nausea like I'm six weeks. If it doesn't stop, I'm going to have to go home."

"Have you tried ginger?"

"Ginger?"

"Ginger makes a soothing herbal tea. Small amounts are safe for the baby and, trust me, it works. Cinnamon also helps. You might add some if you like the taste."

The receptionist smiled dubiously. "Thanks. I'll let Mr. Beauchamps's secretary know you're here."

After the woman slid her frosted window shut, Taki seated herself in the waiting room and glanced at the wall clock. Almost one-thirty. Looking around, she noted sleek and modern furnishings that didn't look all that comfortable. Plenty of magazines littered tables to help pass the time, but she'd rather meditate, if it came to that. Hopefully, she wouldn't have long to wait.

Guru Navi always said waiting was an opportunity to spend quality time with yourself. But would Reese make her wait awhile? Was he that busy?

The only other person in the room was a balding elderly man. She smiled at him, but he didn't make eye contact. Instead, he closed his eyes and shifted uncomfortably in his chair.

Becoming more and more concerned for him, Taki suffered along with the poor man while he twitched and uttered quiet moans. Every few minutes he rose and limped around the small room, sat again, then struggled back to his feet, pressing both hands against his lower back.

She nibbled at her bottom lip. All the signs of a bad lumbar area. She'd helped more than one chronic back patient with either yoga or herbs. Why not assist another while she waited for Mr. Big-shot Lawyer?

"Are you all right?" she asked. She'd learned most people loved to talk about their pain.

"It's my lower back," he said and sucked in a quick bit of air as if it were torture to even breathe. "Hurt it on the job."

"Where exactly does it hurt?" Taki asked, making her voice soothing and sympathetic.

"Right at my belt line. Never goes away."

"I'm so sorry. What does your doctor say?"

The man took a few hesitant steps. "That there's nothing he can do. I'm old and just got to live with it."

"Orthopedist?" she asked.

"And a damn neurologist. Every test in the book."

She nodded. So he'd already consulted the Western medical specialties.

"Damn quacks," he muttered.

"You poor thing." Taki rose and approached the man. Before beginning, she asked what she always asked, even in her yoga classes. "Do you mind if I touch you?"

"What for?" he asked, eyes wide, but now looking at her with interest.

"Maybe I can help."

WHEN THE INTERCOM buzzed, Reese muted the sound on the DVR and rubbed his tired eyes, irritated by the interruption. Agent Rivas was probably correct that no clue to Claudia Romero's location existed in this two-year-old videotape deposition, but he had to try. Perhaps she'd casually mentioned a second home or a place she liked to escape to on holiday.

Where the hell was she? Why hadn't she contacted him? And why had Claudia refused to accept protective custody until her ex's trial? Jury selection would begin in less than three weeks. The woman couldn't possibly think she was safer on her own.

"What is it?" he said into the speaker. Reese reached for a roast beef sandwich delivered twenty minutes ago and loosened the plastic wrap. The sharp fragrance of the horseradish made him realize how hungry he was.

"Taki is here to see you," Joanne said. "Shall I show her in?"

Reese dropped the sandwich and paused the DVR,

already moving toward the long hallway to the reception area. "I'll get her," he told a startled Joanne as he strode past her desk.

Javi Rivas, out in the trenches working seedy pawnshops, reported an hour ago that a knock-out blonde named "Wacky" or "Tacky" had flashed photos of the bowl in some of the worst sections of Miami. He needed to put a stop to that immediately.

What had possessed the woman to search on her own?

She'd already annoyed him by dropping off the photos this morning and disappearing—here and gone before he could inform the receptionist to ask her to wait, that he needed to speak to her.

Taki was obviously in a hurry to make herself the next crime statistic in Miami-Dade County.

Reese opened the door to the waiting area and came to a shocked halt. Taki stood in the center of the room, her graceful hands probing the naked back of Robert Shinhoster.

"Ah. This is the place," she said, stroking her index finger across the bony ridge of the old man's spine.

Reese wasn't sure which surprised him more, the surreal sight of the two of them or his irritated reaction. Taki's hands were all over Robert Shinhoster, an injured federal worker who had been driving the entire office crazy about his case for months, but why should he care?

She was so focused on Shinhoster, she hadn't heard the door open.

"Okay," she told Shinhoster, dropping her arm.

"I want you to mash up a chili pepper, mix it with a white skin cream, and rub it on this spot. But wear plastic gloves when you work with the preparation because it might irritate your hands. And don't use the cream right after a hot bath or shower."

"What will that do?" Shinhoster asked.

"The capsaicin in the pepper confuses the nerves and you focus on a temporary mild burning more than the ache in your back. I also recommend willow tea for its anti-inflammatory properties, massage—lots of gentle massage—and hot packs alternating with cold. When the inflammation goes down, start yoga classes. This time next year, you might be pain free."

"Excuse me," Reese said.

Taki looked over and smiled. "Hi, Reese."

He hooked his hand under Taki's arm to draw her away from a dazed-looking Shinhoster and out of the room.

"Hey, thanks," Shinhoster yelled as the door closed.

"Just what do you think you're doing?" Reese demanded when they faced each other in the long hallway.

Taki's sapphire eyes clouded at his words. "I was helping that man. He's in a great deal of pain."

"And he's trying to squeeze money out of the U.S. government for his supposed pain."

"Only because he thinks he's been cast aside. Poor dear feels disliked because he worked for the Internal Revenue Service. He says no lawyer will believe an auditor could get a bad back."

Reese stared into her earnest face and realized the

woman was absolutely serious. "And where did you get your medical degree?"

"I'm not a doctor," she said, straightening her slender shoulders. "I'm an herbalist."

"Then why are you behaving like a private detective?"

She blinked twice. "What?"

One thing at a time, Reese told himself. He glanced at the openmouthed receptionist who followed the conversation with keen interest.

"Let's go to my office," he said, motioning Taki ahead of him.

The effortless, regal way she moved reminded him of silk flowing over smooth skin. Taki appeared to glide more than walk. She looked curiously around her, her gaze peering into every open room along the corridor.

"Hold my calls," he told Joanne as they passed her desk and entered his office. He closed the door and turned to Taki, whose gaze had zeroed in on his view of the sparkling water of Biscayne Bay.

"Please tell me you're not trying to practice medicine," he told her.

"I certainly know better than that," she said. "I didn't charge Mr. Shinhoster a thing. My advice is always free."

Reese shook his head, imagining the headline on the front page of the *Miami Herald:* Unlicensed Yoga Teacher Caught Prescribing Drugs in U.S. Attorney's Office.

"He can take my advice or ignore it. It's his choice."

She shrugged. "But just think. If I cure his pain, then he'll leave *you* alone. If he listens to me, he could probably return to work soon, but I think he'll probably opt for retirement."

Reese stared at her. "You discussed his future employment plans?"

"He needed someone to talk to. But enough about that. I have news." She waved her hand, apparently intending to leap to a new subject. "I have a lead on the bowl," she announced, excitement shining in her sky-blue eyes.

"A lead?" Reese placed his hands on his hips and leaned forward. "No doubt from one of your pawnshop visits?"

She nodded and flashed a dazzling smile. "I did what you suggested and took a photo to pawnshops. The clerk at Jacques's Hock—" Taki reached in her jeans pocket and handed him a crumpled business card "—says to come back and talk to his boss this afternoon. I thought you would want to know. I was thinking it would be better if you went and did your... lawyer thing."

Reese glanced at the card. "I never suggested that you go to pawnshops yourself."

Unfazed, she continued to smile at him expectantly, obviously pleased with herself and totally relaxed in faded blue jeans and a bulky pale blue cotton sweater. He'd never been less relaxed. He took a deep breath and released it in an explosive whoosh.

"Listen, Taki, your misguided efforts are undermining the work of my field agents."

Her smile faded. "They are? How?"

"The FBI is tracking an extremely dangerous man. Believe me, you don't want this guy to discover you're looking for him. He might come after you to find out why."

"Oh." She bit her lower lip and clasped her hands behind her.

"Let the authorities handle this. You could get yourself hurt."

She shifted her gaze to the floor, looking so disappointed he resisted a foolish urge to make her feel better. Taki desperately wanted that damn bowl back and had worked hard to get what she considered a huge break in the case. He had to give her that.

Still—best not to encourage her. A woman who looked as good as this one shouldn't hang out in the wrong sections of Miami.

Her gaze drifted around his office and stopped on his roast beef and Swiss on rye. "I interrupted your lunch."

"Have you eaten?" he asked.

"No," she said. "I guess I was too busy screwing up your investigation."

"Would you like half of my roast beef sandwich? I have sodas in the refrigerator."

She raised a horrified gaze to his. "Thank you, but I'm a vegetarian."

"Oh," he said, feeling foolish but not sure why.

Her very kissable lips curled into another smile,

and he couldn't help but smile back. What was it about this woman?

"Let me take you out for a healthier lunch," she suggested.

He didn't have time to leave the office for lunch, hadn't gone out for lunch in weeks…hell, maybe a month. The Romero prosecution might be high-profile, but it was far from his only case. He had way too much work to do this afternoon. Her invitation was out of the question.

Unless he could learn more about her bowl and why it had been taken.

"It's a beautiful day," she said in a tempting voice. "The temperature is around sixty-eight degrees, the sky is bright blue and a fresh breeze is blowing. Weather like today's is the reason thousands of people visit Miami every winter."

He hesitated, fascinated by the tip of her tongue moistening her lips. She didn't wear any sort of makeup, and no wonder. Why spoil perfection?

"The fresh air will clear your mind," she said. "I'll bet you'll even be more productive afterward."

"What the hell," Reese said, wondering where his usual sense of urgency had vanished to. The Romero case would just have to wait. A man was entitled to eat.

He grabbed his coat and touched her back lightly. "Let's not invite your new patient to join us."

He'd intended to take his rented vehicle—the Jag was still at the dealer for repairs—but she insisted driving would only stress him out more and he needed to relax. So with a few misgivings, he climbed into the passenger seat and buckled his seat belt.

She bunched her hair into a navy blue beret. "Otherwise it gets hopelessly tangled," she told him, then accelerated into traffic.

He loosened his tie, relishing the warmth of the sun on his face. The cool wind made conversation impossible while she careened way too fast along I-95. He glanced at the speedometer and tightened his seat belt.

And speeding on the interstate in Miami won't stress me out?

He had no idea where she was taking him, but hoped they got there in one piece.

TAKI DECIDED REESE seemed even more familiar today. Much more familiar.

They were seated across from each other at a booth in The Spiritual Kitchen, her favorite restaurant. The sweet fragrance of curry hung in the air, and the faint, peaceful sound of chanting filtered through the sound system.

Reese concentrated on the menu, squinting and holding the paper at arm's length.

She couldn't wait any longer. She had to know if the feeling was mutual. That's why she'd asked him to lunch even though she usually avoided lawyers—as she did all negative influences.

Leaning forward, she asked, "Do I seem familiar to you at all?"

Reese looked up and frowned. She wasn't sure if he reacted to her question or the menu.

"Familiar?" he said. "How so?"

"As if maybe you had known me before."

Reese sat back and rubbed his eyes. "You mean before our vehicles were broken into?"

She nodded.

"As in déjà vu?" he asked.

"Well, something like that."

"No," Reese said with the beginning of a smile. "Believe me, I would definitely remember you."

Before Taki could reply, a turbaned waiter arrived to place a ceramic teapot and two matching cups on their table.

"You honor us with your visit, Taki," the thin Indian man said with a slight bow.

"Thank you, Teshvar," Taki replied, steepling her hands into prayer position and nodding in return. "Do you have any veggie stew left?"

"Always for you."

"Then we'd like two orders, please, and lots of your special whole grain sesame bread."

With another bow, the waiter disappeared. Taki returned her attention to Reese, who now studied her with an amused expression.

"Do you always order for your guests?" he asked.

"But you don't know what's good. Don't worry. I promise you'll love their special, and it won't poison you like the lunch you were going to eat."

As Reese regarded her across the table, she sensed he didn't like losing even the tiniest little bit of control. She decided he was one of those men who needed to dominate everything and everyone around him. The fine tailoring of his charcoal double-breasted suit and cranberry silk tie screamed position and power. *Pay attention to me. I'm important.*

Just like her father.

"How about some peppermint tea?" she asked, disappointed in herself again. Why was she always so quick to judge this man? She didn't really know him, at least in this lifetime, and she wasn't being fair.

She poured them each a cup of tea, then dribbled honey from the jar on the table into her own brew. Her aim was a bit off, so she caught a slow-moving drip on the side of her cup, then licked the thick nectar from her finger. When she glanced up, she found Reese's attention focused on her mouth as if he could taste the sweetness on her lips.

She lowered her gaze and stirred the tea. Steam drifted toward the ceiling between them. Taking a deep breath, she inhaled mint and orange blossoms. Maybe she was quick to judge him because he unsettled her so thoroughly. And because she found him so very attractive, which was of course ridiculous, considering—

"Do I seem familiar to you?" Reese asked, his voice calm and steady in the confusion of her senses.

She took a sip of the tea before answering. "I don't know. I feel some sort of strange connection, but I can't explain why."

"Maybe it's because we both were victims of the same crime two days ago."

"So we're like a victim support group?"

He smiled. "Exactly."

"No. The way I felt was…well, strongest when I touched you the night of the theft."

"When you touched me?"

She nodded. "When we shook hands. I'd like to try an experiment. Do you mind if I touch you again?"

He gave her a lazy grin. "Well, that depends on where you want to touch me."

Heat flooded her cheeks as she said, "I want to touch your third eye."

He blinked. "My what?"

"The third eye is the center of insight and intuition. It looks beyond the physical world."

"And just where is this special body part?" he asked.

Taki bit her lower lip and gazed at the furrowed spot between and just above his dark eyebrows. "Right here," she said, touching the spot lightly with her index finger.

A jolt of his energy rocketed through her, shooting all the way down to her toes. His eyes widened, and she knew the voltage affected him, too. She lowered her hand.

"Did you feel that?" she asked, her voice barely a whisper.

"Yeah, I felt it." He leaned forward with his forearms on the table, holding her gaze. "Does that mean we're attracted to each other?"

"Don't be ridiculous. I think it proves my theory

that you've been harassing me through several life-times," she said, sitting back.

"Harassing you?" Reese narrowed his eyes. "What are you talking about?"

"Well, anyway, we've known each other in a previous lifetime, probably several, and we have some issues to work out."

Reese went still, but continued to stare at her.

"And now I need to help you find your stolen brief-case while I find my bowl," she continued. "That way the negative energy will finally be severed between us and we'll both have what we need, improve our karma."

"Sever...negative...energy." He leaned back in his chair, shaking his head. "And that's a good thing?"

Taki nodded, surprised to be telling him the theory she had formulated last night after calling her guru at the ashram to tell him about the theft and meeting Reese. Navi agreed that the instant connection she had felt to Reese could be because they had known each other in previous lives. Of course that's the only thing that made sense. She couldn't be attracted to a man so like her father, so slick, arrogant and impatient.

Guru Navi had taught her so much, and they'd come such a long way together, how could he be wrong about this?

"I see," Reese said. He tossed back the peppermint tea as if it were a glass of whiskey. "Tell me more about your bowl," he said, with a look that suggested she'd suddenly sprouted wings and might fly like one of her angels. "You said it's valuable because it's one of a kind?"

"Yes," she said. "My guru suggested a difficult task in order to ease my terrible..." She trailed off. Better not to tell the whole story. It was obvious Reese thought her philosophy foolish, and telling him would only further widen the breach between them.

"Your terrible what? Go on."

"The bowl isn't valuable in the sense you mean. There are thousands of similar bowls—even in catalogs. Anyone can buy one."

"Then why is yours so special?"

"I trekked to a secluded monastery in Tibet to have my bowl blessed. The monks suggested I allow it to remain with them for one hundred and eight days, a number with spiritual significance, and then they shipped it back to me." She shook her head, remembering the kindness at the monastery. "My bowl can never be replaced."

"You mentioned the bowl sings? In fact," he said, "I seem to recall something about yodeling."

"My bowl does not yodel," she said, but understood Reese was teasing. "It doesn't rap or sing arias, either."

"Oh, perhaps rock, then?"

She fought a laugh. "When you rub a wand around the interior, the vibration makes the metal hum, producing a clear, peaceful sound. It also chimes when you strike the rim. So, yeah, it sings."

Hearing the lovely, high-pitched tone in her mind, she smiled at Reese, wishing he would pry open his mind just a little. Too bad his head was already crammed full of legal mumbo jumbo. At least he had asked for an explanation.

He gave her a half smile. "Where did you come from, lady?"

"I don't know," she answered. "But I think you were there with me."

"Two vegetarian stews," the waiter said as he placed steaming crocks on the table. Next came a wicker basket overflowing with slices of warm bread.

They both ate for several minutes without conversation. Finally, Taki took a drink of cool water. "I guess we were hungry."

He smiled at her over a spoonful of stew. "You were right. This is delicious."

She took another bite, pleased that he liked her favorite lunch.

"How long have you been a vegetarian?" he asked.

"When I was thirteen, I decided I loved animals so much that I just couldn't eat one."

"I'll bet your mother loved that."

"My mother died when I was nine." Taki almost choked on her water when she realized what she'd said. Why on earth did she insist on babbling her secrets to this skeptical man? Of course, he was partly right. Her decision to become a vegetarian had incensed her father.

"I'm sorry," Reese said.

"That's okay," she blurted, knowing her words only made the moment more awkward. By the kind way he smiled at her, though, she knew his sympathy was genuine.

He offered her a slice of bread and took one himself.

"This soup is really good," he said again.

With peace between them, she decided to tell him her plan. "That pawnshop I told you about isn't very far from here."

He eyed her steadily. "Which pawnshop is that?"

"Jacques's Hock. Where the clerk said to come back about the bowl."

"We are not going to any pawnshop."

She stared right back at him, not liking his dictatorial tone. She took orders from no one.... Well, except maybe Guru Navi, but he never gave orders. Only suggestions. This guy acted as if he were a five-star general.

"Why not?" she asked. "We're right here."

He shook his head as he took another bite of stew. "That's a job for trained federal agents."

"Going to a pawnshop requires training?"

"In this case, yes."

She sat back and folded her arms. "You love giving orders, don't you? And you're used to everyone doing exactly what you tell them."

He dropped a piece of bread on his plate, his dark eyes focused on her. "Have you been following the Romero case in the *Herald*?"

"No." Best not to tell him she ignored newspapers. They were full of nothing but negativity, bad news, sad news, making it impossible to live in the present moment.

"Carlos Romero is in jail awaiting trial on a long list of charges, including first-degree murder for blowing up a post office in Fort Lauderdale and killing four people," Reese explained.

"I remember that," Taki said with a shudder. Even she hadn't been able to avoid the horrifying story of the victims of that violent blast. It'd made national news. Why did people always have to hurt each other?

"Murder comes easily to some people," he said. "They stole my briefcase hoping to discover the location of an important witness. Fortunately, they found nothing."

"Well, I'm glad of that. But why would murderers take my bowl?"

"I was hoping you might know."

"I don't," she said.

"Then maybe a diversion, to throw us off track, or just an opportunity to make a quick buck. But I'll send an agent to check out your pawnshop. I promise."

"When?"

"May I finish the lunch you ordered for me?"

"Of course," she said and took a sip of her tea.

Good thing peppermint is excellent for indigestion, she thought, because Reese looked as if he was in for a serious case of heartburn.

BACK AT THE federal building, Taki smiled at Reese's secretary as they walked past her cubicle. She had a pencil stuck behind one ear and a pen behind the other. The poor thing looked totally frazzled.

"Sorry I'm late, Joanne," he said and grabbed a stack of messages from her desk.

"Romero's attorney is trying to reach you," the secretary said. "And Agent Rivas has phoned twice. I canceled the three o'clock conference when you weren't back. It's rescheduled for tomorrow at four."

"Thank you," Reese mumbled as he entered his office.

"Wow." Taki moved to the front of his massive desk as he stepped behind it, reading his messages. "I made you miss a meeting."

"It wasn't important," he said, still shuffling through the pink papers in his hand.

As she sat in a well-padded chair, Taki watched Reese morph back into Mr. United States Attorney. He'd relaxed slightly at lunch, but on entering his office he reverted to all-business. Just like her father. Never enough time to get everything done.

He'd insisted she accompany him upstairs so she could hear him dispatch an FBI agent to the pawnshop, although she figured it was really because he wanted to keep her away from the place. But since that meant he was worried about someone besides himself, maybe there was still hope for Reese Beauchamps. She hoped so. Despite his arrogance and love of barking orders, she liked him, although she couldn't figure out why.

She hated to think it was because he was so good-looking. What did that say about *her?* But he did have the most gorgeous dark brown eyes. If she let herself, she could stare into them all day. And she liked the way his thick brown hair sported just a little wave. If he let it grow long, it would be magnificent.

"Call your agent Rivas," she said, disgusted with herself. "Then I'll let you get back to work."

"Right." Reese dropped the messages on the desk, pulled a swivel chair toward him and picked up the phone.

To give him space while he spoke to the agent, she wandered around his large office with the fabulous view, examining various diplomas and certificates adorning the walls. Could pieces of paper tell her anything about the man?

She admired elegantly framed degrees from undergraduate school at Princeton and law school at the University of Florida. Her father had once wanted her to attend Princeton.

Without reading, she focused on the Old English script in a dignified plaque as a sickening realization shot through her.

That was the third or maybe fourth time in one afternoon that Reese had caused her to think of her father. Before today, she couldn't remember the last time she'd allowed the soulless monster to creep into her thoughts. Being reminded of the past never did anything but cause her pain.

The two men didn't resemble each other at all physically, but both attacked life as if it were an opponent to be wrestled into submission.

She resisted the urge to run out of Reese's office.

She needed to stay far away from this man. It didn't matter how good-looking he was. He behaved too much like her father and would destroy the serenity she'd fought so hard to create.

CHAPTER THREE

"GET BACK TO me on that right away, Javi. Yeah, thanks." Reese deliberately made his voice loud so Taki could hear him. She'd been staring at his Juris Doctor degree for five minutes as if it held the key to the secrets of her quixotic universe.

When he replaced the receiver, she turned. Reese smiled at her, liking it much better when they were friends.

"He's ten minutes from the shop and will call me right back. Do you want to wait to see what he finds out?"

"No," she said. "I no longer think anything will come of that."

"What?" Reese pushed back in his chair, causing it to squeak in protest. "But you insisted on checking out the lead immediately."

"I know. The thing is…" She paused and looked out the window. "Well, after we left the restaurant our path took us by Jacques's Hock, and I got a strong feeling that my bowl wasn't there."

"You drove by the pawnshop? Why didn't you tell me?"

She met his gaze again. "You'd have just fussed about it," she said with a graceful shrug.

"And you got a…a feeling that your bowl wasn't there?"

She straightened her shoulders. "Yes."

"What kind of a feeling? Explain."

"How can you explain a feeling? I just sensed my bowl was not inside that building."

Reese rose, thinking Taki the most illogical person he had ever encountered. How could she change her mind so quickly? "My investigator is already on his way."

"Sorry. I was wrong," she said, blue eyes troubled. Then she brightened. "But at least I admit it."

"Yeah, at least there's that." Reese fought an impulse to warn her about relying on irrational feelings. "Taki, in my experience, facts work a lot better when searching for the truth."

"Oh, I'm sure you think so," she said, moving toward the door. "But I've learned facts can be manipulated. Twisted into something ugly."

Reese came around his desk and stood beside her, wondering why he felt the urge to touch her, however inappropriate such an action might be. Would that be considered harassment in one of those previous lifetimes where they'd known each other?

Previous lifetimes? Yeah, sure. No doubt they'd known each other during the Civil War. Or maybe ancient Rome.

"Thanks for lunch," he said. Taki had insisted on

paying, reminding him that he was her guest. "I'll let you know if anything develops."

"Thank you."

"Please don't go to any more pawnshops, Taki. And I'm not ordering. I'm asking."

She cocked her head. "And you even said 'please.'"

"I'm serious," he said, doubting she would listen. Taki existed in some mystifying world of her own creation where dangerous men like Romero didn't exist. Too bad that world was total fiction.

"I promise." She smiled, dimples appearing in her smooth cheeks, her face so serious and open that he knew she considered her promise a sacred vow. Without warning, she rose to her toes and brushed a kiss on his left cheek, her lips as soft as her promise. Her fresh scent, maybe jasmine, filled his senses, reminding him of sunshine and a gentle spring breeze.

"Thanks for worrying about me," she said, hesitating an instant too long before pulling away, her breath warm and sweet on his chin. Reese closed his eyes against the thought of crushing her to him.

What the hell is wrong with me?

With his fingers pressed to the spot where her lips had touched, he watched Taki exit his office in her strangely elegant manner.

Talk about a breath of fresh air. Taki had blown into his life and shaken it up like nothing ever had. Treating what he knew to be fact as fiction, she made the impossible seem somehow believable.

Negative energy? Third eyes? Mysterious feelings? Ridiculous.

As his buzzer sounded insistently behind him, Reese felt as if he was coming out of a trance. The woman was sincere in her quirky beliefs, but a total fruitcake. He shook his head to clear it.

Damn, but she was a huge distraction, one he didn't have time for.

Reese sat at his desk and prioritized the phone calls he needed to return. Thanks to his little time-out with Miss New Age Wonder, he wouldn't get home tonight until after ten o'clock.

Better stay far, far away from Wacky Taki or he'd never get any work done.

"Yes, Joanne?" he said into the intercom.

"Agent Rivas is on line two."

Reese punched the speaker. "What have you got for me, Javi?"

"Dead end, Reese. Some crackhead pawned a silver cup from a horse race, nothing from Tibet. But the clerk practically got religious when talking about your friend Taki. When do I get to meet this knockout blonde?"

"She's a little hard to reach," Reese said, realizing with a groan that he still didn't have her phone number or address.

Taki might be a nut job, but she was also damned elusive.

AT HOME THAT evening, still unsettled by the loss of her bowl—not to mention her lunch with Reese—Taki tried to calm her mind by sitting for meditation. But her restless thoughts looped over and over one thing: Reese made her think of her father—actually, reminded her of her father—and she hated her father.

Maybe Reese could help her find the bowl, but she had no business coming within a square mile of him if he dredged up thoughts of the soulless monster. She should never look into Reese's eyes—no matter how dreamy those particular eyes. No matter how dark, how aware. She sighed.

Longing to regain serenity, Taki rose and opened her back door to gaze out on her small herb garden. The sight of vigorous plants bursting with life out of their neat rows immediately improved her mood. The natural world always soothed her. Other than practicing yoga, her happiest times were spent with Mother Nature, either hiking or watching beautiful things grow.

She moved down the steps, feeling as if she were transitioning into another world, a better place, a quiet and simple space where no problems interfered. With the property bordered by tall oaks, she always felt as if she were entering some secret garden as she entered the backyard of the estate where she lived.

Inhaling deeply, she was rewarded with the delicious scent of the rich earth she'd worked so hard to create—Miami Beach actually had pretty lousy dirt—and, yes, there it was: a hint of lavender.

Her gaze zeroed in on the row of lavender, shiny green leaves and tiny purple buds. So hard to grow in South Florida, but with the cooler temperatures of winter, her third attempt had finally met with success. Lavender encouraged relaxation, and soon she could create her special scented bath oil. She often gave samples to new students, recommending long, soothing soaks after class. Maybe she should give some to Reese.

The image of a bare-chested, dark-eyed Reese easing his muscled body into a steaming tub made her anything but relaxed—in fact, it instantly destroyed the tranquility she'd come outside seeking.

Closing her eyes, she released a slow exhale, forcing her traitorous mind away from a naked Reese Beauchamps. It would certainly help if she didn't find him so darned attractive.

She slipped off her shoes and stepped into the soft damp dirt between rows. Glorying in that sensation, she wiggled her toes and hugged her elbows. The plot might be small, but it was all hers, and she was perhaps too proud of these happy, healthy herbs.

And how could she call herself an herbalist if she didn't grow her own product? She'd been on the run so much lately, this was the first time she'd been able to grow her own crop in what seemed like forever. She frowned, thinking back. How long had it been since her last real garden? One where the plants sent their roots straight into the earth and not some plastic pot.

Bending her knees, but keeping her upper back flat to protect the fragile lumbar area, Taki yanked weeds from between her plants. Working steadily down a row of Saint-John's-wort, she considered her next step to locate the missing bowl. Where was it?

She didn't have any luck with the pawnshops. Could Reese's logical methods find it?

She sighed, realizing her thoughts had once again circled back to Reese Beauchamps. Certainly didn't take long.

A mockingbird chirped, flitted into a pine tree, then onto the iron railing of Victoria's second-floor balcony where he began to sing in earnest. No lights were on in the master bedroom, so likely her landlady wasn't home. Taki hoped Victoria was out having a good time at one of her clubs, maybe playing bridge.

Victoria Van Buren, who'd just turned seventy, had once been her mother's best friend and mentor. After returning from Asia, on what was meant to be a brief trip to see Navi six months ago, Victoria offered free lodging in a converted garage behind the main house for as long as Taki wanted, promising never to reveal her true identity to anyone. While waiting for the bowl to arrive, Taki had accepted Victoria's hospitality.

But now with the bowl stolen, everything had somehow changed.

Taki loved her cottage, but definitely did not want to talk to Victoria tonight. Truthfully, she didn't want to talk to anyone. That's why she was pulling weeds in her herb patch, hoping to figure out what to do about her bowl and Reese.

Because the universe in all its wisdom had linked Reese with her bowl. Once that connection was made, there was nothing she could do about it—no matter how much she wanted to never think about him again.

Of course, it would be a lot easier to forget about Reese if she didn't enjoy fantasizing about him in his bath. Maybe she needed to meditate more often. Or longer.

What would Navi tell her to do? Spotting another weed, she bent over to extract it. No doubt Navi would teach something about seeking the truth, tell her that she needed to "do the work." And, yeah, that actually did make sense.

So she'd seek the truth. She'd continue to do what she could to find the bowl.

But she needed to avoid Reese while she did so. She didn't want to be reminded of her scheming father's miserable world of excess, a place she'd vowed to never live again.

TAKI SMILED AT Benny in his usual front row space as she spread her mat for her Thursday evening class at SoBe Spa.

"How is your shoulder tonight, Ben?" Before starting her classes, he'd had a frozen shoulder that he could barely move, the result of an old injury.

Benny slowly rotated his arm and grinned. "Look at that. You're a miracle worker, Taki."

"No, you did the work," she told him, pleased by his improvement.

She taught her most serious students in private sessions, the way yoga was meant to be learned, but she always found good energy with the friendly spa members. She enjoyed teaching here, and hoped she wouldn't have to move again too soon.

To think she'd actually been thinking maybe she could stay in Miami. She should have known better. Getting attached always led to suffering.

For everyone, but especially for her.

After three sun salutations to warm up, she settled into half lotus and surveyed the room on the lookout for curious aerobic or step class students who ventured into her class. They tended to overdo the poses, sometimes harming themselves. Once a personal trainer had almost blown out a knee. She'd warned him to be careful, but he wouldn't listen, and had to wear an elastic brace for a month.

Nobody new tonight, though, except— Recognition sent a startled thrill into her belly. Balancing on his buttocks, his arms wrapped around his knees, Reese sat in the back row, staring at her.

She inhaled deeply to calm herself, surprised by her reaction. She'd been teaching yoga since she was eighteen years old, and never had such a disturbing response to a new student.

But the sight of his bare arms and legs created a long, slow pull on her center.

"Assume a comfortable seated position. Close your eyes and allow your attention to focus on your breath, inhaling and exhaling through your nostrils," Taki instructed, relieved her voice didn't waver. *Yeah, that would inspire confidence in my students.*

"You've been in your head all day at work," she said. "Now it's time to come into your body."

A class opening she frequently used, but a bad choice of words for tonight, she decided, trying to block the image of Reese's well-toned arms and shoulders. She regained her concentration by filling her lungs with oxygen and exhaling with a controlled, even release.

She remained aware of Reese's total attention as she led the class through warm-ups, sun salutes and the various poses she'd selected for tonight's practice. Long used to students watching her, she couldn't fathom why his intense scrutiny made her aware of herself as never before. The energy in the class felt sharper tonight, cutting through her distraction with a laserlike quality.

Only Reese's presence explained the difference.

Why hadn't she realized he might come to class? She'd encouraged him to try yoga, believing the practice would be therapeutic for him.

"And when you're ready, you can come out of deep relaxation," Taki said softly, alerting her students that class time had expired. Sitting with her back against a mirrored wall, she watched Reese, who still lay in corpse position. She hoped he'd been able to relax. Buddha knew the man needed it the way he was always rushing around.

Taki sighed at her ridiculous oath. When had she picked up that saying? Buddha certainly knew no such thing. In her never-ending search for a quiet mind, she'd managed to confuse the different philosophies she'd studied. Now with everything muddled inside her head, she'd never find the path to enlightenment and happiness.

If only her bowl hadn't been stolen.

But she was probably putting too much faith in that remedy. Hadn't Navi told her there was never one sure answer?

With her hands steepled in prayer position, she nodded and smiled at her students as they streamed from the yoga studio, and waited for her last student to leave. Reese.

He sat up, appearing more than a little dazed. But new students frequently reacted to their first savasana and deep relaxation the same way. Most people, definitely including Reese, were so stressed by a fast-paced life that their nervous systems remained in a constant state of agitation, which inevitably led down a path to one of the deadly modern diseases.

He'd recover in a few minutes. Tonight was likely the first time he'd managed to truly relax in years.

"How did you like the class?" she asked when his gaze sharpened and focused on her.

He rotated his neck left and right. "Wow. I haven't been able to do that in a long time. What'd you do to me?"

"Nothing. You did it for yourself."

"Listen," Reese said, rising and stepping beside her. "I need your cell number in case something comes up on the bowl."

"I don't own a cell phone." Taki rose and slipped on her sandals.

"Seriously?"

"Refusing to be at the mercy of a machine isn't against the law." She eased a loose gray sweatshirt over her camisole, feeling a slight chill now that she'd stopped moving.

"Then give me your home number. You do have a landline, right?"

Without replying, Taki removed her digital player from the spa's sound system and stuffed it and other personal possessions into her class bag. She didn't want to give him any phone number. She had good reasons to keep it private. Plus, it would be hard to avoid Reese if he could just call whenever he wanted.

But what if, like he suggested, he needed to speak to her about the bowl? Well, if she gave him her number, he had to respect her privacy and promise not to share it. She needed to make that clear.

When she faced him, his thick eyebrows were drawn together in puzzlement. No doubt he was used to women throwing their numbers at him without being asked.

"Will you miss another meeting if we go upstairs for a cup of herb tea?" she asked. "Before I give you my number, I need to explain something to you."

He hesitated. "I don't have a meeting, but…"

"But you have work to do," she finished for him. Of course. She should have known that he'd feel compelled to use every second of the day to work. Even at night. So Mr. Workaholic could just wait to learn her phone number until he had a spare second.

He took a quick glance at his watch and sighed. "I guess I can make time."

"THE PAWNSHOP DIDN'T have your bowl," Reese told Taki as he relaxed onto a comfortable cushion. Until tonight, he'd never enjoyed this cozy nook of the spa where casual futon-style couches faced a picture window on the Atlantic Ocean. Five miles offshore, the lights of huge freighters glowed on the horizon.

At the service bar, she examined various boxes of tea, selected one and poured steaming water over tea bags in two white foam cups. Always in a hurry to get somewhere else, on occasion he'd grabbed a cup of coffee at this free beverage station, but never knew they provided herb tea. No doubt Taki's doing.

"Lourdes promised she'd order biodegradable cups," Taki said, frowning at the tea. "I'll have to remind her again."

"All Jacques's Hock had was a silver chalice from Hialeah Race Track," Reese said. "Sorry."

She nodded. "I no longer believe my bowl is at a pawnshop. Honey?"

"What?" he asked, startled.

"Do you want honey in your tea?" She turned to him, eyebrows raised. "Or would you rather add another sweetener yourself?"

They stared at each other across the tiny area, and Reese wondered at the uneasiness in her eyes. In the soft lighting, their startling blue color appeared subdued, but her fair skin glowed. What was she worried about?

"Please," he said. "And thank you."

"In fact," she said, while dribbling the thick liquid

into the cups, "I'm not at all certain that your bad guys even took my bowl."

When Reese accepted the tea from Taki, his hand brushed her slender fingers. She lowered her eyes at the contact.

"Why is that?" he asked, enjoying the connection between them. Hell, for some demented reason he enjoyed himself whenever he spent time with Taki.

"It's a feeling I have," she said. She parted her lips as if to say more, then pressed them firmly together.

Wishing he knew what she was about to say, he said, "Do you always rely so heavily on your feelings?"

She leaned back on the sofa. "What are you relying on to believe that Romero's people took your briefcase?"

"Clear, logical assumptions supported by indisputable facts."

"Well, my feelings may not be logical, but they're usually right. Are your assumptions always correct?"

"Not always," he said, smiling at her perceptive question. "Okay. Then what happened to your bowl?"

She stared into the white cup. "I don't know yet."

"Well, I do. Believe me, Taki, I'm trying like hell to get my briefcase back. If I do, I'll locate your bowl."

"Thank you," she said.

But Reese could tell she didn't believe he would find her lost artifact. He looked forward to witnessing her pleasure if he did. He took a hesitant taste and found the brew sweet and refreshing.

"What kind of tea is this?"

"Rosemary. It improves the memory, so it'll help you with your work later."

He stared into the amber liquid and shook his head at her constant attempts to help everyone. Then he grinned at her.

"Maybe you drink too much of this stuff and that's why you think you remember me."

"It doesn't work that way."

"Do I still seem familiar to you?"

"I don't know." Using her fingers as a comb, she absently swept her hand through her long blond hair. He wondered if the strands felt as soft as they looked.

"Sometimes I tend to get a little carried away," she continued, throwing him a quick glance. "Perhaps we did meet previously, and I just don't remember."

"That's much more likely than our introduction occurring in another life," he said. Good to know she occasionally came back to earth.

"But where?" she asked. She took another sip of tea, watching him over the rim of the cup.

"In court maybe?" He raised his eyebrows, hoping she'd treat his next question as a joke. "Have you ever been up on federal charges?"

"Heavens, no. Is federal prosecuting the only legal work you've ever done?"

"Yes. I became an assistant U.S. attorney right out of law school."

"So you don't take private clients?"

"Never."

"Why is that?"

Wondering where she was going with this conversation and why, Reese watched Taki nibble on her lower lip. She obviously wanted some information but didn't want to ask directly.

"If you need a lawyer, Taki, I can recommend several."

Her eyes widened. "I can't imagine what would ever cause me to hire a lawyer," she said with an emphatic shake of her head.

Her response told him a lot. "I guess you don't like lawyers."

He watched her suck air deep into her lungs, and then slowly release the breath.

"What if someone sues you?" he asked when she didn't reply.

"Why would anyone sue me?" Taki balanced the tea as she tucked her bare feet beneath her on the couch.

"What about that blot on your soul? That might cause a lawsuit."

"Maybe you don't need my tea." She grinned and shook her head. "You never forget a thing, do you?"

Not about you, he thought, imagining a thousand ways a woman as beautiful as Taki could place her soul in jeopardy.

"Lourdes says you want to run for political office," Taki said.

"Who knows?" He shrugged, caught off guard by her comment. His future political career must be the subject of widespread speculation if even Taki had heard about it.

"So that's why you're a prosecutor, to get a reputation?"

"I became a prosecutor because I want to put criminals like Romero in jail where they belong. I hate it when people break laws and get away with it. Justice has always been important to me." Reese paused. Where had that disclosure come from? Something about Taki required honesty.

"Or perhaps I secretly wanted to irritate my father," he continued. "Dad believes that public service is for suckers and the way to practice law is behind a desk."

"So your father is a lawyer, too?" she asked.

"Everyone in my family is."

"Everyone?" Her face fell, as if his entire family had been diagnosed with tuberculosis.

"Well, almost everyone. My mother is a doctor."

"Oh. Do you have any brothers or sisters?" she asked. He thought her voice sounded wistful.

"Two brothers and a sister...all attorneys working for my dad."

"Are you from Miami?" she asked.

"Born and raised. How about you?"

"I'm an only child."

"So why all the questions, Taki?" he asked, needing to get moving. "I thought you wanted to explain something to me."

She nodded. "I was trying to get a better sense of who you are. I'm a very private person and have good reasons for not giving my phone number to just anyone."

"I'm not just anyone. I'm a United States attorney, one of the good guys."

"Are you really?" she asked softly.

"I put bad guys in jail," he said, wondering about good reasons for not giving up a number. And why didn't she have a cell?

She nodded, looking away. "The thing is, you remind me of someone who isn't very nice at all."

Startled, he asked, "How so?"

She met his gaze again. "Always barking orders, always in a hurry."

That's how she sees me? He groaned inwardly, knowing there was some truth in that description. "That's how I get things done in my job."

"If I give you my phone number, do you promise you won't give it to anyone else?"

"If you don't want me to, I promise I won't."

She didn't immediately respond. Instead she chewed on her lower lip again. Feeling uncomfortably like a teenager asking a date to the prom, he waited.

TAKI GRABBED A pen and a napkin from the service bar and jotted down the number of the phone Victoria kept in the cottage. How could she say no? Otherwise Reese could start prying into her life to find out where she lived. Didn't the government snoop on everyone these days?

She had no doubt he could learn anything he

wanted through federal high-tech computers and gizmos, and there was no telling what he'd come up with.

She thrust the napkin toward him.

He accepted it with a long look at her scribbles. When he folded the paper and stuck it in the pocket of his gym shorts, she got the curious sensation that he'd memorized the numbers.

"I'll be in touch if I get any news." With a wave, he disappeared inside the men's locker room.

Should she believe him? Would he keep her number private?

But maybe she shouldn't worry. Unless he had info about their stolen property, why would he call? And in that case, she wouldn't mind hearing from him.

Assuming the news was good.

On her way to the parking lot, she passed Hector and Lourdes working at the front desk and gave them a weak wave.

"Hey, Taki," Lourdes said. "Don't forget about the staff meeting next week."

"Okay."

"Any luck with your bowl?" Hector asked.

"Not yet," she said and pushed open the door, glad for the rush of fresh air.

What was it about Reese's dark, intelligent eyes that seemed so…aware? She shivered, recalling the force of his gaze as he stared directly into hers. It reminded her of the times Guru Navi tried to look deep into her soul. Funny, but it felt as if Reese saw her more clearly than her teacher.

Too bad Reese hadn't become a healer like his

mother instead of a lawyer. That would be so much better for his...

She slowed her crisp steps across the well-lit parking lot when she spotted a figure leaning against the Jeep's driver door. Her pulse kicked up a notch, but she relaxed and resumed her pace when she recognized Benny.

"Hi, Ben. I'm sorry. Were you waiting for me?"

When Benny smiled, the wrinkles in his weathered face grew even deeper. "Yes. I have some interesting news."

"What's that?"

"Remember I promised I'd ask around the spa about your missing bowl?"

Taki nodded, a rush of excitement making her belly tingle. Reese would of course discount it as a worthless *feeling*.

"After your class, I found this stuck in my locker." Benny produced a white envelope and handed it to her. With odd-size letters cut out from a magazine, "Taki" was pasted to the front.

"Did you see anyone around your locker?" she asked.

"I have no idea where it came from."

"Have you opened it?"

"Of course not."

She ripped open the envelope and withdrew a photograph.

"Oh, my God," she said, staring at a bowl sitting on a sheet of newspaper with a wand propped against the rim.

Was it hers?

She peered at the image closely to make certain that the— Yes, there was that tiny crescent-shaped mar on the base. She pressed the photo to her chest and closed her eyes. This was definitely hers.

Who had sent this? And why to Benny?

"Are you all right?" he asked.

Taki opened her eyes, feeling silly about her reaction. "Yes, yes. I'm fine."

"What is it?"

With a sigh, she passed him the photo. *Now what?*

"Proof of life," Benny said. "Although of course the bowl isn't actually alive, but that's why they included the paper, to show a date." Ben held up the image to examine it more closely. "That's the front page of today's *Miami Herald*."

"Wait," she said, grabbing the photo from Ben. "There's something on the other side."

On the back of the photograph, with those same mismatched cutout letters, someone had pasted directions.

BE AT PUERTO SAGUA TOMORROW AT SIX P.M. FOR INFORMATION ABOUT THIS ITEM.

AT FIVE FORTY-FIVE the next night, Taki slid onto a stool at Puerto Sagua and smiled at a waiter behind the broken-tiled counter. Smoke from the grill floated upward, billowing and obscuring the ceiling.

With a nod, the heavy-set server placed a menu and a plastic glass of water before her and moved on.

Taki took a slow drink while she surveyed the crowded Cuban restaurant. Maybe twenty-five diners sat at tables or at the long U-shaped counter that cut the room in half. Their noisy chatter and laughter bounced off the tiled walls, making her ears ring.

No one looked familiar. Not in this life or any other.

When the wall clock ticked down to six, the frowning waiter approached her again. She'd have to order something or be asked to leave. Black beans and rice seemed safe, but she was too nervous to eat.

After placing her order, she laid a hand on her queasy stomach. If only Reese had returned her calls. So much for her plan to avoid him, but of course he needed to know about the note.

Reese was always so confident and self-assured, she had no doubt his presence would bolster her faltering courage. She'd left messages at all his numbers revealing her intention to attend the meeting. She'd even spoken with his secretary. Joanne had been sweet, had promised to contact some agent named Javi and all but begged her not to do anything before she talked to Reese.

Forget that nonsense. She couldn't miss the chance to recover her bowl. Benny knew she was here, as did Victoria, plus she had pepper spray tucked in her purse. She'd never used it and wasn't sure if she could harm anyone with it, but just in case she slipped the small cylinder into her pocket for easy access.

And so many people crowded this restaurant, she was beginning to feel too warm. She fanned her face with the menu.

She wouldn't leave with anyone, and even Reese's bad guys wouldn't drag her off from such a public place. What could they possibly want with her?

More important, why would anybody want her bowl?

CHAPTER FOUR

REESE HAD NO problem spotting Taki when he entered the raucous atmosphere of Puerto Sagua. Seated at the counter, long blond hair partially braided and secured with a clip, her stillness was an oasis of tranquility in the center of chaos. In a warm, lively restaurant filled with the essence of garlic and onion, she made him think of the cool freshness of a deep forest.

If he weren't so damned annoyed with her reckless behavior, he'd be glad to see her.

"You don't know me," Reese murmured as he slid onto the stool next to hers. He threw her a quick look. "Pretend we're meeting for the first time."

When she flashed a grateful, relieved smile, his mood improved. At least she was glad he'd come to her rescue.

Spotting Javi on the other side of the counter, Reese nodded. She followed his gaze and then looked to him in surprise.

"Who's that?" she whispered.

"FBI."

Her eyes widened, and her gaze swung back to Javi. "Quit staring at him."

When Taki refocused on her plate, which contained a mammoth serving of black beans—she couldn't have touched a bite—Reese asked, "You really received a photograph of your bowl with a note instructing you to come here?"

"Not exactly. Someone left the photo with Benny, one of my regular students." With a graceful movement, she tucked a strand of hair behind her shoulder.

Reese made a mental note to question Benny. He knew all about Benny. The old man practically lived at SoBe Spa, or anyway, he was there every time Reese worked out. So what was his involvement with Taki and her magic bowl?

"Why him and not you?" Reese asked.

The waiter arrived before she could reply.

"*Cafecito* to go," Reese requested. The potent Cuban coffee was like mainlining caffeine, but he still had hours of work to do tonight.

"I asked people around the spa if they knew anything about the bowl," she said when the waiter moved away. "Benny did, too. I guess he asked the right person."

"That doesn't make any sense. Do you have the photo?"

She reached for her purse.

"Wait. I'll look at it later."

Reese surveyed the room, searching for a familiar face. His initial response to Taki's message had been that someone was playing a joke on her, but Puerto Sagua just happened to be Izzo's favorite place for breakfast, and nobody in law enforcement believed in coincidences.

"Whoever sent the note has my bowl and maybe you can recover your briefcase, too," she said, her voice low and urgent.

Reese stared at Taki's animated face. Why did he find this nutcase so compelling? She certainly had guts. More courage than sense, apparently.

"You shouldn't have come here alone, Taki. It was a foolish thing to do."

"But you didn't return my calls. I had no choice."

Reese shook his head at her stubbornness. Why was this damned bowl so important? Something else had to be going on. He'd find out what tonight.

"I was in trial all day," he said. "I didn't get your messages until five-thirty."

"Well, I didn't want to miss the chance of getting my bowl back. Now quit talking to me or nothing will happen." She smiled sweetly and extended her hand to dismiss him.

Reese grasped her fingers and squeezed. When she released her grip, he picked up his coffee, dropped a bill on the counter and moved to an empty table where he could keep an eye on her.

He pried open the lid of the foam take-out cup, shaking his head as he remembered Taki's disapproval of the nonbiodegradable material. The woman wanted to save the world.

Steam floated up to his face, bringing with it an aroma of coffee.

Letting the brew cool a bit, he waited before taking

the first sip and continued to observe the crowded room. He noted Javi did the same, but the agent blended in with the casually dressed clientele a lot better than Reese did in his tailored suit.

He probably stuck out as obviously as Taki.

What the hell was he doing here? He had too much work for these kinds of games. When he'd received Taki's messages, he'd been torn between outrage and worry. Unable to let her face unknown danger alone, he'd called Javi and asked him to meet them at Puerto Sagua.

Outside the winter light faded to darkness, but no one approached her, although more than one male customer openly ogled her ethereal blond beauty.

Izzo certainly wasn't in sight. Not that Reese thought this meeting had anything to do with him. Just another dead end, another wild-goose chase courtesy of Wacky Taki.

Reese sipped the strong coffee. She might be a little nuts, but he had to admit she was plenty easy on the eyes. Taki barely touched the food she'd ordered. She did drink four glasses of water, however, and occasionally would wrinkle her cute nose and wave off smoke from the grill that drifted her way.

At six forty-five, she scanned the back of the room and gave a disappointed shrug when their gazes locked. She picked up her check and slid off the stool.

Agreeing that it was time to give up, Reese pushed through the front door while Taki dealt with the cashier. He noted she used cash.

The night seemed oppressively dark when he exited the restaurant. Fast-moving clouds obscured the moon, and a brisk wind sent leaves scattering across the sidewalk. He buttoned his jacket against the crisp evening air. A cold front had swept into South Florida, and the thermometer would dip into the forties tonight. A rare event.

Wrapping a wool cape around her slight frame, Taki stepped onto the sidewalk.

"Where are you parked?" he asked when she moved beside him.

"I'm in the public lot over on Washington." She glanced at his rented Ford sitting in a no-parking zone in front of the popular restaurant.

"I was late, remember?" Reese said, wondering why he felt defensive.

She raised her eyebrows, but said nothing.

"Come on. I'll give you a ride to your car." He opened the passenger door and motioned her in.

When Reese pulled his door shut, the quiet in the interior of the sedan made him feel as if he'd just locked out the world and had Taki all to himself. Not a bad feeling.

"Thank you for coming," she said in what had to be the most sincere thanks he'd ever received.

"You're welcome."

"I'm sorry you wasted your time."

"I'm sorry no one showed."

"Me, too." She sighed, obviously frustrated. "What went wrong? Why didn't they come?"

"Good question."

"The note didn't say to come alone," she mused. "Although they couldn't have known you were with me."

Reese suppressed a chuckle. He'd think she'd been watching too much television, but doubted she watched the TV much, if ever, what with all that negative energy emanating from the screen. *Wouldn't be good for that karmic debt.*

"Maybe you'll be contacted again."

"I sure hope so," she said.

"I hope you understand why I couldn't return your calls?"

"Your secretary explained. I know you're a busy man."

Her voice sounded sympathetic, as if he had terminal cancer.

"Let me see the photo," he said.

She dug in a multicolored fabric bag that featured images of an elephant, its strap snug between her breasts, and produced a color picture of a brass bowl with swirling patterns etched into the metal.

Reese studied the image, briefly disappointed there was no sign of his briefcase in the background. He recognized the headline of today's newspaper. Definitely a recent photo.

"You're sure it's your bowl?"

"Positive."

He flipped the photo and read the note, finding nothing that would lead to its author. The way the note had been created screamed amateur. Or again, maybe too many TV crime shows. No way was Romero involved.

He lifted his gaze back to her serious face. "Is there any chance your student was playing a mean trick on you?"

She reacted to that idea as if he had struck her. "Ben would never do that."

He studied her. *We'll see about that.* "Okay. Can I keep this?"

"I guess."

"I want to send it to the FBI lab. Maybe they can find a clue to our mystery."

She brightened at his plan. "Good idea. Thanks."

He started the engine and pulled onto Collins Avenue. She remained silent, probably lost in mystical thoughts as they drove the short distance to her Jeep. He needed to learn why the bowl was so damned important to her.

"I'm going to follow you home," Reese told her when he pulled behind her vehicle.

"That's okay," she said too quickly. "You don't need to."

"Yes, I do."

"But—"

"We don't know who was in that restaurant, but they know who you are."

"Oh." Her eyes widened, and for the first time he noted a hint of worry.

"I need to make sure you get home safely."

"Okay. Thanks."

"Just don't break any speed limits this time."

She nodded, exited the car and climbed into her Jeep.

After driving a few blocks, Reese called Javi, who followed him, checking for a tail.

"You see anything inside the restaurant?" Reese asked.

"Nada," Javi said. "I had another agent posted outside, and she didn't notice anything, either. None of Romero's known people were there. Other than the usual South Beach freaks, no one suspicious."

"Do I have a tail?"

"You're clear."

"Thanks, Javi. Appreciate the help tonight."

"Hey, no problem, Reese. Anytime you need help with that blonde, you just let me know. I'm your man."

"I'll check in with you tomorrow," Reese said, refusing to react to Javi's comment, and disconnected.

When Taki turned into the brick driveway of an impressive Miami Beach home, Reese pulled in behind her and released a low whistle at the affluent surroundings. Soft illumination highlighted a three-tiered flowing fountain in the center of a landscaped oval. Overgrown red bougainvillea lined the facade of a handsome coral-colored villa beneath a clay tile roof. He estimated the gated estate covered at least two acres directly on Biscayne Bay.

He'd pictured Taki in some sort of rustic commune, or perhaps even a tent, not in an exclusive waterfront mansion. Well, well. Wasn't this an interesting turn of events.

She jumped from her Jeep and walked toward him. He now recognized the relaxed way she moved, a fluid lilt to her slim hips he found mesmerizing. But the expression on her face told him she debated some huge problem.

Reese lowered his window, the motor issuing a quiet hum.

She bent her knees to bring her face level with his. "Thanks for following me home."

"You're welcome."

"Were we followed?" Eyes wide, she glanced toward the quiet residential street.

Reese smiled. "I don't think so."

Taki returned her gaze to his face and released a big sigh. "Well, then—"

"You wouldn't have any herbal tea, would you?" he asked.

"Um…well…sure," she said. "Lots of it." She nodded toward the house. "So would you…like to come in?"

"I'd love to."

Reese set the rental's alarm with a shrill beep, thinking, *Why bother?* It hadn't kept Izzo out of the Jag. Truth was, car alarms sounded so frequently in Miami everyone ignored them. Taki grabbed her bag from the Jeep and slung it over one shoulder. He followed her to a small building behind the main house that had probably once been a free-standing garage.

In another life, of course, he thought to himself with a chuckle.

TAKI MENTALLY ZIPPED through an inventory of her living room while unlocking the door to her cottage. Was there anything in open view that would give Reese a clue to her birth name?

The Spencer Trust lawyers hadn't yet traced her to this address, but they might be getting close. Reese had her phone number and now knew where she lived. He could easily give her away without even knowing he'd done a bad thing. Far better that no one know anything about her history. Mistakes could be made, the wrong thing mentioned to the wrong person. Her father had minions everywhere looking for her.

She needed more time to square things with the universe. She needed to find that bowl before her father located her and she was forced to move again.

"Do you have a favorite tea?" Taki asked as she stepped through the entrance and flipped on a switch. "Or will any flavor do?"

"Whatever you have will be fine," Reese said.

As she'd expected, he scrutinized her front room as if they'd entered a Ripley's Believe It or Not! museum. She couldn't tell if he was amused or taken aback by what he saw.

She allowed her gaze to roam over the eclectic collection of furniture and curios from her Eastern travels and secondhand shops. She was especially fond of her collection of statuettes of Lord Ganesha, the Hindu elephant god, a deity so powerful it was said he could remove any obstacle. Now, that was some symbolism she really liked.

Everything had meaning to her, although her possessions probably looked like a bunch of old junk to Reese.

But there were no trappings from the Spencer fortune, she realized with relief. Even if he had heard of a runaway heiress, he'd never make a connection to her.

"Make yourself comfortable," she said, "and I'll put on some water."

Taki poured distilled water into a kettle and placed it on her stove. With a quick push of a button, she ignited the flame, and gas burned with a quiet hiss. Reaching for two mugs from wooden cabinets, she mentally kicked herself for letting Reese in when she knew she should avoid him. How could she keep a calm mind when the man stirred emotion she was better off burying?

He'd been sweet to meet her at Puerto Sagua, but she could have just said she was tired, that she needed to get some sleep. That wasn't a lie, not at all. She hadn't slept well since she'd met Reese. She frowned. Since her bowl had been stolen.

But oh, no. She'd been entranced by the color of his eyes, by the shape of his lips, by the rich timbre of his voice as he'd asked about tea. It was beyond foolish to allow Reese inside her home, and dangerous because she found him so absurdly attractive. And why did she? The man represented everything she'd run away from four years ago. She should stay away from him, as she did all negative influences.

So how to explain her intense rush of pleasure

when he showed up at the restaurant? Her reaction had nothing to do with her bowl, much less any past or future karma. She'd been thrilled from her crown chakra to the tips of her toes that he had come to help her.

Definitely beyond foolish.

Waiting for the water to boil, Taki rejoined Reese in the living room. He stood with folded arms squinting at a print of Buddha hanging near the door to her bedroom. Sensing he was chilled in her unheated home, she turned on a rectangular space heater by the ancient pink brocade sofa.

He's from Miami, she remembered. Miami natives took great offense whenever the temperature dropped below sixty.

"It'll warm up in a minute," she said. As she closed the door to the bedroom, Taki smiled at her dangling angels and prayed for luck.

"Is this also from Tibet?" Reese asked, indicating the colorful print.

"No, a secondhand shop on Lincoln Road." Taki admired the peaceful scene of Buddha seated beneath a leafy tree. It was one of her favorite images, one that usually put her in a serene frame of mind. But not tonight with Reese standing right next to her.

"Tell me about your bowl," he said, "why it's so important that you'd risk your life."

She continued to stare at the bright colors in the print. "I didn't risk my life."

"If Romero's people are involved, you did."

"But why would Romero's people want my bowl?"

"I keep hoping you'll tell me."

Taki leveled her gaze at Reese. Something in his voice made her uneasy. He observed her steadily, a hint of five o'clock shadow on his chin and cheeks. Did he think she knew something about his stolen briefcase?

"I don't know any more than you do about the theft, Reese."

Before he could respond, the kettle issued a shrill whistle.

Reese followed her into the tiny kitchen and less than an inch separated their hips. Not for the first time, she noted how small her kitchenette was. He was so near, she could sense every movement, every shift of his weight on his feet.

"It's amazing what someone did with this old garage," he said, loosening his tie and looking around. "How did you find it?"

"I give private lessons to Victoria Van Buren, the woman who owns the estate. She was a friend of…" Taki trailed off, realizing she'd almost told Reese that Victoria was a friend of her mother's. Better not reveal anything about her history.

"Years ago," Taki continued after clearing her throat, "Victoria's husband converted this garage to an apartment and loaned it to friends in need. Since his death, she's continuing that tradition."

"How long have you lived here?"

"Almost six months," Taki said as she poured steaming water into a ceramic teapot. Of course she couldn't tell him an outright lie. She had to be careful. *Satya,* truth, was an important yogic principle, one she believed in.

"It's nice," he said. "Cozy."

"I really love this cottage. It's full of such good energy. I think old buildings retain the souls of all the people who once lived inside."

Reese blinked. "Like ghosts?"

"No, not exactly. Just some part of their essence—or spirit maybe left behind."

"Come on, Taki," he said with a laugh. "You don't really believe drywall and wood retain dead souls?"

She nodded, again confused by the strange connection she felt to Reese, which made no sense. He was nonreceptive to her beliefs and plainly had a lot of lives yet to live, a lot of issues left to resolve.

Not that she didn't, she reminded herself. Maybe she should be more open to his way of thinking.

When she didn't answer, he said, "Seriously?"

She ought to push him far, far away, but couldn't since he could help her find the bowl. She stared into the brewing tea, knowing that now she wasn't being honest with herself. Her interest in Reese wasn't all about the bowl anymore. Maybe it never was.

"Do you really want this tea?" she said. She dropped her hand to her side, brushing his arm.

With a grin, he raised his eyebrows. "Do you have anything stronger?"

"Wine. Red or white?"

"Red might warm us up," he said.

Reese stood close enough that she could feel his breath on her cheek. Between his overwhelming presence and the steaming water, she didn't need to warm up. She felt as if the flames from the stove would consume her any second.

For a crazy moment she wanted to touch him. She wanted to take the palms of her hands and glide them up the sleeves of his jacket, pressing firmly enough to feel the hard muscle she knew lay beneath the fine blue fabric.

"Taki?" he said, a soft question in his voice.

"You'll have to move so I can reach the wine bin. It's overhead." Her voice sounded strained to her own ears.

"I'll get it for you," he offered.

When Taki met his puzzled gaze, her breath caught in her throat. She, a woman who prided herself on fabulous breath control, could barely inhale because of swift, overpowering physical desire. Reese no longer seemed familiar. He was now a stranger who awoke a hunger she'd thought buried beneath mounds of guilt and sadness.

She swallowed and pointed to the cabinet. "The far corner," she said.

Reese's eyes searched hers, but he raised his arm and easily withdrew a bottle of California Cabernet Sauvignon from the high cupboard.

"How's this?" he asked.

"Perfect."

When she accepted the bottle, she placed her hands over Reese's long fingers. For a brief moment he didn't let go, and she felt his cool hand beneath her warm palms.

"Thanks," she said.

"Sure." His gaze locked on hers, he released the wine and took slow backward steps out of the kitchen.

Trying to regain her focus, Taki took deep inhalations as she searched for the corkscrew in a messy kitchen drawer. Why could she never achieve order in her life? Guru Navi always lectured about order and cleanliness, *saucha,* another essential of a good yoga practice. She located the chrome utensil, grabbed two wineglasses and moved into the living room.

Out of the kitchen, the temperature dropped several degrees. Relieved by the sudden chill, she headed toward the orange glow of the space heater. She placed the bottle and glass on a table and collapsed onto the sofa.

Reese sat beside her, leaning forward to retrieve the wine. She relaxed into the cushions, happy to let him do the honors. She needed to recover from what had almost happened in the kitchen. Had he noticed her ridiculous reaction to him? She'd almost attacked him. How could he not notice?

"You still haven't told me about your bowl," Reese said as he opened the wine. "Let's see. So far I know you have a terrible blot on your soul. Because of that blemish, your guru sent you on a difficult journey to Tibet."

"Right," Taki said, surprised by Reese's quick recitation of the small bits she'd told him. And he didn't appear to be making fun of her. He sounded seriously interested.

"The pilgrimage itself was cleansing," she said.

"But I had a task to complete. I failed that task."
A wave of sadness washed through her. She'd also
hoped the bowl would cleanse her soul of the anguish
created by her mother's death.

Reese nodded. "You were to deliver the bowl to
the—" he paused a moment "—Paradise Way Ashram."

"Good memory." Why in heaven's name had she
told Reese all these details?

He nodded and poured wine into each glass. When
she raised hers, he tapped his against it with a gentle
clink and said, "To getting your bowl back."

"And to you getting your briefcase."

She took a swallow of the heady liquid and let its
warmth slide down her throat. She needed to relax.
Her usual methods hadn't calmed her so far. Maybe
the wine would.

After taking a sip of his own, Reese said, "So tell
me about this blot on your soul."

She smiled in spite of her unsettled mind. "That's
just the way Debbie interpreted my explanation of
rotten karma."

"Maybe you'd better explain karma to me. I'm not
quite clear on that concept. You're doomed somehow
because…?"

"Because of previous bad behavior, maybe even in
another life. Every person is the result of their past
actions and present doings. It's the universe's way of
evening things out."

"What goes around comes around," Reese said

with a nod. "Got it. So what is it you've done that's so awful?"

She knew from his tone of voice that he would probe until he got an answer. She couldn't tell him the whole truth, but she couldn't lie.

"Not me exactly. Let's just say that my family has done some really...bad things that I'm trying to atone for." She shook her head. "Unfortunately, the way things are going I'll never be forgiven."

"But you can't be blamed for what your family has done."

"Yes, I can. I benefited from their greed." She took a slow sip of her wine. "Are you warm enough? Do you mind if I turn down the heater?"

"I'm fine."

When she rose, a quick series of questions snapped through Reese's mind. Could her rotten family be in trouble with the law? Maybe already incarcerated? Is that why she'd asked if he took private clients? What sort of crime had they committed?

Exactly what would he find if he pulled Taki out of the county database?

But she wasn't a witness for him to cross-examine, so he remained silent. During that quiet, a bewildering rapport with her blossomed. No one understood wanting to distance yourself from an overbearing family better than he.

"Families can be a real pain in the ass, can't they?" he said when she'd returned.

"Yes." She paused, then asked, "So you're not close to your family?"

"Oh, we're close. We just don't get along. My dad never stops harping at me to resign from the U.S. Attorney's Office so I can join him in his private practice. He takes it as a personal affront that I won't."

She swirled her wine. "And you don't want to go into private practice?"

"Especially not with him. But we were discussing your problem with the missing bowl."

Before he could stop himself, Reese tucked an errant lock of hair behind her ear. The blond strand was as soft as he'd imagined.

"Tell me if I've got this straight," he said.

She picked up her wine again and took a cautious sip, then leaned against the sofa, raising a wary gaze. He wondered what worried her.

"You believe that by giving the bowl to the ashram, you somehow erase all the previous sins of your family?"

"I hoped it would erase at least some of them, even if just symbolically." Taki stared into the deep red liquid in her glass and sighed. "But, oh, no. I had to leave the bowl in the Jeep, so certain no one would want it, that the security guard would prevent any theft. What was I thinking after traveling all the way to Tibet?" Concern wrinkled her delicate brow. "I wonder if that carelessness makes the whole situation worse." She looked up. "What do you think?"

Reese crooked his arm on the back of the sofa and leaned against it. "My first thought is to argue mitigating circumstances."

She flushed, and he wanted to touch her cheek and

tell her she was delightful. He took a swallow of wine as Taki threw him a challenging look.

"This is all a big joke to you, isn't it?" she asked.

"No. I want my briefcase back as badly as you want your bowl of salvation."

"But you think I'm completely bonkers."

"I think you're lovely." Reese entwined his fingers in hers and lifted. He kissed the back of her hand, finding it soft and smooth. "And, yes, maybe just a little bonkers." Fascinated by the stubborn expression that washed across her flushed face, he released her fingers.

"Should I contact you if I get another message from the thief?" she asked.

"Definitely. And don't meet anyone again without backup."

She wrinkled her nose. "Backup?"

"Call it what you want, just promise not to go alone."

"Sorry," she said. "I can't promise. That would be a lie. I want my bowl too much, but I'll take extra precautions."

He wondered what extra precautions she had in mind. "I'll give you Agent Rivas's phone number," he said, removing a business card from his wallet. "If I'm not available, call him. He can send an agent."

She accepted the card. "You're giving orders again, General Beauchamps."

"Sorry. Bad habit." What did it matter? Reese thought, suspecting she disregarded orders as easily as he gave them.

"That's okay," she said. "I'm getting used to it."

"Yeah, I know. You just ignore me."

"I always ignore lawyers."

"Have you had a lot of experience ignoring attorneys?"

Her face closed off to him then, and he wondered why. What had happened in Taki's past that she hated lawyers? Had she been involved with her family's crimes? Is that why she was so protective of her phone number?

"Any experience is too much," she said.

Good dodge, he thought, and searched for a neutral topic. "Tell me about your name."

"My name?" she asked in a voice he could only describe as cautious. Again he wondered about her secrets.

"I know you weren't born with the name Taki. How did you come by it?"

"Oh," she said. "My guru gave it to me."

"Your *guru?*" Reese shook his head. "You have a guru?"

"Yes, I do. Guru Navi. He's been my teacher since I was eighteen when I met him following a lecture."

"Okay. Go on. Your guru changed your name because…"

"As a symbol of a new beginning. A new name, new beginning. Navi is my spiritual guide."

"How old is he?" Out of nowhere, Reese irrationally hoped that this guru she spoke of with such affection was Shinhoster's age at least. Even older would be better.

"I never thought about it." She grinned. "Ageless, I guess. Or timeless anyway."

"He lives at this ashram?"

"Half the year here, half the year in India. He's in Miami until June."

"Smart guru," Reese said. "He jets out just when the weather starts to get nasty and buggy."

"It's just as hot in India," she said. "Hotter in some places. And you're wrong about Navi. He has helped me more than you can imagine."

Reese decided to run a check on the ashram to make sure the place was legit. It seemed strange that a well-meaning spiritual guide would send a woman with no money on an expensive trip to Tibet. Could the guru have had something to do with the meet at Puerto Sagua?

He took a drink of the delicious wine, wondering if he was actually jealous of a guru.

"This is excellent," he said. He picked up the bottle, but the print was too damn small, so he couldn't read the year. Working twelve hours a day had ruined his eyesight.

"It was a gift," she said.

"Does the name Taki mean anything?" he asked, replacing the bottle.

She gathered her long hair behind her, then draped it across one shoulder. "Navi calls me his little seeker because I'm always searching."

Without thinking, Reese lifted a lock of her blond hair and rubbed his thumb across the silky strands.

"What are you searching for?" When their eyes

met, Reese wondered at the emotion he read there. She moistened her full lips with the tip of her tongue.

"Happiness," she said softly. "Forgiveness."

"How could anyone not forgive you?" he murmured, cupping her cheek. He stroked his thumb across satin-smooth skin, thinking her the most enigmatic woman he'd ever met, full of enchanting contradictions. Her blue eyes widened, but she didn't pull away.

When Reese lowered his mouth to hers, she closed her eyes. Her soft lips were warm and willing, and Reese explored her mouth hungrily, tasting fine wine and enjoying the tiny noises issuing from the back of her throat.

Kissing Taki was a lot easier than trying to figure her out.

CHAPTER FIVE

EVEN IF REBORN a thousand times, Taki knew she would never forget the power of this kiss. Reese took possession of her mouth the way he dominated everything in his path, and his intimate, velvet warmth sent shivers of desire dancing through her.

She made a small sound of protest when he released the pressure on her lips. Reluctantly, she opened her eyes and focused on the area just above his loosened collar. Inhaling his spicy aftershave, a scent she knew she'd forever associate with him, her gaze traveled to his mouth barely an inch away. She lifted her face, wanting to kiss him again, to go on kissing him until...

"Taki, I..." His breath feathered across her cheek as he trailed off, seeming unsure of himself for the first time.

She dropped her chin and pulled back. Reality checked in again, and with it came tons of baggage. For a brief time-out, though, while his mouth made love to hers, nothing had been important but him.

"Should I apologize for that?" he asked, searching her eyes. "Because I'm really not sorry."

"Me, neither," she whispered. And she wasn't. Reese really knew how to kiss.

She averted her eyes, not wanting him to see what she was feeling. She couldn't let anything romantic get started with Reese. The man set her emotions on fire, and such turmoil was all wrong for her. She required tranquility in her life. She'd had enough upheaval.

An awkward silence stretched out.

"It's getting late." He placed his wine on the rattan table but made no motion to rise. Neither of them knew what to do now, she thought, where to go after that amazing kiss. Or at least it had been amazing for her.

"Am I that bad of a kisser?" she asked in an attempt to lighten the mood. Everything had gone all serious between them.

"God, no." He shot her such a startled look that she felt a little better.

"Another meeting, then?" she asked. After beating herself up for letting him in, now she didn't want him to go.

He frowned, and the ever-present wrinkle between his thick brows deepened. She wondered if that worry line ever totally went away. Did he ever relax? Their sensual kiss had generated a glow of tenderness for this driven, ambitious man, and she worried his work schedule would eventually make him sick. Or mean, like her father. Oh, she hoped Reese wasn't totally like her father. Reese might be impatient, always in too much of a hurry, but she saw no sign of cruelty.

And now she was thinking of her father again.

"Not a meeting, but I still have some things to do tonight," he said.

"Then you'd better go." Looking down, Taki ran a finger over the frayed brocade fabric of her sofa. "Guru Navi says we all have to follow our own path."

"Guru Navi says a lot of things," Reese muttered.

"He's a very wise man."

"Listen, Taki—" Reese hesitated.

"Yes?"

"Have you considered the idea that your guru could have set up the meet at Puerto Sagua?"

"What?" Horrified, Taki stared at Reese. Where had he come up with that absurd idea? That was worse than accusing Benny. "Navi didn't steal my bowl. Why would he? I was going to give it to him."

"I don't think he stole it, but maybe…"

"What?" she demanded.

"Maybe he's throwing you another challenge to purify your…blighted soul. Don't you believe that by completing difficult tasks you can work your way into heaven? Or is it nirvana?"

"That's ridiculous," she said, her surge of affection for Reese evaporating. "Navi knew how upset I was over the theft."

"Well, someone is playing games and—"

"It wasn't Navi." She stood, outrage mushrooming that Reese could accuse sweet, gentle Navi of such hateful actions. "You don't know him."

"Okay. Calm down." Reese rose beside her. "You have to admit that the circumstances of the meeting tonight were strange. I'm merely considering all the possibilities."

"That Navi would deliberately make me feel any worse is not a possibility. Lawyers are the only people who enjoy making my life miserable."

Reese's face tightened at her words. "I'd better go," he said, his voice cold. "Thanks for the wine."

"You're welcome." She clamped her lips together so she wouldn't babble anything else. Why had she said that? She knew better. Yoga had taught her not to react, to stay calm. But Reese did something to her insides, a sensual something that disrupted her serenity and made her act in a not-so-nice way.

As she followed him to the door, she wished she could grab her angry words and stuff them back into her mouth, a mouth that still throbbed from the intimacy of their kiss. Reese wasn't one of her father's conniving lawyers. Reese worked for the good guys. He wanted to provide justice in the world, his own version of karma.

But maybe it was better this way.

She locked the door behind him and leaned against it, closing her eyes, wallowing in misery. But why? Because of her argument with Reese, or the fact that he'd left?

No. Of course it was her bowl. She needed to find her bowl.

REESE DECIDED TO go for an early run the next morning, an old habit he'd gotten away from as his workload had increased. Rain or shine, he used to jog every day before the sun came up, but now he used that time either to work at home or go in to the office early.

As he laced up his old running shoes, he thought about how that had happened. The change had been gradual because of deadlines or emergencies. He'd skip one morning and then another, and now he couldn't remember his last predawn run.

But Taki was right about one thing, anyway. He needed an outlet to blow off the stress of his job.

He spent most of the jog thinking about her, reliving their strange evening at Puerto Sagua and later. But pounding the pavement, even the sweat running down his chest, felt damn good, energized him. He promised himself to buy new shoes and resume this ritual.

Even though it was Saturday, after a quick shower and breakfast, he drove into the office to continue preparing for the Romero trial.

Seated at his desk, his attention too often wandered to the mystifying encounter he'd had with Taki the night before.

Although there'd been no mystery about how much they'd both enjoyed that kiss.

He wanted to see her again. No, he wanted to kiss her again. Hell, he wanted to do a lot more than just kiss her.

With a groan, he refocused on the edition of the *Southern Reporter* open before him, trying to recall the reason he'd looked up this old case. Pretty dry stuff. Taki was a lot juicier.

Reese swiveled to his computer and entered "Paradise Way Ashram" into the search engine. The image of a graceful, domed white building known as the "Temple of Tranquility" materialized on the screen. Oriental-style text informed him that yoga and meditation retreats were offered here—for a price—every week. But considering that vegetarian or vegan meals and lodging were included, really not a bad deal.

Clicking through photographs of the grounds, he found sheltered gardens where guests could go for silent meditation, other secluded areas with hammocks strung between trees. He had to admit the place looked peaceful, even inviting. Just where was this Temple of Tranquility located?

He checked the address and sat back, thinking. Previously a private home, the ashram was situated next to a state park, one of the few areas in Miami Beach where single family homes still existed directly on the Atlantic Ocean. Off Collins and hidden behind landscaping, he'd never realized this beautiful sanctuary existed. Probably few people did.

Was a commercial enterprise legal in this location? He checked the zoning and found that Paradise Way Foundation had legally been grandfathered in over forty years ago. The ashram had been functioning without any violations or complaints since. How rare was that on politically volatile Miami Beach?

A few more keystrokes gave him the information he wanted on Taki's Guru Navi. Navi had started his foundation and built the refuge on Miami Beach at the same time. Any profits from the Miami Beach property supported a sister ashram in Pune, India, as well as a health initiative for children at risk in the province. Navi had studied directly under some celebrated yogi master—a complicated Indian name Reese didn't recognize, but knew Taki would. The county database revealed no wants and no warrants.

So her guru appeared to be a good man and totally legit.

Even better, looking at his photograph, which wasn't even recent, he had to be closing in on ninety.

AFTER A FULL day of legal research, Reese joined his mother for dinner at the Bellini Bistro located in the mezzanine of her Bal Harbour condo, an event that occurred at least once a month no matter how absorbed either was in work.

When he arrived, she'd already ordered a bottle of her favorite red wine, which was open and breathing while she chatted with a man standing beside her he didn't recognize.

"Hi, Mom," Reese said, giving her a quick kiss on her cheek, inhaling the pleasant floral scent she always wore.

"Raul, this is my son, Reese. Raul lives on the floor above me," she told Reese, handling the introduction in her usual skillful manner.

"Good to meet you." Reese shook the man's hand and sat across from his mother.

She continued her conversation with her neighbor while Reese poured wine and took a sip. Good, of course, as always, but he didn't enjoy it nearly as much as the wine he'd shared with Taki the night before.

When he'd wanted to rip off her clothes and take her right there on the sofa in the midst of her quirky artifacts. And then he'd infuriated her by daring to besmirch the good name of her exalted guru.

How could he blame her, though? From what he'd learned, the man was practically a saint. Reese frowned. Wrong religion. Or was yoga even a religion?

"What's bothering you tonight, Reese?"

Something in his mother's tone had altered. That change rather than her words finally pulled Reese away from thinking about Taki.

"What?" he asked, refocusing on his mom, realizing Raul the neighbor had returned to his own table.

"You haven't heard one word I've said," she said with a gently chiding smile.

"Sorry. I have a lot on my mind."

"The Romero case?"

Reese nodded.

"When does the trial begin?"

"Two weeks from Monday."

"Any word yet from your missing witness?"

"Nothing."

"So." His mother drummed her manicured nails on the tablecloth. "I take it you don't want to discuss your work."

He sighed. "Not really, Mom."

When her arched eyebrows rose gracefully, Reese knew his mother was formulating another battle plan to determine what was distracting him. A youthful sixty, Katherine Beauchamps power-walked the beach boardwalk every morning. She possessed more than the normal ration of energy, and Reese believed he'd inherited his ambition from his M.D. mother, not his lawyer father.

"There's definitely something different about you tonight." Katherine took a sip of wine, then blotted her lips with a linen napkin. "You're not...focused. What's going on?"

"Probably too much work." *Hadn't Taki told me as much?*

"No, that's not it." His mother smiled, and Reese sensed she understood something he didn't.

"You know, darling," she said as she buttered a roll, "if you're really serious about running for office, you'll need a proper wife. You may think it old-fashioned, but voters don't often trust bachelors."

Again his thoughts strayed to Taki. He smothered a grin as he pictured her in the role of a proper political wife...then caught himself in amazement. Where had that ludicrous notion come from? Taki was the last woman he should ever consider for a partner. As if she'd be interested, what with the negative energy involved in politics.

He shook his head. "I won't need a wife until the time is right to run. Marriage is at least five years in the future."

"I see. What about children? You'll be thirty-five in five years."

"You know that I don't have time for a family right now. Where is this coming from, Mother?"

The waiter arrived before his mother could continue her inquisition.

"I'll have the lobster tonight, Julio," his mother requested. "Reese?"

Reese ordered a salad, filet mignon, medium rare, and a baked potato, thinking Taki would definitely disapprove of his menu selection. *Unhealthy and unexciting. When did I become so boring?*

When the waiter stepped away his mother said, "Reese, life does not always flow on a carefully thought-out schedule."

He took a sip of wine. "There's nothing wrong with making plans."

"And does everything always unfold just as you planned it?"

"Not always," he admitted, "or I'd know Claudia Romero's location."

"Remember that when you meet someone." She leaned toward him. "Have you met someone?"

With his hand still on the wineglass, he eyed his mother steadily. "I meet people every day."

"I meant a woman. The level of distraction you're displaying can only be the result of a romantic entanglement."

"Mom, you're a great neurologist, but not a shrink."

"I'm your mother. *Is* there someone new in your life?" she asked with what he realized was a touch of hope.

"No," he answered with a sigh, giving up. "The last woman I met can't stand attorneys."

"Ah," his mother said. "Someone above your usual selection, then. A woman with character."

"You married a lawyer," he said and immediately regretted the words.

His mother rolled her eyes. "Don't remind me. How is your father anyway?"

"The same," Reese said cautiously. He usually made a point of never discussing one divorced parent with the other. Such a conversation always led to trouble. The acrimony that existed between his mother and father was a large part of the reason he'd avoided a serious relationship. Even after ten years, the fallout from his parents' bitter divorce could still sting.

"No doubt your father remains more interested in his golf game than—" Katherine paused and smoothed her palm across her hair, tucking errant locks into a bun. "I'm doing it again, aren't I?" She reached across the table and squeezed his hand with a strong grip. "I'm sorry, Reese."

He smiled at her, wishing he could ease the hurt she'd endured because of his father's betrayals.

"So why doesn't she like lawyers?"

When his mother sat back with her own wine, he briefly considered that her flash of remorse might have been staged, a devious method of learning what she really wanted to know.

"I'm not sure," he said. "Taki is actually quite secretive."

"Oooh, a woman of mystery. How did you meet her?"

"She teaches yoga at SoBe Spa."

Katherine's eyes widened. "You're taking yoga lessons?"

He didn't like his mother's incredulous tone. "I've been to one class."

"Good Lord, Reese."

"What's wrong with yoga? I rather enjoyed it."

"There's nothing wrong with yoga," she said. "Of course it's a wonderful idea, exactly what you need, but completely out of character for you. You're more the racquetball or solitary long-distance runner type."

"I still play racquetball," he said. *Long-distance runner? I used to be, but that was a long time ago. Or, as Taki might say, in another life.*

Another life? He groaned inwardly at his thoughts. Did she truly believe she'd lived through a previous existence?

His mom remained silent when Julio arrived with their Caesar salads, sprinkled parmesan cheese, then completed the ritual by grinding pepper onto the crisp romaine.

"A yoga teacher, my, my," Katherine said. "Where have you taken her to dinner?"

"Nowhere. She's a vegetarian."

"It's my understanding that vegetarians do eat. The Unicorn is a lovely vegan restaurant. Delicious food. Invite her there."

"No point, Mom. I don't have a prayer with Taki. Like I said, she hates lawyers."

"Well, I'm liking her very much already," Katherine said as he took a bite of the savory salad.

The Unicorn? he wondered. Would Taki agree to

go out with him? Maybe he could offer dinner as an apology for daring to insult the great guru.

What he ought to do was focus on finding her precious bowl. That's what would earn her forgiveness.

"TAKI? ARE YOU home, dear? I have news."

Taki terminated a futile attempt at meditation when she heard the high, breathy voice of her next-door neighbor and landlady. Delighted by the unexpected visit, Taki blew out her candle, flipped on a light and flung open her front door. Victoria Van Buren was her favorite person in the entire cosmos and definitely better for her frame of mind than trying—and failing—to focus on anything other than Reese Beauchamps.

"Hey, Victoria. How's your hand?" Last month, Victoria had taken a nasty fall at her seventieth birthday party, a grand gala held under moonlight in the formal gardens of Villa Vizcaya, the old Deering Estate.

Rotating her right wrist clockwise, then counterclockwise, Victoria stood in the doorway.

"No pain, no gain," she said.

"That's a terrible philosophy," Taki said, hands on her hips. "You need to be more careful."

Victoria swept into the cottage. "Such a nag. Really, Taki."

Taki considered Victoria beautiful—a regal, genuine lady with prominent graceful cheekbones and eyes that still retained a flirty tinge of green. A soft halo of elegantly styled white hair surrounded her deeply lined face. Taki was certain Victoria had once been the most popular belle of every ball, and her friend's infectious energy immediately cured Taki's restless mood.

"Do not offer me any of your horrible tea, dear," Victoria said. "Have you got any of my bourbon left?"

"Of course. You always keep me well stocked."

"I prefer my deep relaxation the old-fashioned way," Victoria said with a wink.

Taki laughed and moved toward her tiny kitchen. "Right, and tonight I'm going to join you."

"Really, dear? That's lovely." Victoria frowned. "You must not have had any luck with the pawn-shops."

"None."

Victoria sighed. "Such dreadful places."

Taki pushed a chair to the kitchen to retrieve a bottle of bourbon from the cabinet over her sink. "Guess what?" she said as she stepped onto the chair. "I had lunch with the attorney I told you about, the one who lost his briefcase."

"Really?" Victoria's voice rose a few decibels while her faded green eyes grew round. "Part of my news concerns him. I asked around my club if anyone knew him. Amy Ann says Reese Beauchamps is going places in Florida politics, that he comes from an established family."

"A politician. Just what I need." Taki grabbed a bottle of Victoria's favorite whiskey and jumped off the chair.

Victoria handed Taki two crystal tumblers.

"Damn," Taki said, picturing Reese's full gorgeous mouth as it had descended on hers. "I can't see him anymore."

"You're seeing him?"

Victoria's excited voice brought Taki back to the present. "No, I'm not seeing him the way you think."

"Dorothy says he's extraordinarily handsome."

Now an appealing image of Reese in his gym clothes flashed through Taki's mind, but she shrugged away the memory. "Not my type."

"No, you prefer ancient, bearded holy men."

"Navi is not ancient...just old. Besides, I'll never be able to bond with a mate until I do something to equalize this rotten karma I'm lugging around." Taki poured shots of amber liquid into the crystal, thinking it wouldn't be fair to wish her horrible luck on anyone.

"Taki, Taki." Victoria shook her head as she accepted the whiskey and sat at a small rattan table. "I'll never understand how you can blame yourself for your family's wealth. You did nothing to create it."

"That doesn't matter, Victoria."

"Of course it does."

Taki sat across from her friend and tried once more to make her understand. "I had the best of everything. I lived a life of such total luxury that I can't even..." Taki shook her head. "Anything I wanted, I could have just like that." She snapped her fingers on the last word. "You were at my fourteenth birthday party at the Palm Beach estate, remember?"

Victoria nodded. "I recall it well."

Taki shuddered at the memory. Her father had hired an entire circus. An entire circus! With elephants, a high-wire act, and clowns and—and everything, although *her* party had of course morphed into a social event for her father's business contacts. She'd been forced to curtsy her thanks in front of stuffy old men for whatever extravagant gift they'd brought.

"All that privilege came off the deaths of thousands of people," Taki told Victoria.

"You did not buy the tobacco stock, Taki. Your great-great-grandfather did. You didn't make anyone light a cigarette."

"Don't forget the chemical factories that pollute rivers and lakes." Taki closed her eyes against often-imagined horror. "No one can force me to have anything to do with that money."

Victoria issued a snort. When Taki opened her eyes, her landlady gazed at her steadily. "You Capricorns are all alike—you glory in taking on all the guilt in the world."

"Spare me an astrology reading tonight. I'm too busy trying to figure out what to do next."

"Very well, dear, but I have more news. It's the real reason I came."

"Go on," Taki said, unease creeping into her thoughts.

"I received a call from the venerable law firm of Winslow & Winslow this afternoon," Victoria announced.

"Uh-oh." Taki sat up in the wicker chair, dread now knotting her belly. Her father's favorite New

York law firm. "I'm afraid to ask, but what did they want?"

"They've traced you to Miami."

"Oh, no," Taki whispered. What she'd been dreading had finally occurred. She'd known it would happen eventually.

"A Mr. David Winslow," Victoria continued, "wanted to know if I'd heard from you lately."

"How did they find me?"

"It seems Josh Winslow, David's uncle, remembered that I had been your mother's friend."

"Wow." Overwhelmed by the awful news, Taki slumped back. "I can't believe anyone would make that connection after so many years."

Victoria nodded. "Josh is a sly old buzzard. I remember him well. But don't worry. I told David the last I heard you were hiking through Nepal."

"Oh, Victoria," Taki said, releasing her breath with an explosive rush.

"Now, don't you worry about my karma because I lied." Victoria waved her hand. "It was for a good cause."

"Thanks." Staring into space, seeing nothing, Taki said, "Why won't they leave me alone?"

Victoria patted her hand. "Taki, your father will never stop trying to find you. You're all he has left."

"Don't try to make me feel sorry for him. All he wants is my signature so he can move his money around. You know he's a soulless monster."

"Yes," Victoria agreed. "And he treated your mother horribly."

As Taki swirled the liquid in the crystal, fumes from the strong alcohol confused her senses. She should do her gypsy routine, pack what few belongings would fit in the Jeep and leave Miami right now. Her possessions were merely material things. They didn't matter. She could always find new "things."

But she was so weary of starting over, so tired of leaving everything behind. She thought sadly of her beautiful herbs. Oh, and the lavender was almost ready.

What would it hurt to take just a little more time and keep searching? She'd be careful. She couldn't bolt. Not yet. Not until she found the bowl and presented it to Navi.

"Are you seeing him again?" Victoria asked.

Taki glanced up. "Who?"

"You know who. Reese."

"I hope I never see him again," Taki said, which was true, but also a lie since part of her wished he would knock on her door right this second. Never see Reese again? That seemed so final, so depressing.

"That's probably for the best if you don't want him to learn your true identity," Victoria said.

Taki took a sip of bourbon, thinking she was less worried about Reese learning her identity than how he affected her, stirred up her emotions, made her think about things she wanted to forget.

But what if he came to her yoga class? Of course she couldn't stop Reese from coming to her classes.

Any member of the spa was free to attend. She swallowed the liquor, which burned as it traveled her throat.

If he came, she'd talk to him, and that's when she got into trouble. Maybe she should resign her position at the spa.

No, she couldn't do that. She needed money to eat, to buy gas so she could leave when the time came. She had to be practical and keep teaching. Since he'd been angry over what she'd said about his noble profession, he probably wouldn't come to her class anyway. And if he did come, she'd treat him like any other student.

"You're safe for a while longer, dear," Victoria said, patting her arm again. "I've made certain the Winslows are looking for you on the other side of the world."

REESE NODDED AT the woman seated next to him at the conference table. Mrs. Carol Taylor, an attractive thirty-four-year-old mother of two, had seen Carlos Romero running away from the post office in Plantation the day of the bombing, making her an important witness in his prosecution.

"Can you remember the make of the car?" Reese asked her.

"A silver late-model Buick. I'm sorry, but I didn't get the license plate. I mean, I knew the man was acting odd—that's why I paid attention—but who looks at license numbers?"

"That's fine," Reese said, pleased because her

description matched one of Romero's known vehicles. It'd be easy to make that link to the jury. "Anything else?" he prompted.

She shook her head. "The last thing I remember is Romero leaping into the Buick's backseat and the car screeching away. After that, I—" She shuddered. "There was a horrible, loud *whoosh* when the building exploded. I was thrown back, off my feet. I remember being just so surprised." She swallowed hard, clearly trying to hold back tears. "And then I woke up in the hospital."

"You're doing great," Reese said, pretending to make a note to give her a moment.

"Now I'd like you to look at a series of photographs," Reese told his witness. "Are you up to that?"

"I've identified that man several times already," she said. "I will never forget his face."

"I know that. But please understand the defense will do everything they can to confuse you. I just want you to be very clear in your own mind."

She nodded. "Go ahead. I suppose he'll be in the courtroom, anyway."

Reese spread six photographs on the conference table, all of them resembling the dark-haired, dark-eyed Romero. All men in their forties or fifties, all tall and lean.

Mrs. Taylor jabbed her finger on Romero's photograph without hesitation. "That's the son of a bitch," she said, her voice trembling. She picked up a tissue and dabbed her eyes. "Sorry," she murmured.

"Good job," Reese said with an encouraging smile.

"We're almost done, but do you want to take a break? Are you sure you don't want some water?"

"I think I would like something to drink after all," she said.

"Of course. I'll be right back."

Reese left the conference room and hurried to the office kitchen where they kept soft drinks and bottles of water. He could have asked for Joanne's help, but he wanted to stretch his legs and give Mrs. Taylor a moment alone to compose herself. Would she be able to face down Romero in court without falling apart?

He found Javi Rivas in the kitchen, rummaging around in the refrigerator.

"Looking for someone in there?"

Javi stood up, grinning. "Reese. Just the person I want to see. You got a minute?"

Reese reached past Javi to grab two bottles of water. "I'm in the middle of prepping Carol Taylor."

"I heard." Javi nodded. "This won't take long. My team finally got a lead on your briefcase."

Reese placed the water on the counter and faced Javi. "You've got my attention."

"Bruce Mayhugh, a well-known fence in Homestead, claims Izzo is coming to unload some hot jewelry later this week. We're going to wire the fence and wait for Izzo to show. You good with that?"

"I like that plan," Reese said.

"It could go nowhere," Javi said. "I have my doubts, but at least we can question Izzo and determine once and for all if Romero put him up to the theft." Javi grinned again. "Hey, maybe we can get your beautiful yogini's property back, too."

Reese nodded, his mind now swirling around Taki, how distraught she'd been the night of the theft. Damn, how he'd love to return her bowl to her.

He gave himself a swift mental kick. What the hell? He was more worried about Taki than his own possessions. He'd been considering going to her class tonight, but decided he needed to stay away to keep his head clear. He had an important trial to prepare for, and he still couldn't find the linchpin for his case, Claudia Romero.

Claudia was the woman he should be obsessing about, not Taki.

Javi turned back to the refrigerator. "I know Joanne said something about leftover birthday cake in here."

"I hope Mayhugh gives us something," Reese said on his way out. "Keep me informed."

Was his witness even still alive? If Claudia didn't contact him soon, he'd have to let his boss know.

Now, that's an interview he was definitely not looking forward to. No prosecutor wanted to tell their boss they couldn't find the most important witness in a case.

CHAPTER SIX

THURSDAY NIGHT, REESE pushed open the door to SoBe Spa's yoga room, grabbed a mat and took a seat in the back row. He usually planned everything days in advance, sometimes weeks, so how did he suddenly find himself in Taki's class again?

Smiling serenely, she sat cross-legged in front of the twenty or so students in the room.

He'd managed to avoid her on Monday by burying himself in trial prep, but she'd been on his mind constantly. Tonight was an effort to preserve his sanity. He ached to touch her again. He needed to clear the air with her.

"Close your eyes," she said to begin the session, "and allow your attention to focus on your breath."

Reese did as she instructed and listened to her soothing voice coax the class into that all-important present moment.

"If your mind generates a thought," she cautioned, "and it probably will, just let that thought float away and return to your breath."

During class, watching Taki maneuver her supple yet powerful body into amazing positions, Reese decided he could not be any more in the present moment than he already was. As he followed her simple, helpful instructions into the various poses, his usually churning thoughts gradually ratcheted down. With each stretch, the tension in his limbs released, making him looser and freer, more at ease than since… Damn, he couldn't remember when he'd ever felt like this.

She remained the complete professional, treating him as she did all the other students, no more attention, no less. Now, with his nose buried in a towel and his arms along his sides—she called this "child's pose"—he could no longer observe her. He could hear her gentle, encouraging voice, though, as she circulated through the room, assisting her students. She moved closer and began working with the middle-aged woman on the mat next to him.

Then Taki's bare feet with cute pink toenails were beside him. He held his breath when she placed her warm hands on his back. For days he'd been longing for her touch.

"Inhale," she murmured. He did as she instructed and her fingers slid down his spine to his lumbar area and she said, "Exhale."

As he released his breath, Taki applied gentle, steady pressure to his lower back. He closed his eyes, enjoying the deep stretch and the fleeting touch of her soft breath on his neck.

When she pulled back, her fingertips trailed across his torso with a light touch, and he didn't want those pretty pink toenails to step away.

But they did. She continued to move from student

to student, adjusting when necessary, offering support, teaching the class in her calm, serene manner.

After leading them through a final twist, she said, "Now prepare yourself for the most important asana we'll do tonight." Taki guided them into what she called "savasana," the last pose, the one that allowed deep relaxation.

"Allow your attention to again focus on your breath," she said. "Make your exhalations longer than your inhalations."

Reese settled onto his back and closed his eyes, remembering how great he'd felt after his last yoga session with Taki. He'd slept better that night than he had in years. He sucked in a deep breath and let the air out slowly.

"Roll over onto your right side and assume a fetal position for a few breaths. When you're ready, you can come out of deep relaxation. Stay in the room as long as you like, guys. See you next time."

Reese heard Taki's calm voice as if from far, far away and wondered where he'd been and how long. Not exactly asleep...but not wholly awake. Deep relaxation? Felt as if he'd been floating in midair.

But when Reese rolled over and came fully alert, he caught a glimpse of Taki's tight rear end as she hurried from the yoga room.

She wasn't waiting for him this time.

He jumped to his feet and caught up with her halfway to the parking lot.

"Taki, wait," he called.

She paused beneath a streetlight and turned to look at him questioningly.

So she wasn't going to make it easy for him. He would have walked away from any other woman.

"I'm sorry if I insulted your guru," he said. "I had no right."

Her eyes widened, and he could tell the apology surprised her. Flustered, she lowered her gaze and shifted her stuffed yoga bag from one arm to the other.

Knowing it had to be heavy, he took the bag from her and slung it over his own shoulder.

"Thanks," she said, meeting his gaze again, now smiling.

"So am I forgiven?"

"Of course. You don't know Navi."

Reese didn't correct her, but Taki was wrong. Courtesy of a second, more thorough search of government computers and databases, he now knew her guru probably better than she did. And from everything on record, Guru Navi was an honest, holy man.

"I did it again," she said, shaking her head.

"What?" he asked, trying to follow her train of thought but distracted by the light reflecting off her blond hair.

"Judging you. I expected you to say something mean about Navi, and then you apologized. I have to remember not to prejudge people. Especially you." As she arranged her long hair in front of one shoulder, Reese remembered the feel of her supple hands on his back.

"May I walk you to your car?" he asked. He quirked an eyebrow. "Just in case there are thieves lurking in the night."

They took a few steps in silence while he wrestled with whether to tell her Javi had uncovered a link to Izzo, but decided not to raise her hopes about recovering the bowl. The lead could go nowhere.

"Did you enjoy class?" she asked as they strolled across the lit parking lot.

"Very much," he said. "I think you're right about my need to relax. Lately I've been unproductive at work."

She nodded, her hair catching the glow from the streetlight again. "You need balance in your life, not all work and not all play."

"I know a way you can help me with that."

"Me?" she asked. "How?"

They'd arrived at her Jeep, and Taki rummaged through her cloth purse. Reese smiled at her confusion. She seemed to be having a great deal of difficulty finding something.

He saw what looked like a ball of keys in a pocket of the hoodie she wore and poked the lump with a finger. "Is that what you're looking for?" he asked.

She slipped a hand into the pocket and withdrew her keys. "Thanks. Someday I'll get organized."

Reese reached out and clasped her other hand, giving it a gentle squeeze. "I've heard about a vegetarian restaurant in Aventura called The Unicorn. Would you like to have dinner with me tomorrow night?"

"Oh." Taki opened, then closed her mouth, and

looked away. "No, I'm sorry. A fellow yoga teacher asked me to substitute-teach his class Friday night."

He released her hand, knowing she wasn't telling the whole truth. Prosecutors studied body language to identify the tells when a witness was evading or hiding something they didn't want to reveal. Taki probably had a class to teach—he couldn't imagine her lying outright—but that was only an excuse. She didn't want to have dinner with him.

Disappointed on a number of levels, he handed her the gym bag. "Too bad. Maybe next time."

"Yeah, sure," Taki said, still avoiding his gaze. "Maybe another time."

STRANGELY DEFLATED, TAKI slid behind the wheel of her Jeep and watched Reese's purposeful stride until he disappeared inside SoBe Spa. *Just like my father. Always in such a hurry.*

Darn Reese Beauchamps. Now she was forced to teach Peter's class tomorrow night or else have told a lie. In a way, she'd already fibbed since she hadn't committed to subbing yet.

Inhaling the salty breeze, she strained to hear the roar of the nearby Atlantic Ocean, wave after wave crashing against the sandy beach behind the spa. Like her life, smashing into constant conflict no matter what she did to alter the tumultuous pattern.

Tomorrow would be another perfect day and night in paradise. It would have been lovely to spend the evening with Reese. She wanted to have dinner with him. She shivered as she considered running after him to accept his invitation and wherever it might lead.

When she'd touched him during class, the heat from his body had flowed through her fingers into her arms, creating a unique bond she'd never before experienced with a student. And just now when he'd clasped her hand, she had simply forgotten to breathe.

She remembered the sensation of his touch, reliving the charged, pleasurable shock of the contact. She'd wanted him to kiss her again. She wanted him to pull her into his arms and crush her against his chest.

Disturbed by the erotic flush that warmed her to her fingertips, she glanced at the keys dangling from the ignition and wrapped her hand around the sharp ridges of cold metal.

She'd hated the tight look on his face when she'd turned him down. But she couldn't go out with Reese. They were all wrong for each other. He made her feel too much, caused her to think about the past she'd run away from. Reese threw her normally placid mind into chaos.

He made her think of her father, of how her father had treated her mother and how destructive her parents' relationship had been. Just like her mom and dad, she and Reese were too different. They couldn't help but end up hurting each other.

Taki collapsed against the seat. Victoria was right to caution her to avoid Reese. Refusing his invitation had been the right thing to do.

Taki closed her eyes. *I need help.*

Since their kiss, she thought more about Reese than her missing bowl. Maybe she should make a trip to Cassadaga and consult her psychic. In fact, she probably should have visited Robin first thing. Even if she couldn't help locate the bowl, Robin might have some insight about Reese.

Determined to push away negative thoughts, Taki opened her eyes—then froze when her gaze fell on the corner of white paper barely jutting from her gym bag. With a mounting, excited sense of déjà vu, she flipped on the Jeep's inside light and withdrew a sealed envelope with her name handwritten across the front in block letters.

Where had this come from? Had it been there before Reese took the bag from her? Could he have stuffed the envelope inside?

Another message about her bowl?

She ripped open the envelope and read stiff capital letters, written as if someone were trying to camouflage their writing.

IF YOU WANT TO RECOVER YOUR MISSING PROPERTY, COME TO THIS ADDRESS. DO NOT CONTACT THE AUTHORITIES. COME ALONE.

An address in Homestead, Florida, appeared in bold black ink.

Taki considered and rejected the idea of driving to Homestead immediately. Not a good idea to make the trip at night. She started the Jeep and turned north onto Collins Avenue toward home.

Was it a good idea to go at all? Should she tell Reese?

Yeah, great way to avoid him.

Obviously someone at the spa was responsible for the notes. That much was clear to her now. But who? Benny? He was always around, but so was Debbie. Who else had she seen tonight? Hector? Lourdes?

And of course Reese.

A sick feeling crept into her belly. Couldn't be.

Reese slipping her this message made about as much sense as Navi tricking her, but Reese had a better opportunity to place the envelope in her bag tonight than anyone. She took a deep breath.

What did she really know about his character, anyway? Maybe he wasn't what he seemed. She'd heard of plenty of government officials on the take in Miami. He could have some hidden agenda.

No. Not Reese. She refused to believe that.

Anyone who attended her class was suspect. Hadn't she babbled endlessly about the trip to Asia and her quest for the bowl? Yeah, and everyone also understood she had no money for ransom, so what was this about? And why didn't the notes ask for anything? Why was this message made differently? Did the communication come from two different people? Nothing made any sense.

As she drove home, with the cool breeze rushing against her face, knotting her hair into tangles, Taki wondered if Reese had created the note in order to test her, to see if she would contact him.

No, that was ridiculous. The man didn't have time for silly games. And why would he? But what if he did? What if Reese had some hidden motivation she didn't understand? Could he somehow be working for her father?

No way. That idea was preposterous. He didn't know who she was.

At a red light, she bunched her hair into the beret, still thinking about Reese and any possible motives.

That's all she did—worry about Reese. Victoria was right. To protect her peace of mind, she needed to stay away from him.

Besides, if she told Reese about the second note, what would he do? No question about that. She nodded as she pictured the scene. He'd stop her from driving to Homestead. He'd lock her up if he had to, and she'd lose this chance to recover the bowl. Maybe her last chance.

She'd be extra careful, make sure Victoria knew where she'd gone, take the pepper spray she used when alone in the woods.

Yeah, if he found out, he'd be seriously pissed. She pictured his gorgeous eyes flashing fury, and wished she could smooth away that worry line between them rather than always making it deeper.

She sighed. Reese blurred her focus, and she could no longer permit that. Plus, however unlikely, the timing of this second message made him a suspect.

Taki pulled into the cottage's driveway confident of her decision. She wouldn't tell Reese about the second note since she couldn't totally trust him. She wouldn't call his FBI agent, either, because Javi would immediately inform Reese. Hadn't she already raised one false alarm at Puerto Sagua? Anyway, she didn't have time to wait for an FBI operation, which could take days to coordinate.

She was running out of time. Her father was closing in on her, could locate her any day now. When he did, she'd be forced to pack her Jeep and flee before finding the bowl.

THE NEXT AFTERNOON, Taki pulled her Jeep off a dusty road and braked beside a battered mailbox. She'd gotten lost, had to ask for directions twice, but she'd finally found the address. Or at least she had according to the numbers peeling off the mailbox's metal housing.

Her gaze traveled the long gravel driveway leading to an old coral-rock house. A trickle of unease traced her spine. Towering royal palms and red hibiscus bordered the entrance. Lush landscaping that hadn't been trimmed for years isolated the small structure from the roadway.

Planning her next move, she carefully observed the surroundings. South of the driveway sat run-down shade houses, screens torn, some flapping in a gentle breeze. Row after row of tomato plants had been planted in a huge field to the north. Across the street were more rows of another crop where huge, traveling plumes of water glistened in the afternoon sun.

Definitely rural, and not a soul in sight. The lively, crowded atmosphere of Puerto Sagua had been much easier to deal with.

No one except Victoria even knew she'd come here. Was she being foolish?

Taki inhaled deeply, hoping a breathing exercise would calm her pounding heart. She closed her eyes and allowed the rich smell of farmland to fill her senses, the familiar earthy scent transporting her back to her childhood in Rhode Island. Maybe someday she could stay in one place long enough to plant a real vegetable garden again—not the tiny plot of herbs she managed in Victoria's backyard.

An automobile whizzed by, its speed causing the old mailbox to sway and rattle from the vibration. She eyed the driveway and squared her shoulders. *Come into the present moment, girl. Quit worrying about the unchangeable past and an unknowable future.*

This was Homestead, Florida, in broad daylight, not some scary nighttime Gothic setting.

A hundred yards to the north a perfectly normal blue van was parked beside the tomato field, apparently broken-down, because the hood was propped open as if someone had been working on the engine. The owner was probably somewhere close by.

She was letting Reese's paranoia make her crazy. Besides, his bad guys didn't have anything to do with the disappearance of her bowl. Someone at the spa had taken it, and whoever lived at the end of this driveway knew why. They hadn't asked for money, so maybe Reese was right that someone was playing a mean trick on her. Why, though? And who'd taken Reese's briefcase? It was difficult to believe he was involved, but maybe…

Well, she'd just have to ask whoever answered the door. She'd learned to trust her intuition, and instinct told her no one inside that structure would harm her.

Still, she had promised Reese she'd be careful, take extra precautions. She wanted him to open his mind to new ideas. To be fair, maybe she ought to do the same thing. He wanted her to be more practical, so she'd start right here.

She inched the Jeep forward, the tires crunching along the gravel driveway, still wary. At the first sign of trouble she'd throw her transmission into Reverse and zoom backward out of the property.

When she reached the rock house, she turned her vehicle around 180 degrees so the front faced the driveway. Reese would be proud that she'd planned ahead for a quick getaway.

Turning off the ignition, she leaned over the wheel and listened carefully…for what? Birds chirped. A dog barked. A lawn mower sputtered somewhere in the distance.

Did evil make noise?

Disgusted with her hesitation, trusting her gut feelings, she jumped from the Jeep and climbed two steps onto the front porch of the farmhouse. Just in case, she reached in her bag and removed the tiny vial of pepper spray she carried when she foraged for herbs alone.

A heavy wooden door stood open behind an

aluminum screen. After two unanswered knocks on the metal frame, Taki yelled, "Hello?"

No answer.

With a backward step, she took a quick peek through the front window. Lace curtains shielded the interior. She couldn't see a thing.

"Is anybody home?" she yelled.

A nervous cough caught her attention. She looked back to the door, and a heavyset, balding man appeared wearing a loose beige sweater.

"May I help you?" he asked.

With a sigh of relief, Taki reached into her bag and withdrew a photograph. *What was I worried about? This is going fine.*

"I understand you have some information about this item."

When the man opened the door and accepted the photograph, Taki stepped into the house beside him.

His eyes widened and darted from the picture toward his right. "Now is not a good time. Please come back later."

"I can't," she said. "I have to get back to Miami and teach a class tonight."

The man silently mouthed some words and tapped a small bulge on the right side of his chest.

"Are you all right?" she asked, fearing he could be having a heart attack. No time for any herbal remedy. Thank goodness she knew CPR. Was he going to collapse?

"I'm sorry," he said, way too loudly. "You'll have to

come back another time." He jabbed a thumb toward his right and raised his eyebrows.

She turned in the direction he pointed and saw nothing but a closed door. When she returned her gaze to the agitated man, he'd become deathly pale.

"I think you should sit down," she said.

The instant she reached forward to support him, the closed door burst open. Four clean-cut men ran into the room, their hands wrapped around large guns.

"FBI," one of them yelled. "Hold it right there."

Taki shrieked and stepped back, causing the man to lose his balance. As she caught him, she recognized one of the men rushing forward as the FBI agent who'd been with Reese at Puerto Sagua.

What in the world?

"She's not Izzo," the man said quickly.

All four men lowered their weapons.

"Who the hell are you?" one demanded roughly.

"She's Taki." Reese's agent holstered his gun.

"You know her, Javi?"

"Yeah," Javi said, staring at her with a hard look. "She's come about a bowl."

AFTER WORKING OVER an hour on his opening statement, Reese rubbed his eyes and pushed back from the computer. He was getting nothing accomplished, and that was completely unlike him. Normally, he could focus no matter the circumstances.

But waiting to hear from the FBI, his mind constantly drifted away from the evidence in the Romero trial. He was more concerned about the man he hoped to have in custody any minute.

Javi's sting on the fence in Homestead was happening today. When Izzo showed up to unload hot jewelry, the FBI would be there to question him.

Now maybe he could get Taki's bowl back. He swiveled away from the screen. No...of course he meant to get his briefcase and its contents back, find out if Romero was involved in the theft. How he'd love to generate more evidence against the terrorist.

He shook his head. Thoughts of Taki were seriously interfering with his work. The biggest trial of his career loomed in ten days, and he couldn't stop smarting over rejection by a New Age moonbeam with hair softer than a cloud.

He saved his file to a thumb drive, stretched and moved toward the large window on the bay. A gray mist obscured the view. It had started raining two hours ago, the opening salvo of another cold front that would drop the temperature close to freezing tonight.

Damn, but he needed to focus. Rubbing a hand across his forehead, Reese tried to concentrate on facts. He needed to find Claudia Romero. Yeah, he had her original journal locked up safe in an evidence vault. With her testimony, no question that smoking-gun diary was crammed full of enough dates and names to convict her ex-husband.

But without Claudia to authenticate the pages, the journal was worthless to him as evidence. He had a signed statement, but the court might not allow the jury to consider it.

Where the hell was she? Would she resurface in time for the trial? No way could he get another continuance. If he didn't hear from Claudia by tomorrow, he'd have to pay a visit to his boss and give her the bad news.

He'd studied the journal, picked it apart day by day, had read every deposition she'd ever given and then sent agents to possible locations she could be hiding. But so far nothing had panned out.

His cell phone rang and Reese hurried to the desk. Yes! Javi's number.

Reese grabbed the receiver. "Yeah, Javi?"

"We've got a problem."

Disappointment forced Reese into his leather chair. "What went wrong?"

"Your friend Taki showed up and scared Izzo away."

Certain his mind was again betraying him, Reese didn't immediately reply. He scrubbed fingers across his tired eyes. Javi couldn't have said that Taki scared Izzo away.

"Did you say Taki?"

"You heard me. I'm following her home so she doesn't get into any more trouble. Why don't you meet us there?"

DRIVING TOWARD TAKI'S cottage, Reese went crazy imagining what she'd done. And even though she hadn't promised not to, a smoldering sense of betrayal ate at him because she'd gone looking for the bowl without telling him.

It was a damn good thing it took twenty minutes to drive from his downtown office to Miami Beach because he needed every bit of that time to wrestle his temper under control.

She was doing everything in her power to push him away, and it made him angrier by the minute because it didn't make sense. As she'd refused his invitation to dinner, her eyes had told him she really wanted to say yes. But yet… He shook his head.

He believed her incapable of telling a lie. Even with all her secrets, he'd never met anyone more giving in his life, more eager to help everyone she met. His office receptionist was thrilled because some remedy Taki had suggested had cured her morning sickness. Robert Shinhoster, the IRS employee with a bad back, hadn't showed up at the office lately, either.

Reese frowned as he recalled her words. She searched for "happiness" and "forgiveness." Shit. Everyone wanted happiness. No surprise there. He sensed some inner sadness about her, that she was afraid of something. Did that sorrow have anything to do with her criminal family? Was fear the reason she was so private?

And forgiveness for what? Terminal stupidity?

Right now he wasn't sure he could forgive her for what he considered incredibly reckless behavior.

When he pulled into the estate where Taki lived, an older woman struggled to push a lawn mower through thick grass in the front yard. She wore earbuds and didn't glance his way, so he kept driving to Taki's rear cottage where he exited his Jag and slammed the door with a satisfying *bang,* noting her Jeep and Javi's government-issue Crown Vic were both covered in dirt.

Javi met him at the door. It didn't improve his mood that the agent didn't try to suppress an amused grin.

"Where is she?" Reese demanded, stepping inside.

"Calm down, man," Javi said. "She's waiting on the sofa."

Taki met his gaze unflinchingly when he walked toward her. She lifted her chin, as she released a huge sigh.

God, she was beautiful. Reese tore his gaze from her and swiveled to Javi.

"Tell me what happened."

Cold fury closed in on Reese as he listened to Javi's clipped, professional recitation of the afternoon's events. If Romero's man Izzo had shown up even close to the time Taki had ventured to Mayhugh's den, she could easily have been killed.

Romero didn't like witnesses. His ex-wife had gone into hiding, believing it was the best way to stay alive.

With her usual excellent posture, Taki remained quiet on her couch, attentively listening to Javi, occasionally nodding her head.

The second note lay on the rattan table before her. Reese glared at it and wondered if she'd already had the message when they'd spoken at the spa last night—when she had refused his dinner invitation. Had guilt been the reason she'd said no? Why hadn't she told him about the message?

"Mayhugh believes Izzo will try to set the buy-up

again tomorrow," Javi concluded. "I doubt it. Izzo hasn't eluded arrest this long because he's stupid, but maybe we'll get lucky. I'll let you know."

"What did Mayhugh have to say about this message?"

Javi shrugged. "Mayhugh insists he had no knowledge of the note or any singing bowl. He says the whole thing is a joke or a mistake."

"Yeah, right," Reese said.

"We'll keep working on Mayhugh, but I don't want to press him too hard until we see if Izzo shows tomorrow. I want to keep the fence cooperative."

"That makes sense," Reese agreed.

At the door, Javi grinned and patted Reese's shoulder. "Try to keep that loose cannon in there out of my way."

Reese nodded. *As if I have any control over her.*

Taki's blue eyes regarded him warily when he returned to her. She ought to be nervous, he thought, begrudgingly admiring her undaunted spirit. Loosening his tie, he paced her small living room.

"What were you doing at Mayhugh's?" Years of trial work had taught Reese how to control his voice, how never to reveal his thoughts. But tonight, as he glared at Taki sitting serenely on her couch, he didn't care that he sounded angry. "I thought you had a yoga class to teach."

"I did." Taki pulled her feet up on the sofa and wrapped her arms around her shins. "But the FBI wouldn't let me leave. They thought the Izzo guy might still show. They wouldn't even let me make a phone call." She laid her cheek on her knees. "I can't believe I let Peter's students down."

Startled, Reese stopped his restless movement. She wasn't the least remorseful about causing him to lose Izzo and a shot at the stolen goods. She was only upset because she'd missed a damn yoga class.

"They finally called the whole thing off. Javi decided Izzo probably took off when he saw my Jeep." She sighed. "This is just awful."

"Let me get this straight…" Reese stared at Taki when she lifted her face, but for the moment he was too furious to continue. Furious at her and at himself for his obvious blind spot when it came to this bewildering enigma from another dimension. She'd managed to thwart his chance to locate his briefcase and who knows, maybe his witness, yet he was glad to see her.

He took a deep breath. And damned glad she hadn't been harmed.

One thing was for sure. He was definitely in the present moment. And he was trying to figure out why she always insisted that was such a good thing. He felt pretty damn crappy.

He loomed over her with hands plunged deep into his pockets. "I was in my office all day today. Funny thing. I never received a phone call from you concerning another note."

"No." She didn't look away, blue eyes steady on his. "I decided not to call you."

"Why?"

"I didn't want to be the girl who cries wolf."

Once again Reese knew she wasn't telling the whole truth, and he wanted to know why. Why was she pushing him away so hard and so fast? It baffled him, especially since she insisted they had some sort of cosmic connection. He doubted it had anything to do with the cosmos, but she pulled him with a draw that grew stronger by the minute.

"You know what you've done, don't you?"

She nodded, looking miserable. "I scared away the man who has your briefcase."

"And your bowl," Reese pointed out.

"No. Mr. Mayhugh has my bowl."

"I don't think so. The FBI turned his home inside out. They didn't find any of the stolen items."

"Well, Mayhugh knows where my bowl is. Because the FBI were—" she rolled her eyes "—everywhere, we weren't able to have a discussion, but I know he has it. I'm going back tomorrow."

"What?" Reese moved swiftly to Taki and sat beside her. He grabbed her upper arms. "Don't be a fool."

Before he knew what he was doing, his thumbs caressed her soft skin, stroking the muscle that lay beneath. But touching her only intensified his frustration. Her moist lips parted, and he instantly knew she welcomed their physical contact as much as he.

"Haven't you heard anything I've said?" he demanded. "These people are ruthless. Bruce Mayhugh is one of the most notorious fences in Florida."

"But he—" she began.

"You heard Javi. He's going to reset the meet."

Reese released her and sat back. Being close to Taki muddled his senses.

"You can't go down there tomorrow. If you get in Izzo's way, he won't think twice about getting rid of you. He won't care how beautiful you are, how gentle—" Reese sucked air deep into his lungs "—how naive."

Taki's eyes widened in surprise, and then she shook her head, looking sad. "Believe me, Reese, I'm not naive."

The sound of his name on her lips shot a tiny thrill through him, made him wish she spoke his name more often. And the regret that tinged her words intrigued him. Damn, but she had her secrets.

"You're too trusting," he said finally.

"It's just that—and I know you'll think this is crazy—but I believe that we make our own reality. If we think negative thoughts, then negative events will follow."

"You can't believe that thinking positive thoughts will make everything turn out the way you want." He shook his head. "Surely you know that's not true."

"But it's what I believe."

Reese wanted to grab her again and shake some sense into her, but knew that if he touched her, he'd kiss her and never stop.

"Or anyway, staying positive can't hurt," she continued.

"Taki, please."

"On the practical side, thanks to you, I took my pepper spray." She withdrew a small cylinder from her pocket and showed it to him. "I'd have used it, too." She lowered her gaze. "At least I think I would have. And my landlady knew where I was. I didn't feel any danger going into that house today."

"You didn't *feel* any danger? Listen to yourself."

After a pause, she said, "Okay. I won't go back until you tell me it's safe."

Relief flooded him until her eyes opened wide again.

"Or maybe Mayhugh will contact me again. Believe me, he knows something about the bowl. Before the FBI burst in he was trying to tell me something."

Before he could stop himself, Reese grasped her hand and interlaced their fingers. "Just wait until I tell you it's okay. Javi will interrogate Mayhugh again about the second note. I agree he must know something. We'll find out what."

"Hmm." When she lowered her eyes, he felt the heat of her gaze as she studied their joined hands. Suddenly it seemed as though the entire world centered on that small area where they were in contact. She inhaled deeply, her breasts rising with the movement.

"Was that a yes?" he asked softly. "You promise not to go?"

"Why am I starting to listen to your orders?"

"When did you start that?" Reese asked, swallowing hard against desire that was building to unmanageable intensity. "Clearly, not earlier today."

"No." She sighed and looked up, blue eyes bright. "I'm sorry if I scared off Izzo and ruined your stakeout. But communication works both ways, you know. You could have told me about your plan."

"I couldn't," Reese said, thinking her maddening, impossible and fascinating. "It was an FBI operation."

She continued to study him, a tentative smile curving her lips.

"Momma said there'd be days like this," he murmured, remembering the words to an old song. Her smile deepened.

Neither of them spoke for a moment. "I feel so close to you right now," she whispered. "Do you feel it, too?"

Reese sucked in a quick breath, then released it. "Yes."

And it was true. He did feel somehow connected to Taki. What had happened to his common sense? His usual levelheadedness must have fled at the same time as his sense of balance. And that had all occurred when he'd met her.

She raised her hand to his cheek, stroking his face as if caressing a precious keepsake.

"I know I met you for a reason," she said, her voice full of wonder.

"Taki, I…" He cupped her neck with both hands and pulled her toward him, never wanting to let her go.

He groaned as her soft, warm lips parted beneath his. His breath caught in his throat when she slid her hands up his chest, probing the flesh beneath his shirt with gentle pressure, leaving a wake of aching need. As her hands smoothed behind his neck and into his hair, Reese slanted his mouth against hers and pulled her closer. She arched into his embrace, and he thought of nothing but making slow, sweet, endless love to Taki. He wanted to bury himself in her and never—

"Taki? Are you home, dear?" An elderly, feminine voice penetrated his sensual fog.

CHAPTER SEVEN

TAKI HEARD VICTORIA'S breathless voice and the kitchen door opening but chose to ignore it. Right now she definitely wanted to make her own reality. She wanted to make Victoria go away. She wanted Reese to continue kissing her.

But he pulled back, and his hand slid down her shoulder. In the confusion of her senses, she shivered from emotion she dared not explore.

"In here, Victoria," Taki said, her voice barely rising above a whisper, her gaze lingering on Reese's beckoning mouth.

He cursed and exhaled roughly.

"There you are. I've confirmed your— Oh." Victoria halted midsentence when she entered the tiny living room. A sly smile softened her face.

"I'm sorry, dear. I didn't know you had company."

"Victoria, this is Reese Beauchamps," Taki managed, her thoughts clearing way too slowly.

Reese stood and nodded respectfully to Victoria. He cleared his throat. "Ma'am," he said, his voice husky.

"Sit down," Victoria said, eyeing Reese with a knowing smirk. "I'm so sorry I interrupted."

Taki took a deep breath as Reese rejoined her on the sofa, her stomach clenching as she faced the reality that once again Reese's kisses had sucked her into mindless passion.

They'd be in her bed right now if her friend hadn't dropped by. Good thing Victoria had used the side door. If her landlady had come around front, she would have seen Reese's Jag and probably gone home. To think she'd actually wished Victoria would disappear!

"Have a seat...please." Taki used her eyes to beg Victoria to stay, not daring to look at Reese. Not that she needed to. Even though no part of her body touched him, she could feel his heat, as if his lips still devoured hers. And, Buddha help her, she wished they still did.

What kind of pull on her did Reese have? How could a kiss make her totally lose herself, forget everything? All she wanted to do was climb inside him and never come up for air.

"What...what did you say, Victoria? You've confirmed something?" Taki asked.

"Robin is expecting you at four tomorrow afternoon for your reading," Victoria said, perching on a tapestry-covered footstool, her green eyes bright and amused.

In an attempt to ground herself, Taki noted Victoria was dressed in loose shorts and a grass-stained blouse. She'd probably been in her yard or working with her roses.

"She's looking forward to consulting with you again," Victoria continued.

Expecting me? Consulting? Oh, right. Robin. The reading.

"Excellent," Taki said, relieved to have something to focus on besides Reese. "I'll leave early tomorrow morning."

"She said to be sure to bring a photograph of the bowl," Victoria said, "and anything it might have touched."

"What's this about the bowl?" Reese demanded. "What kind of reading?"

Taki dared to shoot him a quick glance. Of course he'd recovered more quickly than she. He was already frowning, the worry lines in his forehead deeply furrowed. Just great. Now she had to tell him she was consulting a psychic, and he'd object. Or worse, laugh.

Why did she find it so difficult to explain anything to Reese? And why should she even care if he believed in her methods?

"I've thought of a new way to locate the bowl," she began. "I know an excellent psychic in Cassadaga that I consult on difficult matters."

"A psychic?" Reese's frown intensified. "Seriously? Like a palm reader?"

"Well, sometimes Robin does read my palm," Taki admitted.

He stared at her. "Have you received another message that I don't know about? One from another dimension?"

"No, no," Taki said, knowing she probably deserved his sharp question. "I just want to ask her if she has a sense of where the bowl might be. She can be wonderfully insightful."

"I see." Reese rubbed fingers across his chin, and Taki heard the scratch of his five o'clock shadow. She traced the determined set of his jaw with her gaze. What was he thinking? Probably that she was a complete whack job.

"And that's all there is to it?" he asked. "You're sure?"

"No," Victoria said.

Taki threw Victoria a look to shut her up, but she just smiled.

"She was going to ask about you, too," Victoria announced importantly.

If Taki weren't so furious at Victoria for her outrageous remark, she would have laughed at the mystified expression blooming across Reese's face.

"Me? What about me?" he asked.

Taki glared at Victoria, thinking her white hair didn't look at all like a halo anymore. When Taki returned her attention to Reese, she felt as if he were looking into her soul again. She wondered what he could see.

"I need to know whether or not I can trust you," she explained.

"I should be going." Victoria came to her feet with exaggerated determination.

Taki sent Victoria the most imploring expression she could muster, but her friend merely laughed, waved and left the way she'd come.

Taki folded her arms across her chest. Why had she told Victoria anything about Reese? And why did she ache all over for him to touch her again?

"Why don't you trust me?" he asked quietly.

Taki swallowed hard. "It's just I've had some… problems with lawyers in the past."

He nodded. "Legal matters can be rough, but we're not all sharks."

"And, well, don't get mad again, but I found the note buried in my yoga bag right after you so nicely carried it for me."

Reese narrowed his eyes at her. "Yeah? And?"

"So I thought maybe you had—" She paused. "So, I'm sorry, but that made you a suspect in my view. I thought maybe the note had come from you."

His jaw dropped, as she had known it would. Good. He was no longer thinking about any past legal problems.

"You cannot be serious." He enunciated each word as if it were heavy as stone.

"I no longer believe that," she said in a rush. "But remember you told me I should be more logical."

"I do recall that. So by suspecting me you were being logical?"

"I was trying to not rely on my feelings, like you suggested. If I relied on my feelings…" She met his gaze and again felt herself sinking into the depths of his mesmerizing brown eyes. Reese had such beautiful, fascinating eyes.

"If I relied only on my feelings, I would never

suspect you." She reached for his hand and squeezed. "Never."

He placed his hand on top of hers, and she was comforted by the connection. She loved touching Reese. If only things were different.

STARING AT HER lovely face, Reese couldn't decide whether to be insulted or mollified. Her skin glowed in the soft light, making her appear radiant.

But her logic was so convoluted he gave up trying to follow such a twisted labyrinth.

"Thanks," he said finally. "I think."

"You're welcome." She withdrew her hand, and he felt the loss keenly.

"Where is Cassadaga?" he asked.

"Near Daytona Beach," she replied. "About a five- or six-hour drive."

He rubbed his chin again, sudden inspiration sprouting to life, although he wasn't quite sure where the idea came from. "Is Victoria going with you?"

"No."

"So you're going to drive to North Florida alone in that rusted heap?"

She shrugged. "Yes."

"Do you really think that's wise?"

"I've done it many times before."

Reese marveled at the defiance in Taki's voice. Maybe she did create her own reality.

The more he thought about her trip, the more he knew he had to accompany her. He ticked off the reasons in his mind one after another: her old Jeep was unreliable; a woman traveling alone was always a tempting target; and there was a good chance she could be meeting someone about the bowl again and not telling him. Worst of all, if Javi was right, Izzo now knew her license plate and she could be in danger. There had to be more of a connection between his briefcase and her bowl than she was admitting.

For sure she was hiding something. The question was, what? Why was she so secretive? He needed to find out. The sooner, the better.

Reese knew if he worked on it long enough, he could come up with several more excuses. All he had to do was find one that would convince her.

"This psychic has been helpful in the past?" Reese asked, not believing the words coming out of his mouth. Was he actually considering a consult with a fortune-teller? "So you recommend her?"

Taki nodded. "Robin is absolutely awesome. Amazing."

"And you believe she can pinpoint the location of the bowl?" He hoped he managed to sound interested. No reason to antagonize Taki again.

"Pinpoint? I don't know about that, but she might give me a clue." Taki leaned toward him. "Once, out of nowhere, she warned me that my—" Taki halted midthought and bit her bottom lip, making him wish they did have an otherworldly bond so he'd know what she'd been about to reveal.

More secrets.

"Let's just say Robin has saved me from several disasters." Taki sat back, plucking at the hem of a royal-blue Paradise Way Ashram sweatshirt, which featured the image of an opening pink lotus flower. As usual, she looked totally comfortable in casual clothing, while his pin-striped suit and tie made him appear ready for a day in court.

"She sounds great," he said. "Do you think she could help me find my briefcase?"

"Possibly." Taki threw him a suspicious look. "Why do you ask?"

"You scared away my only lead. I'm thinking why not ask your psychic for some help."

"Yeah, right. Mr. Assistant United States Attorney for the Southern District of Florida consulting a spiritualist?"

Reese winced as she emphasized each word of his title.

"I don't think so," she concluded.

"You're wrong, Taki." Reese modulated his voice to sound reasonable. "Law enforcement personnel have often found the services of these specialists useful."

She held up one hand. "Wa-ait a minute. I know you don't believe in psychics."

"But I've lost personal property that's very important to me, a briefcase containing trial notes for an important case. I need to avail myself of all possible remedies to get those notes back. We'll drive up together in the Jag. I've got a new back windshield and trunk lock."

Her mouth fell open. "No way."

"Why not? I guarantee you'll find the trip a lot more comfortable than your Jeep."

When her blue eyes widened, they also glimmered with a hint of mischief. At that moment he would have given up his corner office to know what she was thinking.

"I always spend the night," she said. "It's too far to drive back the same day."

"No problem. I'm sure there are motels in the area," he said. "Or we could always drive to Orlando for lodging."

He waited for the obligatory insistence on separate rooms, but she remained silent, continuing to eye him thoughtfully. "Are you sure you don't have to work?"

"Tomorrow is Saturday. Besides, I will be working, remember? I'm consulting an expert about missing evidence in a case. And I'll bet your psychic will be pleased to have extra business."

He suspected Taki wouldn't be able to resist throwing a friend some unexpected work. She'd think it good for her all-important karma.

"Yes," Taki said, drawing the word out slowly. "No question Robin will be very happy about another reading."

"Good. What time do you want to leave?" Reese stood, deciding to make a quick getaway before Taki changed her mind. She could get a "feeling" at any moment and cancel the trip, and he suddenly wanted very much to drive with her to Cassadaga. If nothing else, he intended to convince her she could trust him. Having his integrity questioned was a new and unsettling experience.

"We have to leave no later than ten to make it by

four." When she rose in her fluid, effortless manner, he knew she'd decided to accept the ride.

"I'll pick you up at ten."

"I'll leave a message for Robin that you want a reading at five," she said.

"Sounds good. Thanks."

"Sure." When they reached the door, she paused. "Um...are you a safe driver?"

"Safer than you. I don't speed."

As he smiled into her troubled eyes, the prospect of waking up next to such a fascinating face rendered him speechless. Maybe he could stay the night right here. Images of Taki's limber body in very unyoga-like positions sprang into his mind, blotting out any other thought. Desire rose with a swift intensity. He wanted to crush her to him.

She moistened her lips, and he wondered if her brain waves traveled down the same erotic path as his. Maybe she wanted him to stay. She liked their kisses. Why not more? He lifted his arm and touched her hair. He could swing by home in the morning to pick up what he needed.

"It won't work if you don't believe," she said softly before he could pull her into his arms.

"What?" The husky word hung in the air, and he allowed his hand to trail down her arm.

"The reading won't work if you don't believe in it."

He remained silent a moment, suppressing disappointment that her cosmic connection didn't work any better. But of course she hadn't known what he was thinking. He'd lost his freaking mind.

"You have no idea how much I want to believe," he said finally, resisting the urge to suggest he spend the night.

She nodded, as if pleased.

He squeezed her hand. "See you tomorrow morning."

"Good night, Reese."

He released her fingers reluctantly, hearing uncertainty in her voice when she spoke his name.

The brisk evening air hit him like a splash of frigid water. Two shrill beeps confirmed that he'd clicked off the Jag's alarm. He slid onto a cold leather seat and buttoned his jacket.

Was he really going on a road trip with Taki tomorrow? How had that happened? He hadn't taken off an entire weekend in over six months.

He started the engine and shifted into Reverse. Well, it was about time he got a life again. What was it Taki espoused? Live in the present moment, don't worry about the future or the past; your life was what was happening right now.

Fine. He'd do as she recommended. Why not? With a smile, he remembered the taste of her warm, sweet mouth. He hadn't felt this alive since before law school.

If only he knew what she was hiding.

TAKI WAITED UNTIL certain Reese had left her neighborhood, then grabbed her cape and ran to the Jeep. The duct tape she'd used to seal the cut in her canvas top had worked its way loose, so she smoothed it down, the chilly night air numbing her fingers.

At the first red light, wishing she had gloves, she rubbed her hands together and blew on them. Even she had to admit it was chilly tonight.

She glanced at the Jeep's clock. Only 9:00 p.m. Navi usually meditated until ten. She could easily catch him before he retired. She wanted to talk to him about tomorrow's trip.

She desperately needed her guru's advice.

How had she let Reese maneuver her into accompanying her to Cassadaga for her reading? And why was she now looking forward to the journey so very much? She could fool herself into thinking it was because she didn't have to drive for five hours, but knew that wasn't the reason. Although, not driving was definitely a good thing.

No, she was excited about spending the whole blessed day tomorrow alone with Reese, getting to know him better away from any interruptions from his work. The whole night, too. She swallowed at the thought of what could happen tomorrow night.

This was an extremely bad idea. A dangerous path to plunge down. Yes, that was the right image. Like falling off a cliff. But didn't Navi always tell her she had to follow her own path? That's likely what he'd say tonight.

She'd have to be careful, watch every single word the entire day, and not let anything about her true identity slip. Yeah, that's what she always promised herself, but Reese still managed to get past her defenses and ferret out details. Damning details that would come back to haunt her if he ever put them all together.

Tomorrow she'd be extra vigilant, always on her guard.

But what would happen if she just told Reese who she was? He'd promised never to reveal her phone number to anyone. Why would he give her away? He had no loyalty to the Spencer Trust. She'd see how the weekend went, get to know him better, and maybe she'd tell him the truth.

After the turn onto Alton Road, Taki spotted an open drugstore ahead on the left. Impulsively, she turned into the almost-empty parking lot. She needed a few things for the trip. This store sold a delicious all-natural trail mix for snacking. She preferred to make her own, but didn't have time tonight. She hated that time had become her enemy. Not very yogic.

Stepping inside the store's warmth, she grabbed a plastic basket. She paused before a display of disposable cameras, and after a moment placed one in her bin. Now she could have a photograph of Reese to take with her when she had to leave. The thought of leaving deflated her good mood a little, but she found the trail mix and threw several packages into her container. She didn't have to move just yet.

She passed a rack of reading glasses, then turned back to examine the display of frames. Why didn't Reese wear glasses? When he'd squinted at her note this evening, it wasn't the first time she'd noticed he needed help with his vision. She reached for a masculine style she liked in a weak magnification.

Smiling at herself in the tiny mirror, she imagined Reese's dark eyes behind the lenses instead of her blue ones. She tried on two other pairs, tilting her chin, viewing herself from straight on and profile. She placed her first selection in the basket.

Wouldn't Reese be surprised tomorrow when she gave him her gift.

"Excuse me," a brusque female voice said close to her ear.

Taki moved out of the way, realizing she'd blocked the path. "I'm so sorry," she said, giving the woman an apologetic smile.

Taki decided long ago to make every chance encounter with another being a pleasant one. That way both people ended up feeling better for the rest of the day.

"I guess I was daydreaming," Taki told the woman with a grin. A big smile did wonders to lighten anybody's mood.

Looking surprised, her fellow customer smiled back and said, "No problem. I do that all the time."

As the woman continued on, Taki glanced across the aisle and spotted three rows of condoms.

She scanned the labels on brightly colored boxes and stepped closer. Was this something she might need tomorrow night? Or would Reese be prepared? Startled by her thoughts, Taki's face grew warm, and she understood exactly why she was thrilled about this trip with Reese, why she'd come into this drug-store, in fact.

Everything happened for a reason.

Deciding she didn't need to talk to Guru Navi after all, Taki tossed a box that promised "Ultra Pleasure" into her basket and stepped toward the cashier.

CHAPTER EIGHT

THE NEXT MORNING, Taki was ready to go by nine-thirty, an overnight case packed and sitting by the front door beside the lunch she'd prepared. Humming a peaceful chant under her breath, she stepped outside to check her garden, and a blast of chilly morning air enveloped her.

As she descended the steps, she decided her lavender would love the cooler temperature, then raised her arms overhead to greet the sun. After a deep, glorious breath, Taki spun in a circle, listening to the cry of a blue jay as it flew into one of the oaks. What a perfect day!

She stuck a finger into the soil to check the moisture, finding the deep earth warmer than the air, and decided not to water. She plucked a few stray weeds, then moved back inside to warm up.

If she needed another reason to be traveling to North Florida with Reese, the heat in her Jeep barely worked. But who needed another reason?

She stepped over to the shelf where she kept the infusions she'd already prepared and stored in amber-colored bottles to protect the contents from light. What oil did she have ready that would relax Reese?

She intended to give him a massage tonight that he would never forget.

She paused, wondering why today felt like a fresh start with Reese when, in a way, it was likely more of an ending. She pushed away that depressing thought. She had this one day and night to spend with him, and she wanted to enjoy every moment.

At the sound of a car braking out front, she grabbed a bottle and hurried to the front door. She spotted Reese's Jag and a blue SUV on Victoria's driveway. She stuffed the oil in her bag and carried it outside just as Reese stepped from his sedan.

She caught her breath at the sight of him, and felt a slow pull in her center. Tall and handsome, he wore khaki slacks and a navy turtleneck sweater that displayed his wide shoulders and flat abs.

"Good morning," he said with a huge smile.

"Hi," she said, suddenly overwhelmed by what she'd planned.

He took her bag and placed it in the trunk, while she slid into the passenger seat, where the distinctive bouquet of fine leather catapulted her to chauffeur-driven days of long ago. Lost in bittersweet memories, she ran her hand across the smooth, cool seat and thought of Ivan, her father's driver, a sweet man from Russia who'd picked her up after school and always asked what she had learned that day, if she made any new friends. He'd cared more about her than her father had. Sometimes he—

"Earth to Taki. Hello?"

Reese's impatient words were spoken as if he'd

been trying to gain her attention for several minutes. And he probably had, while she'd been wallowing in painful history.

"I—I'm sorry. What did you say?" How long had she been time traveling? They were almost to the interstate, at least a ten-minute drive.

"What's the matter? You act as if…" He frowned, and she waited for the wrinkle between his eyes to deepen. It did.

"As if what?" she asked.

"Like you've just seen a ghost."

"Well, we are going to see a psychic, remember?"

He threw her a questioning glance, and she grinned to reassure him. "Kidding."

"Are you all right?" he asked.

"Yes. I just had an MCR."

Reese accelerated onto I-95, and the Jaguar sprang forward. Taki relaxed into her seat, barely feeling any vibration from the road, the sedan as tight and quiet as a submarine. Nothing like her rattling Jeep.

"Are you going to explain an MCR?" Reese asked when he'd reached the far-left lane. He kept his eyes on the road ahead. "I don't know yoga-teacher code."

"It's a mystic crystal revelation, but it has nothing to do with yoga. MCRs are one of the few things I remember vividly about my mother."

"I'm still lost. Can you elaborate a little?"

"When Mom had an MCR, she would stop whatever she was doing and hug me tight. It didn't matter where we were. Once we were in the middle of an antique car auction. When she released me, she would announce she'd had a mystic crystal revelation, and her face would be transformed by this really pleased smile." Taki held her hands out to demonstrate the width of her mother's grin. "MCRs made her very happy."

Surprised by her outburst of childhood memory, Taki fell silent. But it felt good to talk about her mom. She didn't do that often, even with Victoria who'd been her mother's friend and mentor.

Reese nodded. "So it's like a sudden insight into life? An epiphany?"

"Yes," Taki said. "Where something becomes totally clear for the first time. Mom said sometimes what you figured out was as plain as the nose on your face but you just couldn't see it until the MCR."

"Your mother doesn't sound so awful," he said after a moment. "Didn't you tell me your family had committed some... What was it? Really bad but as yet undefined crimes?"

Taki froze, too late realizing her blunder in broaching the off-limits topic of her family when she'd promised herself to be supercareful. Not a great start, and she couldn't even blame this on Reese. Actually, she realized, definitely another MCR, it would be so much easier to just tell him the truth.

"My mom was wonderful," Taki said softly, never wanting Reese to think her mom was some criminal. Her father was the problem, not her mom.

"So what MCR did you just experience?" he asked.

"Oh," Taki said. "Well, it was about you."

"About me? You just had an epiphany about me?"

She smothered a smile at his curious, husky voice. Surprising Reese was such fun, and it leveled the playing field since she spent most of her time around him feeling off balance. Actually, she'd had this particular MCR last night, but she needed it to cover her unexpected reaction to the luxury of his car—and to keep him off the subject of her mother.

"I understand now why you put up with me even though you think I'm...unique," she said.

She watched him turn over her words in his quick mind. "And what did you decide was the reason?"

"Because you subconsciously realize I'm here to help you."

"You're here to...help me?" His voice sounded deliberately neutral, as if feeling his way through dangerous territory. "That's an interesting theory."

"I can tell you don't agree."

He tossed her another quick look. "Well, so far you've made my life more difficult."

Taki shifted sideways, lifting the Jag's shoulder strap behind her. With his gaze fixed on the traffic, she could take her time to examine his profile. She'd never seen him this early in the day when totally clean-shaven. He looked different, more unguarded maybe. Or maybe it was because he wore casual clothes rather than his usual stuffy business suit.

She enjoyed looking at Reese, and had never felt this intense attraction to any other man. What a surprising twist from the universe that she would feel this way about a man so much like her father.

"I know I may have caused a little…confusion in your investigation—" she began.

"A little confusion?"

"—but if you allow yourself to believe, Robin will help you find your briefcase."

"I hope so." After a moment, he said, "How often do you consult this psychic?"

"Just when weird stuff starts happening."

The corners of his mouth twitched. "And does weird stuff happen to you often?"

"Not like this," she said. Taki shook her head. *Never like this*.

"Like what?"

Like meeting you, she wanted to say. *Meeting you has changed everything*.

Be cautious, an insistent voice buzzed in her ear. She felt like a moth dancing around the flame in her meditative candle as she reminded herself that Reese didn't know the truth about her. Why not tell him? What would it matter if he knew who she was? But she'd been on the run for so long, the idea of revealing herself frightened her—yet seemed liberating at the same time.

Not yet, she cautioned herself. Not yet.

"For instance, my bowl being stolen," she said. "That's weird. And receiving those notes. Almost getting arrested. Weird."

"When did you almost get arrested?"

"The FBI wouldn't let me leave Mayhugh's."

She expected the accusing glance he tossed her. "That was for your own protection, and you know it."

Taki sighed. "I know. Peter was very understand-ing, but I need to apologize to his students next week and give them a free class."

"Missing the class wasn't your fault."

"Hmm," she said, hoping Reese didn't pursue this. She could try to explain to him why it was her fault. Not that he'd understand. Or even try to. None of her father's attorneys had ever really listened to a word she'd said, even after she'd sent them an extensive reading list.

"Did that Izzo guy ever show up to Mayhugh's?" she asked.

"No, but we'll apprehend him sooner or later."

Reese pushed a button and a drawer with a com-pact disc slid out. "Check that," he said. "See if you like it."

Taki picked up the silver disc and turned it over. "Jazz," she said. "I love it."

"I thought you might."

Reese watched Taki replace the CD with the el-egant, manicured fingers of a pianist. She wore no rings. No jewelry at all. Probably because she'd never had any money to spend on trinkets. As he thought of his own mother's collection of gems, he wondered about Taki's deceased mom. And where was her fa-ther?

What crimes had her family committed that she was so ashamed of? Fraud?

He pushed the start button on the disc player. Taki relaxed into the seat with a dreamy smile while a soft, rising melody from a saxophone filled the car. He intended to learn everything he could about her on this trip, but had to use caution or she'd clam up again. Asking about her mother seemed a safe place to start.

"What happened to your mom?" he asked. "You said you were nine when she died."

"Oh." Her smile faded. She poked a finger into a frayed hole in her jeans, making little circles around the denim. After a fleeting glimpse of her pink flesh, Reese averted his gaze back to the road and waited for her answer.

"She committed suicide. Overdose of drugs."

"I'm sorry," he said, an automatic response as a sharp pang of regret and sympathy shot through him. He longed to ask more about her mother's death, but realized talking about it made Taki uncomfortable. She continued to play with the frayed strands of her jeans. Maybe her mother had died a long time ago, but she still didn't like to discuss that passing, and a suicide explained a lot. Of course he would respect her feelings.

"So how did you become a yoga teacher?" he asked, making a quick decision to shift to a less emotional subject. He wanted to learn everything about her. What did it matter where he started?

"The simple answer is I took a course that trained teachers," she said, appearing relieved by his question.

"What's the complicated answer?"

She thought for a minute. "I guess I wanted to share yoga, so it could heal others the way it helped me. I love the philosophy of never harming anyone, of always trying to be honest. Everything I studied just made sense, so I decided to live my life by yogic principles." She sighed. "Or try to, anyway. It's not easy."

"Then there's more to yoga than the exercises we do in class?"

She smiled. "What we do in class is actually a very small part of yoga, but what most people in the Western world know best. Yoga was created thousands of years ago to quiet our restless minds, to prepare for meditation." After a moment she added, "Yoga helped me cope with my mother's death."

She promised to loan him a book so he could learn more. Music and movies also turned out to be a safe topic. As Reese probed her likes and dislikes, Taki revealed a lively sense of humor and never failed to fascinate him with her comments, many of which he agreed with.

He was surprised to discover that she enjoyed romantic comedies. He'd thought she might favor the more serious art pictures, cinema heavy with spiritual meaning that needed subtitles for interpretation.

"No way," she said. "I like to laugh and escape when I go to a movie, pretend that there really are happy endings."

Her wistful words surprised him again. He'd assumed she'd be the eternal optimist. "You don't believe in happy endings?"

"I'm not sure." She shook her head. "Do you?"

"Sure. I think it can happen."

She sent him a shy, curious smile, and Reese's breath caught. What was it about Taki that made him want to show her a happy ending? His own parents' marriage certainly hadn't turned out well, and they were much better suited, far more alike than he and Taki.

He shook his head, amazed at his train of thought. Was he really thinking about a happy ending with Taki? *Not likely to happen in this lifetime.*

"Are you hungry?" he asked. "We could find a restaurant for lunch."

"I brought a picnic," she said. "Let's find a sunny rest area."

He glanced at his watch, then shrugged. They should have time.

"Don't worry," Taki said. "Robin's a psychic. She'll know if we run late."

He threw her a look.

"Gotcha," she said with a grin.

They found a concrete picnic table at an I-95 rest stop just south of the Saint Lucie Inlet. The sun shone brightly overhead as they ate, but the temperature dipped lower the farther upstate they traveled.

"That was delicious," Reese said, patting his comfortably full stomach. Taki had provided a thermos full of hot homemade vegetable soup, garlicky hummus and the most delicious whole-wheat bread he'd ever tasted. Grapes, bananas and oranges were her choices for something sweet.

"I'll end up healthy if I keep having lunch with you," he told her.

"You're already healthy," she said, her gaze sweeping his chest.

"I'm glad you think so." Reese took a swallow of the sweet ginger tea she'd brought in a second thermos, watching her blush over the rim of the mug. The warm liquid fought the chill of the cool afternoon.

"By the way," he said. "Our receptionist sends her thanks. Apparently you cured her morning sickness." He held up his mug in a toast.

Taki beamed at his news. "Oh, I'm so pleased."

He glanced into the steaming liquid. "Why are we drinking ginger tea? You don't look pregnant, and I know I'm not."

"In case of car sickness."

Reese smiled. No doubt another opportunity to improve her damaged karma. The woman was relentless. "So how does one become an herbalist?"

"My mother was into herbs," Taki said without hesitation.

Reese nodded, encouraging her to continue, pleased she seemed more at ease with him.

"Mom was kind of a latter-day hippie, I guess you'd say." Taki leaned her elbow on the picnic table and placed her chin in her hand. "I took a home study course to learn more and became fascinated by the healing power of nature. After Tibet, I took a detour to Kuala Lumpur because herbalists there believe in using every part of the plant, and I wanted to study their methods." She shook her head. "What an amazing journey."

"How did you communicate with these herbalists?"

"Oh, well, of course I used my extra sensory perception," she said. "You know, ESP."

He narrowed his eyes at her. "What are you talking about?"

"Sorry." She grinned. "Couldn't resist. I learned the words I needed to, plus I used an interpreter. Someday I'm going to publish what I've collected." After a soft sigh, she added, "Much of the ancient knowledge is oral and easily lost."

He hated to ruin her good mood, but felt compelled to issue a warning. "You are aware you need a license to prescribe herbs?"

"Well…"

"Wait." He held up a hand to stop her. "Don't tell me about anything illegal." He paused. Maybe it was best if he didn't know *everything* about her. "You don't do anything illegal, do you?"

"Isn't that what's called 'a leading question'?" Taki popped a grape in her mouth, and he wondered how she knew about leading questions.

She swallowed. "Don't worry. I know the law. I don't prescribe. I educate." Shrugging, she said, "My favorite part is growing my own herbs. I love watching a sprout bravely emerge from the dark earth, reach for the sun and grow into something useful. I really hate leaving my plants behind."

"So you move around a lot?"

When she stiffened, he knew she regretted the unguarded revelation. Why was she always protecting the details of her background? What was she hiding?

"I've been in Miami six months," she said reluctantly. "That's a long time for me lately."

He'd lived in Miami his entire life except for the

years he'd been away at school and didn't think he'd like living out of a suitcase.

"So why not put down roots along with your plants and remain in one place for a while?"

She raised her chin and grinned, a new light in her clear blue eyes. "Maybe I'm a gypsy. How far are we from Cassadaga, anyway?"

Nice dodge, he thought. But he considered himself a patient man, willing to earn her trust.

While Taki repacked their lunch, he retrieved the map from the car. Damn print was too small, though. Even with his arms fully extended, he couldn't bring the lettering into focus. He squinted at the red ribbon of I-95 flowing beside the blue Atlantic Ocean and looked for the Saint Lucie exit.

"Reese." Taki's soft voice caused him to look up.

She held a pair of spectacles in her hand. "These are for you," she said, extending them toward him. "Maybe they'll help."

He accepted tortoiseshell frames from her. "I don't wear—" he began and trailed off. He'd known he needed to purchase reading glasses for weeks, maybe a month, but kept putting it off. Vanity, he guessed.

He placed the glasses on his nose and focused on the map. Not surprisingly, he could now read even the smallest words.

When he looked up, Taki's face was a blurry haze through the magnification of the lenses. He removed the frames.

"Thanks," he said, warmed by her thoughtfulness. She'd noticed his need for reading glasses, which proved how observant she was. Of course she'd call it staying in the present moment. Whatever.

She was the sweetest human being he'd ever met, someone who spent most of her time trying to help others. Maybe she was kooky, maybe her actions were designed to improve that mysterious karma, but her kindness made Taki damn hard to resist. And, hell, why was he resisting?

Because she was also full of secrets.

TAKI TRIED TO relax as they zoomed along in the Jaguar at—she glanced at the speedometer—a legal sixty-five miles an hour. She felt like a passenger on a smooth rocket to some unknown, terribly important fate.

Reese had readily agreed to play the Pat Metheny CD she'd requested. She wanted him to listen to the music and curtail his inquisition. So far he'd spent the whole trip pumping her for information when she'd rather learn more about him.

Why had he asked so many questions about her herbs? Could he bust her for telling his receptionist to drink ginger tea? A few months ago the Food and Drug Administration had raided an herbal shop somewhere in Broward County and confiscated homemade products.

Reese was a Fed. Had he been involved with that disaster?

He hummed along with a familiar melody and glanced at her with the sexiest, most intelligent eyes she'd ever strayed into. Man, she could get lost in those eyes. He grinned, and she returned his smile, remembering his reaction to the reading glasses. She'd worried he might be offended, but he'd been pleased, even grateful.

She was overreacting to his questions. Reese couldn't arrest her. He wasn't even a cop.

Surely Reese hadn't accompanied her on this trip so he could question her. Did he still think she knew something about his missing briefcase?

Well, she'd doubted him for a nanosecond, so it made sense he didn't trust *her* and that's the reason he kept grilling her for information. She rubbed between her eyebrows to stimulate her third eye. Reese had an uncanny ability to worm information out of her. No, that wasn't exactly what happened.

For some bizarre reason, she liked telling him things, sharing things with him. She'd loved explaining yoga, and, oddest of all, had told him about her mom's suicide, an event she'd never willingly mentioned to another human being.

She sat up in the seat, realizing she'd just had another MCR. A really important one. One that could change her life. And, yes, she should have seen it before.

Reese was her soul mate.

Maybe she loved confiding in him, felt this incredible connection to him because only by joining with him could she achieve true happiness.

CHAPTER NINE

THEY ARRIVED IN Cassadaga with just minutes to spare, so Taki led Reese into the seventy-year-old hotel where Robin conducted her spiritual practice. The lobby contained a bookstore full of interesting titles—which she planned to browse during Reese's reading—also a gift shop and comfortable chairs where he could wait if he didn't want to shop.

At 4:00 p.m., Taki ascended a narrow flight of pine stairs to the second floor and lightly knocked on the entrance to Robin's reading room.

"You may enter," came a muffled voice.

Taki pushed open the door and found her plump, white-haired spiritualist seated at a small wooden desk whose top was empty but for a red candle and her well-worn pack of Tarot cards. She wore her usual flowing blue robe. As the candle burned, it released the scent of cinnamon into the room.

"How are you, my dear Taki?" Robin asked with a gentle smile.

"I'm well," Taki said.

"Shall we begin?" Robin asked, lifting her tarot deck from the table.

Taki nodded, hopeful about a clue to the location of her bowl. "Please."

After Robin shuffled the deck, Taki picked ten cards. Robin pushed a button to start a digital recorder, then placed two cards faceup on the oak desk between them. She didn't speak for several moments as she studied the colorful images.

"You've met someone," Robin said, scrutinizing one card closely. "This man is important to you." A note of disbelief hung in cinnamon-tinged air.

Taki blinked when she saw the Lovers card. She usually interpreted the Lovers as a union of opposites, and opposites surely described her and Reese. But of course there were other ways to construe its meaning.

Robin looked up and leveled her gaze at Taki. "I knew something was different about you today." The flame from the candle flickered, and a thin ribbon of smoke snaked high into the room.

"The Lovers can also signify trials overcome," Taki said. "Or emotional growth."

"Just who is giving this reading?" Robin flipped another card, light from the candle shining in her amber eyes. The Nine of Swords.

Taki quickly made her own interpretation of its meaning…a card for deception. But did it apply to her or to Reese? She remained quiet, deciding to analyze the reading later when she listened to the recording Robin always made of their sessions.

"Someone is not telling the truth." The sleeve of Robin's robe swept across the desk when she revealed the next card. The High Priestess. "Ah. I believe we've seen this card before. Once again it is you, Taki, who is not the person she seems to be."

When the next card appeared, Taki swallowed hard. The dreaded Tower, with two screaming human figures falling from its flaming heights.

"You know what this means as well as I do." Robin tapped the card with her index finger, the sound echoing in the quiet room. "Unexpected changes are coming. You need to be careful. I see danger, trouble from a surprising source." Robin frowned, her face tightening. "There is some connection here, but I can't quite…"

The psychic closed her eyes and touched Taki's wrist, becoming still. While Robin concentrated on finding a psychic impulse, Taki's mind wandered to Reese. What was he doing?

When she'd come upstairs, he'd been in the gift shop examining a book on astral projection with his new glasses, a disbelieving frown on his handsome face. The turtleneck sweater displayed his broad, muscled shoulders to perfection, even if they were shaking with silent laughter. Of course he wouldn't buy into what he called her New Age hocus-pocus. If only he—

"Your mind is filled with nothing but images of this new man," Robin said, opening her eyes. She waited, brows raised, apparently expecting a reply.

Taki shifted in her seat and shrugged. "I guess so." What else could she say? She knew only too well that she couldn't stop thinking about Reese. Mostly about his body.

"You said it was important to find your bowl. Do you ever think of *it?*"

"Of course. And I brought a picture." Taki dug in her bag and handed Robin a photograph.

Once more Robin closed her eyes and wrapped her fingers around Taki's wrist. Taki inhaled the cloying fragrance of cinnamon and tried to focus on the bowl. Holding its image in her thoughts, she closed her own eyes, but soon drifted again.

What was the danger Robin referred to? Her father? Reese?

Of course, the cards never lied, and they had revealed her deception. She felt a twinge of guilt about hiding her identity from Reese. The more time she spent with him, the more she liked him in spite of his show-me-the-proof, how-can-you-believe-this-utter-nonsense attitude. The more she wanted to tell him the truth. She hoped Robin found his briefcase. That would show him her beliefs weren't all hocus-pocus.

Taki sighed as she became aware of her thoughts. Reese again. Her psychic was right. She thought about him way too much.

Robin released her wrist. "I'm sorry, Taki. I can't see the bowl."

Taki sighed. "I know you tried."

"Yes, and I can tell you this," Robin continued. "Your bowl has some connection to this new man, but not in the way you think. The situation is muddled, difficult." She shook her head. "That's all I can get for you."

"Can I trust this man?"

"Trust. Ah, now that's something you don't normally ask me." Robin turned over two more cards. After studying them, she focused in the distance over Taki's shoulder, making Taki want to turn and look.

"He will never intentionally harm you," Robin said finally. "Of this I am certain."

Never intentionally, but he could hurt me. Taki nodded, disappointed not to learn more. But the time had come to ask her number one question.

"Do you sense that the monster's people are close to finding me?"

Robin nodded. "I was waiting for that one."

Taki leaned forward. "Tell me. What do you see?"

As long as she'd been running from her father's legal vultures, no matter what city she was in, Taki always asked a psychic the same question: Are they about to find me?

Robin flipped the remainder of the cards Taki had selected and nodded definitively. "I'm sorry, but, yes. I sense his people are very close."

"So maybe that's the danger you see in the cards," Taki suggested hopefully. She didn't want to believe the Tower referred to Reese.

"No." Robin covered the cards with her palm, looking more worried than usual. "This is new danger, something quite different. Something unexpected."

Robin met her gaze with an intensity that startled

Taki, and a chill ran down her spine. "Please, Taki. I want you to be very careful."

WAITING ON AN antique sofa in the lobby, Reese watched Taki slowly descend the narrow flight of stairs with her usual fluid grace. Her gaze remained fixed on the steps, one hand on a railing, lost in thought and looking so dejected he wanted to give her a hug. He'd never seen her this discouraged.

He stood when she trudged into the lobby. "How'd it go?"

"No luck." She shrugged, her blue eyes catching light from the ancient crystal chandelier overhead. "Robin couldn't find any clue to the bowl's location. She believes you have some connection to the bowl, but she can't find the link."

Thinking anyone could have made that observation, Reese patted Taki's arm. Of course he had a connection to the bowl. He traveled with Taki, and she wanted the damn thing desperately.

"Maybe she'll have better luck with my briefcase."

Taki brightened. "Maybe. She's waiting for you. Second room on the right at the top of the stairs."

He glanced up the staircase.

"Just keep your mind open, Reese," Taki said softly.

And my wallet closed, he wanted to say, but didn't. He hurried up the steps and knocked on the door.

"I'm Robin," the spiritualist said as he sat across from her at a wooden desk.

"Reese Beauchamps." He thought she looked

rather like a ghost…round and pale. Hopefully she was friendly.

"I'll be recording our session, then I'll give you a CD to study later."

While she inserted a disc into a small recorder, Reese surveyed the room. No crystal balls. He wondered if there were special effects for floating heads. Maybe he'd have to settle for the plume of smoke wafting toward the ceiling from the red candle near her elbow.

With a click, she pressed the start button on the recorder and looked up, focusing somewhere in the distance. He found the effect disconcerting.

"Have you had a reading before?" she asked.

"Never."

"Well, I'm no fortune-teller. You may not like some of the things I say, but there's a message for you if you listen carefully. Life contains many meanings extending beyond our familiar concepts."

Reese thought the speech sounded canned, like a disclaimer she issued to avoid getting sued.

"Taki tells me you've come with a specific question," Robin said.

"I had a briefcase stolen out of my car. I need to find it."

"Did you bring a picture? I do photo readings."

"No," Reese said, wondering who the hell took pictures of their briefcase.

Robin closed her eyes.

Yeah, Reese thought, *try to catch that good vibration. Maybe Claudia's location will be on it.* His gaze strayed around the room. Posters of women with glowing auras enveloping their heads hung on cracked plaster walls.

"Does the name Marie mean anything to you?" Robin muttered, startling him.

He refocused on the spiritualist. "Yes," he admitted. "Marie is my sister. Also, my grandmother's name was Marie."

Robin clasped her hands before her and nodded. "Your grandmother is with us spiritually. She is pleased you came. You were very close."

He quickly scanned the room, almost expecting to see that floating head he'd just scoffed at. Truthfully, he wouldn't mind seeing his gran, but the idea was preposterous. Sure, they'd been close, but that wasn't unusual. The psychic had made a lucky guess.

With her eyes still shut, Robin clasped her hands together on the desk before her. "Describe the briefcase."

"Black leather, about a foot high, two feet long, six inches wide." *It has my name embossed on it,* he thought during the ensuing silence. *Should be easy to identify among the briefcases in the spirit world.*

Thankfully focusing on his face this time, Robin sighed and settled back in her chair. "Ah, a skeptic. Why did you come for a reading when you are a non-believer?"

"How do you know I'm skeptical?"

"I don't need to be psychic. Look at the way you're sitting, with your arms folded across your chest and your legs crossed in front of you. You're not going to accept a word I say."

Reese checked his body language and leaned forward, placing his arms on the desk. "Let's forget the briefcase for now. I have another question for you."

Robin looked at him expectantly.

"I need to locate a woman, a missing witness. Do you know where she is? Is she in trouble?"

"A missing woman. Ah. Yes." A strange light entered the spiritualist's gaze, and she nodded. Closing her eyes again, she continued to nod and began to mumble.

Reese gaped at her. *What the hell was this?*

Suddenly, Robin's eyes popped open. "Your gran says the woman is safe, that you don't need to know where she is, that she will contact you when the time is right."

He resisted the urge to laugh. "You're saying my grandmother knows where my witness is?"

"Your grandmother is in a place where she can know many things."

He shook his head. *Oh, just great. Very specific.* "How about this—Taki believes we knew each other in another life. What do you think?"

Robin frowned. "Taki did not mention that to me."

"Well, since she believes you're psychic, she probably thought you already knew."

With a sad smile, Robin retrieved a deck of cards from her desk drawer. As she shuffled, she said, "Seven shuffles will remove any existing pattern."

She spread the deck out before him. "Pick ten cards. We shall proceed with your reading."

He did as she asked and placed the cards face-down in a pile. One by one Robin turned the cards over, obviously anxious to earn her fee and get rid of him. Of course she didn't know Claudia's location. He'd only asked to see what ludicrous answer he got. This so-called psychic knew nothing about any past lives he'd spent with Taki. The whole concept was beyond fantastic.

"Stress surrounds you," Robin said, staring at the cards. "You are cautious about career changes, but I see you going in a new direction."

He nodded. Loosely interpreted, that could apply to 95 percent of the people in this country.

She turned another card and grimaced. "Just as I suspected, there is a wedding in your future."

Oh, really. Nothing but bland generalities. But maybe she'd misjudged his relationship with Taki. Just what had she told this woman?

Robin turned over the remaining cards and sucked in her breath when she revealed the final one. Leaning forward, the psychic grasped his wrist with a surprisingly strong grip and searched his eyes. "You must keep very careful watch over the one you love. She is in terrible danger."

Startled by the woman's intensity, Reese stared at the card. A bolt of lightning had ignited a tower and two terrified figures tumbled to the earth.

"What kind of danger?" he asked. Did the psychic consider Taki to be the woman in danger?

Robin shook her head. "Just like with Taki, I can't see the trouble. But it exists."

He examined the colorful spread of cards. *Trouble exists? Oh, how very insightful.*

"Yes," Robin said slowly.

His gaze connected with the psychic's.

"You have known Taki in many lives." Robin turned her head, holding it to one side as if trying to hear something in the distance.

"Nothing else," she said finally. "You are too closed." The woman eyed him with a speculative gaze. "If you'd like to come back, we could try a past-life regression to explore your previous journeys."

"We've got twenty minutes left now," he suggested.

"A regression takes much longer than that," Robin said.

Past-life regression? Reese shook his head, wondering what the hell that involved.

"I'll need to hypnotize you," Robin said in answer to his unspoken question.

"No, thanks. You're sure you don't…'see' anything about my briefcase?" he asked.

Robin gazed into the steady flame of the candle for a long moment, then focused on him again, offering a smile that seemed full of sorrow.

"Stay close to the one you love. She'll lead you to what you want," she said after a moment. Then she added, "Remember sometimes friends turn out to be false."

"Well, thanks. I guess." When Reese stood, Robin stopped her recorder and handed him a disc.

As he descended the stairs, Reese shoved Robin's CD in his pocket and forgot about it. In his opinion, that reading was nothing but a con hybridized with a game of chance. Robin had told him nothing he didn't already know, certainly nothing he could confirm.

As if he would pay good money for a bogus past-life regression to find out about his previous lives. What made Taki buy into this garbage?

He paused on the bottom step when he spotted her. Balanced on one foot, the other propped against her thigh, Taki stood by the old-fashioned reception desk that featured wooden slots for guest messages behind it. She and the clerk were folding some sort of brochure. He recognized a familiar rhythm in her soft voice, but couldn't make out her words. An inexplicable surge of well-being washed over him as he watched her lean into the counter and laugh.

Now what to tell her about his aborted reading?

"That was quick!" Taki said when he joined her by the counter.

"I wasn't on the same wavelength with your psychic," Reese said, hoping to make her smile.

Her mouth turned up in a knowing grin. "What happened?"

He arranged his features to look properly solemn. "I'm afraid I was closed."

"Closed?" She shook her head. "Reese, you're locked up tighter than a bank vault."

He wondered why her words pleased him. He didn't particularly want her to think of him as the proverbial stuffed shirt, but her teasing indicated that she'd grown more comfortable with him during the trip.

"I warned you to keep an open mind," she continued. "So nothing at all on the briefcase?"

"Nothing." Time to put this nonsense behind them and look forward to the rest of the evening.

"Do you mind if we stop by the bookstore?" she asked. "There's a book I've been wanting."

Reese held open the door for her. "Sure."

"And can we eat in the hotel's dining room? I love their vegetable lasagna."

"Sounds great," Reese said. Maybe he hadn't known Taki in a previous life, but he loved spending time with her in this one.

WHEN THEY WERE seated in the dimly lit café, Taki searched for an opening to push her plan into reality. She'd been deciding about how to go about it all day—well, really since last night, if she were honest. But she'd made up her mind and nothing would stop her.

She intended to seduce Reese tonight.

Not that he would require much coaxing. At least she hoped not. But she wanted him, wanted him desperately, and feared tonight would be her only chance to make love to him.

The problem was she'd never deliberately lured a man to her bed before, so really wasn't sure of the best way to go about it. Of course she was no virgin, but she'd never had to persuade anyone into sex. Her previous boyfriends had been more than eager.

In fact, one of the reasons her father had been so strict was because he considered her boy-crazy. And, yes, she had liked boys, or more so the freedom they represented.

But none of them had known how to kiss like Reese. None of them had ever turned her insides into a hot molten mass of pure desire.

As she watched him order, she remembered her reaction to him the night they'd met. Something powerful and mysterious existed between them, something she'd never experienced before. She'd purchased a book on soul mates in the bookstore, and would read that later to gain a better understanding of what was going on.

But she'd enjoy one fabulous, erotic night with Reese, something to cherish as long as she lived. Then she could find her bowl, give it to Navi and leave Miami before her father located her. Her plan was perfect.

She'd suggest they split the cost of a hotel room, a perfectly logical idea considering her circumstances. He wouldn't refuse, and even with two double beds she figured the rest would be easy once the lights went out.

She shifted in her seat as the image of Reese's naked body moving over hers slammed into her mind. Maybe she'd leave the lights on. She'd enjoy watching those well-defined muscles strain with a little effort.

Disoriented by her lusty thoughts, she tried to concentrate on Reese's words and realized he'd stopped speaking.

"Another mystic crystal revelation?" he asked as he raised his water for a drink.

"No MCR." Finally, the opening she needed. She smiled, thinking Reese entirely too good-looking for her own good. Thick dark hair fell across his forehead, not quite reaching his third eye but softening the set of his determined jaw. Once again she marveled at the pull he had on her even while he annoyed her with his skepticism.

"I was just wondering where you want to spend the night," she continued.

"I thought we'd stay with my cousin in Orlando."

"Your cousin?" She sat back and swallowed hard. *His cousin?*

"I know you're always worried about money," he continued, "and Mike's got plenty of room. Plus, he makes a killer breakfast."

Taki nodded. Truth was, after paying Robin, she would be short of cash the rest of the month. But if Reese supplied free lodging, she could hardly insist on a motel room. So much for her seduction.

"Orlando?" she managed to squeak out.

"Well, Casselberry, really. His mom is my father's younger sister. We were roommates at Princeton," Reese said. "Mike's a cardiologist in Winter Park. About an hour drive."

"You sure have a huge family," she said.

"Don't you have cousins?"

"No." She shrugged, hoping this cousin would make certain assumptions and put her in the same room with Reese. Definitely time for some positive thoughts.

REESE'S COUSIN MIKE lived on Lake Monroe, a freshwater lake near Casselberry, Florida. He was shorter and heavier than Reese, but had the same dark hair and eyes.

Mike had shown her to a cozy guest suite on the second floor overlooking the lake, complete with its own bathroom and balcony. After splashing her face with warm water, she'd gone in search of Reese. She'd found him in the kitchen with Mike selecting a bottle of red wine, but no mention was made of his sleeping arrangements. All she knew was that he wasn't bunked with her.

Mike uncorked the wine, Reese grabbed three glasses and they all moved outside to a large wooden deck behind the house with lounge chairs and a huge stainless-steel barbecue. The deck extended out into the water, turning into at least a twenty-foot dock.

Taki watched Reese's cousin take a long draw on a fat, smelly cigar. *Some healer.* The tip glowed in the cool February darkness while gray smoke drifted slowly toward the huge body of water beside them. She shook her head. How could a heart specialist smoke lung- and air-polluting cigars?

And was it his idea or Reese's to put them in separate rooms?

A full moon shone overhead, casting a wide silver beam across the lake's glittering surface. Water gently lapped against the hull of Mike's powerboat at the end of the dock. She took a deep breath, inhaling a hint of night-blooming jasmine…but that sweet scent was soon overpowered by noxious tobacco.

"I only allow myself one of these babies a week," Mike said.

"Joan still won't let you smoke in the house?" Reese asked with a laugh.

"Nope, and she can smell it every time." Mike took another puff, then blew the smoke into the air. "It's just not worth it even though she's visiting her sister to help out for a few days."

Now Taki understood why they were sitting outside when the thermometer hovered around 60 degrees… of course a delightful temperature in her opinion. She relished the light breeze as it flowed across her cheek, but had been surprised Mike and Reese would want to sit in the cool air.

Looking more relaxed than she'd ever seen him, Reese reclined on a cushioned lounge chair, sipping the delicious California Merlot that Mike had opened.

As she listened to the cousins catch up on family gossip, she decided Reese didn't seem quite so buttoned up, so intense and focused tonight. He laughed and joked with Mike, occasionally raking his fingers through his thick hair in an unconscious gesture she found strangely endearing. Maybe because it made him seem less rigid, more human. Less like her father.

From their conversation, she decided neither Mike nor Reese let their family tell them what to do. In fact, she detected a surprising note of independence in Reese's attitude, an unwillingness to be pigeon-holed precisely where they wanted him. Mike dismissed the family edicts even more strongly than Reese.

As she sipped her wine, Taki wondered if she could find his room later. Would it be on the same floor as hers?

"And when I told Avery that you were hell-bent on litigation, on putting scum behind bars where they belong, I thought he would have a coronary right then and there."

Reese nodded. "He still tries to talk me into giving up the courtroom."

"We're probably boring Taki to death," Mike said. He'd just finished telling a story about how, during a golf game, his dear uncle Avery, Reese's father, had tried to enlist Mike's help convincing Reese to join him in private practice.

"Not at all," she said. "It's enlightening to hear how normal families work."

Mike waved the hand with the cigar. "Our family, normal? We're a pretty dysfunctional bunch."

Reese laughed. "What's a normal family, anyway?"

She threw Reese a quick glance, and he returned her gaze steadily. By the look on his face, she knew he was alluding to her own family's deliberately vague history.

"So how did the readings go?" Mike asked. "Reese told me about your stolen bowl."

Reese raised his brows and nodded at her. She had no idea what he was thinking or what outrageous stories he'd told his cousin.

"The readings didn't go well, I'm afraid," she said.

So Reese must have planned all along for them to stay the night here. She pushed away a twinge of disappointment that he hadn't been more eager to share a bed with her.

After a long drag on his cigar, Mike asked Reese, "What will you do now?"

"Same thing I've been doing," Reese said. "Try to find Romero's man, Izzo."

"Izzo might have your briefcase," Taki said, "but he doesn't have my bowl. Mayhugh does."

"Mayhugh?" Mike asked. "Who's this Mayhugh?"

"A sleazy fence in Homestead," Reese answered. "Taki thinks he has her bowl."

"He does," she insisted. "I know he does."

Mike leaned forward. "How do you know?"

She glanced at Reese again, knowing how preposterous the words would sound to these logical, practical men. She'd never convince them that sometimes the universe supplied what you needed when you least expected it.

"Taki is quite intuitive," Reese said softly. "She relies on her feelings."

CHAPTER TEN

WONDERING WHY THE hell they weren't in a Ramada Inn, Reese returned Taki's heart-stopping smile. Her grin could melt the Columbia Icefield.

What had possessed him to act all noble when he'd wanted this intriguing woman since he'd laid eyes on her? Oh, right. He'd been insulted by her lack of trust, thought he'd earn that and save her some money by crashing with Mike. Reese shook his head. He was a reasonably intelligent guy. Surely he could have made love to her first and then figured out some way to earn her trust.

"You rely on feelings, huh?" Mike gave a short laugh. "Well, my instincts have served me well many times. Reese tells me you're an herbalist."

"Yes."

Mike nodded. "A lot of my patients are very interested in herbs. Saint-John's-wort, garlic, echinacea. The American Medical Association is investigating the various claims being made. They want scientifically credible information."

"I'm not convinced that's a good thing," Taki said. "We don't want herbs regulated like drugs, but the

Food and Drug Administration would love to tax botanicals anyone can grow in their backyard."

While Taki and Mike discussed the pros and cons of government regulation, Reese realized Mike took the subject seriously. Apparently the medical community believed physicians needed to get up to speed on herbs or their patients would go looking for information elsewhere—perhaps to unlicensed practitioners like Taki who used homegrown product.

"Yeah, and the big pharmaceutical companies have already moved in on the market," she said. "Have you seen what's on the shelf in drugstores?"

"That's why standards should be set," Mike said.

Reese smiled to himself. Damn, but the woman managed to keep life interesting. But it was time to get rid of Mike. The way she responded to their kisses told him she was equally interested in some time alone.

She sighed and stretched her arms overhead, gazing over the lake. "Your backyard is breathtaking," she told Mike. "So peaceful."

"Thank you, ma'am," Mike said.

Reese gave Mike a hand signal that they'd perfected as college roommates—a sign that he wanted to be alone with his date. Getting the message, Mike flashed an evil grin, then put out his cigar in a ceramic ashtray by his lounge.

"It's too damn cold for me out here. Plus, I've got some medical journals to catch up on. You two can stay and freeze as long as you want."

"It's such a beautiful night," Taki said. "If you don't mind, I would like to remain out here a while longer."

"Be my guest. Reese, you have custody of the wine. See you in the morning."

When Mike disappeared inside, Reese held up the bottle. "More wine?"

"Maybe a little," she said.

When Taki slid her long, jean-clad legs to one side of the lounger, he sat beside her, noting the cushion retained her warmth.

She held out her glass, and Reese trickled wine into the bowl.

"It's nice to have a cousin that's a friend," she said. "Because he's family you'll be friends forever."

Reese heard a touch of longing in her words and again wondered about her mysterious family.

"Mike and I have always been tight." Reese grinned, unable to resist saying, "See, at least I'm on the same wavelength with some people."

Taki's slim shoulders shook with laughter. "Poor Robin. I'll bet she's turning in her crystal ball right now."

The night was too dark to appreciate the vivid color of her eyes, but he saw the reflection of moonlight mirrored in their depths.

"Are you warm enough?" he asked.

She nodded. "But I'll bet you're not."

"I have an idea."

After placing the wine bottle and his glass on the deck, he pulled Taki to her feet and took her seat on the lounge chair, then gently eased her down between his legs, nestling her back against his chest. Nice. Intimate. Her warmth now blanketed him on both sides.

After the switch she held herself stiff for a moment, then relaxed against him with a fluid release.

"I can't believe I didn't spill my wine during that maneuver," she said in a laughing voice.

"I knew you wouldn't. You have amazing grace." He reached for his wine on the deck floor. "You could probably perform on a high wire."

"Sounds dangerous," she said.

"This from a woman who's not afraid of antagonizing a hit man."

Taki shook her head gently, her hair tickling his chin. "You know I didn't mean to antagonize anybody."

"So you say."

She remained quiet for a moment, then said, "You thought we might be followed to Cassadaga, didn't you?"

"It crossed my mind. I saw you looking behind the car, too."

"Only because you were." She turned her head and caught his gaze. "Reese, I've told you everything I know about the theft."

When he didn't respond immediately, she said, "Don't you believe me?"

"Maybe I should have asked Robin if I can trust *you*."

She settled against him again. "I suppose I deserved that."

He placed one arm around her waist and placed

his cheek against her hair. He sensed some part of her couldn't completely relax with him, but she felt delicious in his arms, soft and strong and full of endless puzzles. What was it she held back? And why? Because she'd had legal problems in the past and he was an attorney? But she was too smart, too nonjudgmental for that type of silly bias.

"Did you ask Robin about me?" he asked.

"I sure did."

"And did I get the psychic seal of approval?" he asked.

Taki hesitated, then said, "She said you would never deliberately harm me."

"And that's true." He said his words simply and hoped Taki believed them. "I never would."

They remained comfortably quiet, and Reese listened to the sound of frogs croaking halfway around the lake. Taking his last sip of wine, he placed the empty glass on the deck and wrapped both arms around her, hugging her close.

"Warmer?" she asked.

"Definitely."

"Glad to be of help."

"That's one of the things I admire most about you."

She turned her head, again meeting his gaze. "You admire something about me?"

"I admire a lot about you, Taki. But I'm referring to how you want to help everyone you meet. It's sweet." He cocked his head. "Unusual." Giving her a slight squeeze, he said, "Even when you make things worse, you're always trying to help."

She rolled her eyes and faced front again. "Thanks a lot."

Reese chuckled at her wounded tone, knowing she was teasing. She warmed him inside and out. "Now that you've learned more about my family, what do you think? Worse than yours?"

He felt her withdrawal, a slight rigidity at his words. "Your father sounds like a real character," she said.

"That's one way to put it. He's used to getting his own way."

"How does your mother put up with him?"

"She doesn't. She divorced him ten years ago."

"Oh." Taki's voice was almost too quiet to hear.

"Don't worry, she's a lot happier since they split. He cheated on her constantly."

"The divorce must have been hard on you," she said.

Reese hoped his laugh didn't sound bitter. He intended to keep his saga light, the point being to encourage Taki to become more free with her own family history. No one had a perfect life, certainly not a perfect family.

"My parents separated when I was a senior in high school," he told her. "The divorce wasn't final until my second year in law school. They fought over everything, including whether my father could continue working at the law firm my maternal grandfather founded.

"Does this fall under the category of too much

information?" he asked when she didn't respond. "Maybe I should also be atoning for rotten parents."

"Both of my parents weren't rotten," Taki blurted.

"I assume you stayed with your father after your mother died."

After another pause, she said, "Yes. And he's a soulless monster."

"Ah. So he's the one you have to atone for?"

Taki took a healthy swallow of wine before responding. When she turned her head to gaze over the lake, he knew he'd hit a sore spot.

"Are you cross-examining me, Reese?" she asked.

"Sorry." He tightened his arms around her. "Is it a crime to want to learn more about you?"

She placed her wine on the deck and turned in the chair to meet his gaze. "Does it matter who I used to be? This is who I am right now."

He brushed a thumb across her cheek, finding her skin soft and smooth. "Humor me. Remember, Robin said I would never harm you."

"She said 'never deliberately.'"

"What are you afraid of me finding out? Is there a warrant out for your arrest somewhere?"

She took a deep breath. By now he understood it was her method of calming herself. "I have no doubt you and Javi already know there's not." She raised her brows. "Am I wrong about that?"

"You're not wrong," Reese answered. *Nothing under the name* Taki, *anyway.*

She placed both hands flat against his chest. "I

promise my face is not on the wall in a post office somewhere."

He laced all ten fingers through hers, certain that she spoke the truth. "I have to admit," he said softly, "I found it difficult to believe you were a desperado."

Dipping his head, he claimed her mouth. Taki parted her lips which he took as an invitation and he greedily deepened their kiss. She responded, teasing him with her tongue, sending bolts of desire crashing through him. When he cupped her cool cheeks between his palms, she sighed, and he lowered a hand to stroke the swell of her right breast, tracing its fullness with a gentle finger.

Crushing an unrelenting urge to bury himself inside her, Reese broke the kiss and cradled Taki's cheek against his chest. Her breathing had become as labored as his.

With a moan of disapproval at his retreat, she lengthened her body against his, pressing into his chest, urging him to resume his caresses.

But he wanted to make love to her in a warm bed, not on an exposed deck in his cousin's chilly backyard. He had too much respect for her. If they continued this, they needed to move inside.

Before speaking, he relished the quiet, intimate moment with her nestled willingly in his arms. No telling what would happen when they went in the house. Taki was the most unpredictable woman he'd ever encountered. With a soft kiss on top of her head, he breathed in the sweet fragrance of her velvet hair.

He was about to suggest they relocate, when she raised her chin.

"I was born in Rhode Island," she said, tracing a random pattern across his sweater, near his heart. Her soft, halting revelation intensified his arousal. He clenched against the need to shift her beneath him.

"I left my home because I wanted to see the rest of the world," she continued. "I had no reason to remain in a place full of horrible memories."

"But you're so secretive about your background," he protested softly.

Her breasts pressed against him when she inhaled. "My mother is gone, Reese. I'm better off if I don't think about the way she died."

"Is your father still alive?" he asked.

After a moment, Taki said, "He's dead to me."

"Yeah, I get that." Reese hugged her closer, then lightly stroked her arm to encourage her to reveal more.

"My birth name is Kimberly Spencer," she said. "My father is a man named Howell Atwood Spencer."

Reese didn't dare speak.

"Have you heard of him?" she asked.

"Should I know him?"

"Maybe," she murmured. "He's a very wealthy man."

"So that would be enough for me to know who he is?"

When Taki didn't respond, Reese wondered if this was more new age positive thinking. "Are you serious?" he asked.

"Unfortunately, I am. But he's cruel and heartless.

My grandmother didn't exactly approve of the way her son, my father, raised me after my mother's death, but she was an old lady and didn't have the spirit to fight him. Her will left half of the fortune to me."

Reese went still. "Are you saying you're some sort of heiress?"

"I don't want the money or anything to do with him," Taki said. "I ran away, but my father has people searching for me constantly."

Stunned, Reese needed time to absorb Taki's hesitant revelations. An heiress? People were looking for her? This was bizarre, even crazier than her new age mumbo jumbo.

"I guess that explains why you move so often."

"He always finds me. That's why I didn't want to tell you anything about my family."

"Because you thought I'd tell your father where you were? But why would I—"

"I worry about that with everyone, and I didn't know you," she said. "Now that I do, I know I'm safe. But I was afraid to tell you right away. I've kept my identity secret for so long, that I—" She sighed. "You have no idea how hard this is to tell you."

He had a thousand questions, but sensed she wasn't ready yet to talk more about life with a father she obviously hated, about why she hated him. He placed his chin on her head. He'd just have to give her more time. They had all night.

"Let's go inside," he suggested.

"Okay," she murmured.

Taki slid off the lounge chair, and he felt the loss

of her warmth keenly. They gathered the wine and their glasses and carried them into Mike's kitchen. Reese locked the back door, then took her hand, leading her down the hallway to his room.

When they arrived at the open door, she looked inside to his bed and slipped her hand from his. He reached for her, but she stepped away.

"Good night, Reese," she said. Her eyes glittered with unshed tears.

"Taki. Wait."

She shook her head, and walked away from him.

He wanted to go after her. His lust, his sympathy, his affection for her twisted up inside him, making him crazy with wanting.

But he let her go.

What had her father done that was so cruel?

ALONE IN MIKE'S guest room, Taki closed her book and hugged it to her chest, listening to croaking frogs and crickets serenading each other around the lake. White curtains billowed through the open windows. She knew exactly where Reese was sleeping—on the first floor in Mike's office on a convertible couch.

Reese had made certain that she saw his bed, subtly inviting her to stay. She'd longed to climb into that bed with him and finish what they'd started.

What she'd started.

But she no longer believed one night with Reese, no matter how deliciously intimate and fulfilling, would be enough. No, one night would just make everything worse. She'd want more. Sucking cool air deep into her lungs, she realized she needed to re-think her impetuous decisions. Reese was not good for her.

Talking and thinking about her mother today had reinforced that in some twisted cosmic symmetry, she and Reese, with their opposite personalities, were a repeat of her mother and father. They were destined to make the same tragic mistakes. At least in this life.

So how could it feel good that she'd told Reese about who she was? Well, maybe not the whole truth, but enough so he'd quit probing. Revealing her iden-tity had been hard. She'd hidden her birth name for so long that forming the words and uttering them had been close to impossible. She'd felt like cracking ice, as if she'd melt, just flow away into that lake and dis-appear if she disclosed the truth.

But when they'd kissed, bolts of hot energy shot down her spine, creating a pleasurable ache between her legs. She closed her eyes, allowing herself to re-live the erotic sensations. It was as if a spiral of heat had rushed into every pulse point of her body. She lost herself, sinking past the point of no return into warm, sensual quicksand. At that moment, she would have gladly done anything he asked.

Why did Reese have an effect on her more power-ful than her most incredible visions?

He seemed different tonight with his cousin. Re-laxed. Easygoing. Someone she could grow to love. She sighed and faced the truth.

She already loved him.

If she made love with him, she'd hurt him. She didn't want to hurt him.

She'd been touched by the story of his parents' divorce, imagining the pain of a teenager caught in the middle of a nasty fight. Reese spoke of very old wounds, and she knew more than anyone about old pain from warring parents. She wanted to hug him, press her lips against his heart and visualize it healing, making his spirit whole again.

She lifted her new book on soul mates, which she'd been reading since she was too restless for sleep. She'd learned there were many versions of the legend, including one from Plato, who claimed that Zeus had split androgynous humans in half because of their pride, but then they were so miserable apart they couldn't even eat. Apollo sewed the humans back together, but they remained incomplete and always longed for their other half, their soul mate. When you found your soul mate, you immediately shared an unspoken understanding of all things. When finally joined, there could be no greater joy.

If things were different, she and Reese could have had absolute perfect joy.

Taki turned on her side and pictured him downstairs, his strong body tangled in the quilts on his bed. If they made love, it would be the most exquisite experience of any lifetime. For both of them. She wouldn't be able to tear herself away from him.

But she could see their future all too clearly. They were too different, their personalities opposite. They'd tear each other apart, just like her mother and father had.

She rolled to her other side. It wasn't fair to him—to either one of them—to allow a love affair to begin. Whether they were soul mates or not, had known each other for several lifetimes or not—none of that mattered. If they became intimate, they would only cause each other pain.

She had to end this now with Reese before it went any further, before he fell in love with her.

It was too late for her, though. He was already part of her, the other half of her soul, and she'd never forget him. Never be happy without him.

THE NEXT MORNING, Reese sat with his cousin in Mike's country oak kitchen.

"I'm telling you, Reese, you should get the hell out of South Florida while you still can." Mike spoke with heated emphasis while pouring two cups of coffee.

"Ah, there she is."

Mike retrieved another mug from the cupboard when Taki entered the kitchen.

Reese smiled at Taki, her hair not yet combed, when she sat across the eat-in kitchen counter looking sleepy but sexy as hell. He'd lain awake most of the night hoping she'd come to him. She never had.

Did the shadows under her eyes mean she hadn't slept, either?

"Miami has just gotten too damned dangerous," Mike continued, placing sugar and cream on the counter. "First your briefcase...next someone will take your life."

"All large cities have their dangers," Reese said with a shrug. Mike made this emotional pitch every visit. "I love Miami. It's the most exciting city in the world." He held up his cup of black coffee in a toast. "To Miami."

Mike snorted. "Exciting, my rear end. You just think your connections in Miami-Dade County will provide the best route to the governor's mansion."

"You want to be governor?" Taki asked as if just waking up. Reese shook his head. He'd have to remember she wasn't a morning person.

Before he could reply, Mike said, "Not if he's dead, he won't. How about you, Taki? Are you crazy about Miami, too?"

"Oh, well...I won't be in Miami much longer," she said.

Her offhand statement was a sharp blow to Reese's gut. For a moment, he couldn't breathe. She was leaving? Where was she going?

"But I've visited some gritty developing countries," she continued, staring at the coffee Mike had poured for her. "Miami is a sanctuary compared to some of the cities I've been to."

Reese took a gulp of coffee and burned his tongue. He'd counted on Taki being around for a long time—like, well, maybe for the rest of this lifetime. *This* lifetime? How had that thought snuck into his logical mind? Of course he knew where it'd come from. Taki.

The thought of her leaving filled him with a strange, hollow ache.

"Is this decaf?" she asked.

"Decaf?" Mike grinned. "I never saw the point."

Reese half expected her to pull a box of herbal tea out of thin air. Instead, she just smiled and pushed the mug away.

He didn't question her about where she was going, when she was leaving. She didn't like being cross-examined. Instead he brooded all through Mike's famous breakfast of eggs, pancakes, sausage, toast, grits and potatoes, which he barely tasted. Taki ate everything but the meat.

He didn't want her to go anywhere. Not yet. Hell, not ever.

"You didn't know she was blowing town, did you?"

"What?" Only half listening to his cousin, Reese watched Taki move effortlessly up a circular staircase to finish packing. It was almost 11:00 a.m., time for them to get on the road.

"That was the first you heard of your girlfriend leaving town," Mike repeated, "and you don't much like the idea."

"I didn't know anything about it," Reese admitted. Mike calling Taki his girlfriend startled him. He didn't object even though it was inaccurate. He'd only known her, what—two weeks? Seemed like much longer.

"I can't figure if you're pissed because she didn't tell you or because she's leaving."

Reese remained silent, not certain of his own reaction, either. Taki had told him she was a gypsy. What did he expect?

"I've never seen you quite so smitten, cuz. Good luck."

Reese shook his head. "Smitten?"

"I'd say that about describes it. I can't wait until Uncle Avery meets your gorgeous yogini. You know, he could use a good stretching in her yoga class. That man is strung so tight he squeaks when he walks."

Reese grinned at that image. "Taki would set my father back on his heels, wouldn't she?"

"No kidding. Man, make sure you invite me to that dinner party. Maybe his favorite golfing buddies will be present. I'm sure Taki would explain karma to the reigning state politicos. Someone needs to, considering the way things are going."

Reese chuckled at the thought of Taki explaining her new age theories to the movers and shakers in Tallahassee.

"And since your mom is a past president of the Dade County Medical Society, what will she think about a woman who prescribes herbs without a license?"

"Taki doesn't prescribe. She offers free advice," Reese said, then wondered if Taki would be around long enough to meet his mom. Yeah, his dad might freak out, but his mom would love her.

THEY SAID THEIR goodbyes to Mike and were on the road before noon. Reese waited until he'd accelerated onto the interstate before asking. He wished he could transport them back to the intimacy of last night and the pleasure he'd known as she'd confided in him. Would she remain as open in the harsh light of day?

Maybe the night hadn't ended exactly as he'd anticipated, but other than temporary disappointment he hadn't been overly worried. He'd thought he had plenty of time to get to know her. Maybe he was wrong.

"Why are you leaving Miami?"

She threw him a startled look.

He shook his head. *Seriously. Didn't she expect me to ask?*

"Lourdes Garcia told me you're one of the most popular instructors at SoBe Spa," he added. "And don't you teach at your ashram, too?"

"My father already has feelers out in Miami. He'll find me soon, so it's time to move on."

"What exactly does he want?"

"Not me. He doesn't care about me," she explained. "He only wants me to sign documents—contracts, stock sales, leases, which I refuse to do. He'd love to have power of attorney."

"Why not let me help you with your legal problems? I'm not without resources."

She shook her head. "You talk just like him."

"What?"

"You've always reminded me of my father. So impatient, arrogant, always questioning my beliefs."

Reese tightened his grip on the steering wheel. Shit. What could he say? Yeah, he knew he was impatient. Arrogant? Maybe so, but he'd never get anything accomplished if he didn't push back a little.

No question he'd doubted her philosophy.

"So the person I remind you of that's not very nice is your father?" he asked, remembering something she'd once said.

"That's why I kept pushing you away, but I've come to understand it's not as simple as that. Your personality is similar to my father's, while I now realize I am very like my mother. Believe me, history has shown that's a terrible combination." After a moment she added wonderingly, "You know, I even resemble her physically."

"I thought we knew each other in previous lives," he said.

"I still believe we did."

After a moment Reese asked, "Did your father abuse you, Taki? Is that why you—"

"Not in the way that you mean." She released a deep sigh. "You know, I don't even like to think about him. Can we change the subject?"

Reese ran a hand through his hair. Damn, but she was making this hard. "When are you leaving?"

"When I find the bowl and give it to Navi."

"And if you never find your bowl?"

When she didn't answer, Reese threw her a quick glance. He didn't expect to find her staring out the window with a faraway look in her eyes.

"At some point I'll have to give up, won't I?" she said.

"But not yet," Reese said. Of course he'd voiced

what she'd consider negative thoughts. Never mind that it looked less and less like either of them would ever find their property. He'd given up on the briefcase. After forty-eight hours, stolen property was seldom recovered.

And now he had mixed feelings about helping her locate that damned bowl. If he did, she would disappear from his life forever.

"Where are you going?" he asked.

CHAPTER ELEVEN

TAKI CLOSED HER eyes and swallowed hard. Now what? If she told Reese about her plan to check out Key West, which sounded like an interesting place to live, full of creative people, if also expensive, he might track her down. If he did, she wouldn't be able to resist him.

But if she simply said, "I don't know where I'm going," he would think she was even loonier than he already did.

And of course she couldn't lie outright. Not that lawyers didn't love to lie. Or what had the judge called it? Misrepresentation.

Just thinking the word made her stiffen, brought back her white-hot rage when she'd learned her father's attorneys had misrepresented the facts about her mom, told lies that ensured her dad got full custody of his daughter.

Taki shook her head to clear her chaotic thoughts. Once again Reese had thrown her mind into turmoil.

"I haven't gone anywhere yet," she told him. "Let's figure out how we're going to find our property."

"Any more psychics up your sleeve?"

Matching his lighter tone, she said, "We could always try a séance."

"Why am I not surprised you know a medium? Not that I'm questioning your beliefs," he added quickly.

"Yes, you are, but I'm actually kidding. I still think I should contact Bruce Mayhugh again," she said.

"Taki, please. We've been through this."

"I know, I know," she said. "But you and your FBI people can be in on everything. Isn't it worth a try?"

He seemed to mull over her suggestion. "I'll discuss it with Javi. Would you consider wearing a wire?"

"A wire? You mean like a listening device so you could hear what goes on?"

"Right. We'd be monitoring you the entire time."

While Reese proposed a few scenarios to see what she thought, Taki breathed a sigh of relief that Reese had stopped his probing. She couldn't tell him where she was going.

Then, with a rush of total, gut-churning horror, she realized her half-truths to Reese were exactly the same sort of misrepresentation her father's lawyers had engaged in sixteen years ago. They hadn't told an out-and-out lie, either, just cleverly shaded the truth about her mother's rebellious life as a young woman. The cruel way they'd portrayed her mother to the court left the judge no choice but to deny her custody of a nine-year-old daughter.

And those heartless misrepresentations had resulted in her mother's death.

She'd misled Reese about who she was, hid the

total truth about why she was leaving. She hadn't told him the depth of her father's cruelty.

Tears pricked at the back of Taki's eyes. She sincerely tried to be a good person, one that made a difference in the world, who made people's lives better.

But maybe she was no better than the people she was running away from.

JUST AFTER DARK, Reese pulled into Taki's driveway and cut the Jag's engine. Considering how late they had left Mike's, they'd made good time. Neither of them spoke for a moment.

Finally, he turned to her. Illuminated by a soft glow from a porch light, she gazed at her hands clasped in her lap. Taki had been unusually quiet for hours, answering his questions only with a nod, or a murmured yes or no.

He'd been practicing law long enough to know that meant she didn't want to volunteer anything other than precisely what was asked.

More than once during the long drive home he'd seen her wipe moisture away from sad eyes. Maybe the idea of wearing a wire bothered her. He'd make certain there was no danger, but if the idea frightened her, she didn't have to go through with it.

"What's wrong, Taki?"

She opened her mouth to issue what he knew would be a quick denial but stopped herself.

"I'm tired," she admitted.

"It was a long trip," he agreed. "Didn't you sleep well last night?"

"No," Taki whispered.

"Me, either." And they both knew why.

She glanced up, her eyes moist and bright. "Really?"

"Really."

"I make a special valerian tea blend that would help you sleep tonight. It's got a strong taste, but works very well. Just add honey and…" She trailed off. "That is, if you don't mind being prescribed herbs illegally."

Reese smiled, marveling at her attempt to be helpful even when so obviously upset. "Thanks," he said. "I'd very much like some of your tea."

"Okay, then," she said and pushed open her door.

He followed her into her cottage, wishing he knew what went wrong, how to get through to her. He hated to see her so dispirited. On this trip he'd realized there was an air of loneliness about Taki. Maybe because she was an only child. She hid it well, but he sensed she'd been fascinated by, and maybe a little envious of, his large family.

And what was bothering her now? Had he done or said something to cause the tears she tried to hide? Was she thinking about her move?

"I'll just be a minute," she said. She flipped on a light and went into the kitchen.

As he rubbed his hands together, Reese shook his head. It was almost as cold inside her home as out. He knew the cottage didn't have central heat, only space heaters, which were expensive to run. Taki insisted she liked cool temperatures, but could living in an environment like this really be good for her?

She returned with a plastic bag containing loose herbs and a round, aluminum object he couldn't identify.

"I doubt if you have a tea infuser," she said, "so I've included one with the blend. Just put the tea inside the infuser and insert in boiling water. Allow it to steep for at least five minutes."

When she handed him the tea, he pulled her into his arms, wanting to warm her, himself, and not allow their journey together to end.

"Thanks," he said, breathing the word against her soft, sweetly scented hair.

"You're welcome. Thank you for the ride." Her voice caught, and she ran her hands under his jacket, hugging him tightly.

He hugged her back. "Tell me what's bothering you."

"I can't," she said, her words muffled against his chest.

"If you're worried about wearing a wire when you meet Mayhugh, then—"

"It's not that."

"Is it your father?" He lifted her chin and caught his breath at the tears swimming in her blue eyes. "Maybe I can help."

Shaking her head, she attempted a smile, then lifted onto her toes and lightly kissed him on the cheek. Reese turned his head and caught her mouth hungrily, tasting salty tears on warm, trembling lips that parted willingly for him.

As he explored her mouth, he realized that none of their many differences seemed to matter when he kissed her. Whenever she was in his arms, he felt they belonged together, no matter how different, no matter the obstacles.

Those damn obstacles just kept getting in the way.

He pulled away and located a handkerchief in a pocket. She grinned as she accepted it and blew her nose. Then she laughed, seeming a little embarrassed by the noise.

"Way to spoil the mood, huh?" she said.

"You're too sweet to spoil anything, Taki."

Releasing a sigh of denial, she looked at the floor and shook her head.

He drew her into his arms again. "Let me stay with you tonight."

She sucked in a quick breath, causing her breasts to press into him. His suggestion had definitely affected her. He just wasn't sure how.

She stepped out of his embrace, her eyes now bright but dry, and cupped his cheek with her warm palm. "I don't think I'd be very good company tonight, Reese," she said softly.

"Let me be the judge of that."

She cocked an eyebrow and dropped her hand. "I thought you wanted to be governor. Now it's a judge?"

He wanted to smile at her attempt to lighten their

downer mood, but frustration ate at him. Why did she always push him away?

"Are you sure you're all right?" he asked.

She nodded. "Don't worry about me. I get like this sometimes when I don't get enough sleep."

"Okay." He studied her carefully. There was something else going on, and he hated to leave her alone and unhappy. "I'll call you tomorrow after I talk to Javi."

"All right," she said. She tucked her arm into his and moved him toward the door. "Now go home, make some of my tea and get a good night's rest. You have to work tomorrow."

He didn't believe anything short of a narcotic would provide him a good night's sleep. His thoughts would be filled with her mysterious moods and how much he hated leaving her.

How desperately he wanted to make love to her.

"Good night," he said and kissed her softly.

"Goodbye, Reese."

TAKI REMAINED AT the door, straining to hear the fading roar of the Jaguar's engine. When she heard nothing but the faint ticks of her kitchen clock, she knew Reese was gone and that she would never see him again.

She turned from the door and allowed her gaze to roam over her small, comfortable cottage. Time to start packing. She shivered, unsure if it was from the cold or from the longing that consumed her so thoroughly. *If only, if only...*

But it was time to go. She needed to get away from Reese before she ruined his life. She was glad she'd told him the truth, or most of it, anyway. But they'd never make it work between them. They were too different. He was too much like her father. Or maybe she was too much like her mother.

Bowl or no bowl, she had to leave Miami and make a fresh start somewhere new. But she'd done this so many times. She was so very tired of being a nomad.

She closed her eyes and was briefly transported to another room in a much larger house. A warm room. A room full of love. She was laughing so hard that her tummy hurt while playing a game with her mother and father. She wore one of her mother's huge, floppy hats and a pair of too-big shoes, pretending to be something she wasn't even then.

But why...why couldn't she picture her mother's face? Taki squeezed her eyes shut, trying to bring the image to her mind. Had she forgotten what her mother looked like? How could that happen?

Opening her eyes, she grabbed the tapestry footstool and scooted it across the hardwood floor. At her bedroom closet, she stepped on the stool and reached to the farthest corner for a large, ragged cardboard box. Her treasure chest. She kept it with her always, taking it whenever she moved, but had avoided looking inside for years.

She carried the carton to the middle of her living room, turned on the space heater and sat cross-legged on the floor beside it.

First came letters, depositions, stock certificates,

a copy of her grandmother's will—for years she'd tossed legal garbage into the box and out of sight. Now she had to remove handfuls of hateful documents to find what she wanted....

An old photo album, its yellowing, plastic-protected pages long since ripped from the binder. On the first leaf she found a faded color photograph of her parents standing beside their elegant, three-tiered wedding cake, gazing into each other's eyes with complete adoration. When she flipped the page they were laughing and feeding each other messy gobs of white frosting. Taki smiled and stretched out along the floor with her chin propped on her hand.

How could she forget her mother's face when everyone always said they looked just alike? Her first-grade teacher had even told her mom on back-to-school night, "I don't need to ask whose mother you are."

With tender care, Taki leafed through the only photo album she had taken from Rhode Island, one compiled by her mom. The photos revealed images of happy, carefree days with her parents. Taki ran her index finger across a photograph of the three of them on a swing, grinning at the camera. Who had taken that shot? Where had the swing been located? She didn't remember one on the estate, but there must have been.

Hard to believe she had once been that little and so obviously cherished by two loving people. She remembered few specifics of those times, only vague, haunting memories that could have sprung from these very pictures, rather than from the events themselves. All of this seemed so long ago.

What had been etched painfully in her mind was her father's subsequent harsh rule, a structured life full of strict nannies, starched dresses and standards impossible to live up to. Her father could give her anything on earth she wanted. Anything except love.

Her father had taken love out of a child's life as surely as he had killed her mother. He'd probably torn down that swing set.

Closing the photo album, Taki pulled more mementos from the carton. Anniversary and Valentine's Day cards from her father to her mother. Four goofy pictures of the two of them in a photo booth. Flimsy newspaper clippings about important social events in their lives. A small lock of blond baby hair in a frame. Her hair, she supposed.

Surrounded by keepsakes on her living room floor, Taki began to reread a stack of her parents' love letters.

DURING THE THIRTY-MINUTE drive from Taki's home on Miami Beach to his condo on Brickell Avenue, Reese tried to pinpoint exactly when she'd become unreachable. He must have inadvertently touched a sensitive nerve to cause her withdrawal. Had he somehow hurt her feelings? He couldn't fathom what he'd said, but believed her cool, polite distance had everything to do with her family. No, had to be her hated father, the man she called a monster. He decided to run a search on the name she'd given him tomorrow.

As he mentally combed over every snippet of their conversation for hidden nuance, he always circled back to one disturbing thought. Her parting words sounded like goodbye. Forever. As in, *Goodbye, Reese. Have a nice life. It's been great and I've enjoyed knowing you, but we'll never see each other again.*

The end, *fini,* over and out.

And, damn, he had heard regret. She wanted to see him again. He knew how to read people. That ability was what made him a good prosecutor. Taki was as attracted to him as he was to her.

Or maybe he just wanted to believe that. Maybe he was fooling himself.

As he turned into the concrete garage of his highrise building, Reese wondered how he could possibly read so much into two short syllables. Often he didn't get that much meaning from a two-hundred-page deposition transcript. He eased the transmission into Park and cut the engine.

Rubbing the bridge of his nose where Taki's recent gift had begun to irritate, he realized he already relied on the optical magnification. Maybe the glasses pinched a little, but they were definitely worth the bother.

He relaxed his head against the backrest. A faint click sounded as the Jag's alarm snapped on automatically. A tiny red light over the windshield began to blink.

Regarding himself with pure disgust, Reese admitted he had a feeling—no, much more than a *feeling*. A certainty that churned in his gut. If he didn't go back to Taki right now, he would never see her again. She would slip out of his life as if she'd never been in it.

What was happening to him? He had no facts, no evidence to back up this ridiculous theory. All he had was a softly spoken farewell that sounded moving-day final.

The hell with that shit.

He turned over the key, but the ignition froze because the alarm had engaged, and a shrill siren echoed against the surrounding concrete. Reese killed the noise and backed out of the parking space, refusing to believe she could disappear in half an hour.

Not even Taki could manage that.

TAKI LOOKED UP at an insistent knock on her front door. She'd been rereading a poem by her father, not one of his best, where he begged her mother to forgive him, to marry him, to "ignore the jealous roars of the howling Spencer beast." Taki interpreted the "beast" to be the Spencer money. Good description.

Finding it impossible to follow the sweet but somewhat skewed logic of the poem while someone beat on her door, Taki rose and checked through the peephole, assuming her visitor was Victoria wanting to learn about her reading with Robin. Or maybe about her journey with Reese.

As if her thoughts made him manifest, Reese stood in the doorway with an unreadable expression on his handsome face. She heard herself gasp his name and without thinking, opened the door.

"Can I come in?" he asked.

"Oh…of course." She stepped out of the way and motioned him inside. "Did you forget something?"

"Yes," he said. His gaze swept the interior of the cottage, and he nodded. "I see you've already started packing."

Following his gaze to her cardboard box of memories in the middle of the floor, Taki stepped forward to tuck her mementoes away again, back where they belonged. As she moved past Reese, he shot out his arm and pulled her to him.

"I don't want you to go," he said as he wrapped both arms around her, hugging her tight.

She rested her cheek against his chest, drawing the familiar scent of his spicy aftershave into her lungs. Where did he think she was going? "But I was just going to—"

"I mean I don't want you to leave Miami."

"Oh," she whispered. *Why did he come back? Is he going to ask me to stay?*

He raised her chin with his thumb and searched her face. The room spun during his careful scrutiny, and she focused on a tender light in his gaze that first warmed her with its glow, then consumed her with a fiery surge of heat. She placed her hands on his shoulders to steady herself, and knew she could never let him go.

Taki parted her lips, hoping Reese would kiss her soon.

When he slanted his head and moved close, she raised her face, longing for his mouth to claim hers.

Sweet, desperate yearning engulfed her. Swallowed by a wave of pure desire, she closed her eyes—but he pulled back, just out of reach.

"Stay awhile," he said, his voice intense, demanding, his breath moving a lock of hair against her ear.

She placed her hands around his neck. "You, too," she whispered.

As she pulled him toward her, Taki wondered at her recklessness, why she now needed Reese to touch her more than she needed to breathe. She'd known this would happen. Her attraction to him was too intense, too dangerous, too—everything. A mistake from the beginning.

But it didn't matter, she decided as his lips captured hers. She wanted him. He wanted her. Nothing could stop the inevitable.

When his hands cupped her buttocks, she rotated her hips against his erection, thinking she and Reese had danced this erotic, frustrating tango through countless lifetimes together.

As she half pulled him, and he half carried her toward the bedroom, Taki yanked his turtleneck out of his khakis. She smoothed her hands up the bare skin of his chest, delighting in the way his muscles tensed beneath her touch. God, he was gorgeous. She found his nipple and teased it with her thumb, causing him to issue a throaty moan and drop her to her feet.

They stood at her bed. She looked up at him and smiled into those dark eyes she loved so much. Stepping back, she pulled her sweater overhead and flung it aside. Reese's gaze dropped to her bare breasts.

She sucked in a breath, her nipples already taut in response to an ache only he could alleviate.

"You're beautiful," he said. His long fingers caressed the flesh of her right breast, tenderly circling her nipple. She closed her eyes and reveled in the soft brush of his touch. She wanted to be beautiful for him. Only him.

Never feeling more centered, so absolutely grounded in the present, she unzipped her jeans and slipped them off her hips. Next came bikini panties, and she stood naked before him. No matter what secrets she'd been forced to protect, this night she would give herself to him totally. And she would take whatever he offered. There would be no barriers between them. Tonight they would add another memorable chapter to their dance through time, one she would never forget.

She raised her eyes and met his hot stare as he began to loosen his buckle.

REESE ADMIRED TAKI'S slim body standing proudly before him, knowing this moment would burn in his memory forever. He'd never received a more honest gift nor seen a female form that excited him more.

Her full breasts rose and fell sharply with each breath, her hands clenching and unclenching by her sides. His arousal jerked as he imagined her hands on him, warm and supple.

Her lips parted. She released a slow, shaky breath when he dropped the last of his clothing to the floor.

He stepped forward to embrace her, eager for the

feel of her, the heat of her flesh. She melted into his arms, soft and strong, full of contradictions that made her fascinating and frustrating. Husky sounds vibrated from her graceful throat. The uninhibited way she responded to him deepened his desire, hardened him to the point of pain. Her breasts molded to him perfectly, as did her belly, her hips. He needed her.

Kissing her, loving her, stroking her, Reese pulled Taki onto the bed, pressed his body against her warmth. She met him hungrily, eagerly. Her mouth, her hands, her hips, even her feet caressed him, moved against him with an urgent, sensual message that took him beyond reason, beyond remembering who he was and what he wanted.

He wanted only Taki. Nothing could ever be more important. Nothing would stop him from having her. Keeping her.

Her eyes appeared bottomless in the dark as he smoothed his hand down her velvet skin to explore the moisture between her legs. She purred an encouraging moan, and he rolled her under him. As he entered her, she arched beneath him. Staring wonderingly into her face, he acknowledged a fleeting remembrance of a similar moment from another time. Then any memory was lost to a passion that threatened to tear him apart.

"WHY DID YOU come back?"

Taki's soft words barely penetrated the cocoon of contentment that enveloped Reese. He didn't open his eyes. They were in her bed, somehow sprawled over the sheets, her cheek resting on his bare chest, his arm around her. Beyond that, the boundaries were blurred. He wasn't sure where he began and she left off.

He'd never felt this close to another being in his life.

He'd always believed when people spoke of becoming "one" with someone else, it was in the more, well, graphic sense. Before tonight, he would never have believed he could truly get lost in another person. Or that after having achieved such a unique bond, he would never want it to end.

He felt stronger because of their closeness, maybe even a better person. Certainly he'd never enjoyed this inner wellspring of happiness, a feeling of almost weightlessness.

Taki's breath feathered across his damp skin, creating a pleasurable shiver. Maybe he should turn on a heater for them, but he didn't want to move. Everything was perfect right now.

"Reese?"

"Mmm?" he said, lightly stroking her shoulder, trying to figure out why he felt so complete. He'd had great sex plenty of times before.

"Are you having an MCR?"

Thinking, yes, in a way he was, Reese chuckled and opened his eyes. Then blinked and opened them wider. Dangling from the ceiling were countless dolls—no. As his eyes adjusted to the faint light, he recognized winged angels of every description and size staring down at them in the bed. For an instant, he wanted to cover Taki's naked body from their prying eyes.

"Reese?" she said again.

Finding his voice, he said, "I...I think I'm having a vision."

"What kind of vision?"

"Taki, what's that?" He pointed up.

She raised her head, then lowered it with a giggle and kissed his chest. "My guardian angels."

"Do you need so...many of them?"

"Yes, actually I do. They protect me from negative energy, and as you know there's a lot of that in the universe."

"I see," Reese said, swallowing hard. Would Taki ever stop surprising him? Smoothing her long hair, tangled from their lovemaking, he hoped he would eventually become accustomed to how differently she approached the world. Life with Taki would certainly keep him on his toes. Or, as she'd likely put it, in the present moment.

"They'll protect you, too," she said. "In fact, I think I'll give you one."

"This isn't some sort of Santeria or voodoo, is it?"

"Worried you'll find a dead chicken on your doorstep? You really do need an angel to ward off your negative thoughts."

"No," he said, turning to plant a kiss on the top of her head. "Not when I have you."

She snuggled closer and murmured, "Thank you. That's the sweetest thing anyone has ever said to me."

They lay quietly for a few moments while Reese

examined the suspended angels, wondering where they'd all come from. Some were intricately designed with wings of white lace or satin and brightly painted faces. Others were only vague characterizations of a plump cherub. One looked more threatening than protective to him, but she did feature a lovely golden halo.

"Why did you come back?" Taki asked again. "What did you forget?"

"To ask you not to go."

"Oh."

"I had this overpowering feeling, a certainty, really, that I would never see you again, that you were going to start packing tonight and disappear from my life." He stroked her hair, waiting for her to tease him for relying upon feelings.

But she just nodded, and that slight motion caused her hair to tickle his chest. He kissed her head again, but froze when she spoke.

"That proves we're soul mates," she said. "I'm leaving tomorrow."

CHAPTER TWELVE

"DON'T GO."

Taki closed her eyes as Reese's soft request rumbled against her cheek. What could she tell him that made sense, that didn't make her sound like a lunatic? After the bond they'd just forged, she wanted him to know everything.

She placed her palm across his navel. According to Plato, the navel was the only remnant of humans' original form after Apollo sewed them back together. She let the heat from Reese's center flow into her hand, knowing she would forever long for this man, her other half.

"I have to," she said. "My father is getting close." *More half-truths.*

"If you stay, I can help you."

"But you're part of the problem."

"I am? How so?"

"I can't explain why, but if I remain I'll only hurt you."

"Why can't you explain it to me?"

She released a sigh. Reese wasn't going to give up. "You'll only laugh."

"I promise not to laugh."

She squeezed her eyes tighter, willing the hot tears that pricked her lids to evaporate. How could she leave him now? *Do I have the strength to do what I should?*

He turned, placing her beneath him on the bed. His cool fingers smoothed hair away from her face. "You told me once that you met me for a purpose. Do you remember that?"

She nodded, not trusting herself to speak.

His dark eyes searched hers as he spoke. "Well, maybe I'm supposed to help you. Stick around and let me do that."

"Reese, I..."

"Why are you crying?" he asked as he brushed away a tear that spilled down her cheek. "Tell me what's wrong."

"I can't," she whispered again.

"After the honesty we just shared, you still don't trust me?"

She caught her breath at the yearning in his words. "It's not you."

"Don't you know that the way we are together is a rare, beautiful thing?" When Reese's lips turned up in a half smile, the ache in her heart intensified. "I think I would trust you with my life."

Blinking back tears, she reached up and touched the space between his eyebrows. "No one has ever said such sweet things to me."

"Can you read my mind by doing that?" he asked, his smile turning into a teasing grin.

"No." She dropped her hand.

"Too bad. I'm willing to give anything a try." Placing his thumb in the center of her forehead he murmured, "Nope. Not a thing."

She giggled, twined her fingers into his and pulled their joined hands to her heart center.

"I'd give a lot to understand you, moonbeam," he said.

"Moonbeam?" she asked.

"That's how I think of you sometimes," he said. "Mysterious and mystical, soft and beautiful."

"Oh, Reese," she murmured, squeezing his hands.

After a moment he said, "Let me help you with your father."

"No." Taki placed all ten fingers over his lips to stop his words. "No. But thank you for offering."

He kissed her palm and slid his lips to her wrist, pausing to exhale warm breath on her raging pulse. "If you're in some kind of danger, I can arrange for protection."

Touched by his offer, she cupped his cheek with her hand. "Why do you think I'm in danger?"

His dark eyes continued to search hers. "Something your psychic friend said, some business about a flaming tower. Plus, don't forget Izzo and Romero."

Taki smiled tenderly at him as pleasured warmth surged through her. He *had* paid attention to Robin's reading after all. Reese was growing, changing. If only they could have more than this one night together. She was changing, too, had even managed to open up to him.

"You worry too much," she said, moving her finger

to the line that always creased his strong brow. As she gently massaged, he closed his lids. *If only, if only...*

But at least the generous universe had given them this one night.

"Would you like to know what I'm thinking right now?" she asked.

He murmured, "Sure," but sounded a little doubtful, perhaps undecided about hearing her thoughts.

"If you really want to know, I'll tell you." She trailed her fingers lightly across his cheek, his chest, his abdomen, moving toward his groin.

He sucked in a quick breath. "I really want to know."

"I'm thinking," she said, "that I want you to stay with me the rest of the night."

Reese widened his eyes. "You do, huh?"

"Oh, yes," she said, her hand continuing south. "I really do."

"I like those particular thoughts," he said, staring into her face.

"Good."

"At least tell me where you're going," he said, his voice husky.

"I'm not going anywhere tonight," she whispered, pulling him close.

THOROUGHLY CHILLED, REESE woke the next morning to the smug smiles of hovering cherubs. On his left, Taki still slumbered, snugly cocooned in the covers. *Now, here's a real angel,* he thought as he traced his thumb across her smooth, cool cheek. Her face glowed in the soft morning light.

But he was late, and Monday morning wouldn't wait. Deciding to let her sleep a while longer, Reese swung his legs out of bed and pulled on his briefs and khakis. Shrugging on his shirt, he picked up his shoes and eased Taki's bedroom door shut behind him.

When he turned, the sight of the cardboard box in the center of her living room floor hit his gut like a sledgehammer, a harsh reminder that she was leaving.

Damn, but he didn't want her to go. She was good for him, and he was good for her. He helped ground her. Despite the crazy differences between them, he believed that what they'd started had a chance to grow, could morph into something real and permanent. But for that opportunity, she had to remain in Miami.

How could he convince her to stay? Rubbing his chin, Reese considered who might have influence over Taki. Victoria, the landlady? Ah. Where did the great guru weigh in on her change of address? Could he enlist the swami's help to convince her to stay? Reese decided to ask Taki to speak to her teacher before she left. That ought to buy him a day, at least.

Why wouldn't she tell him where she was going? Was it possible she didn't know? He shook his head. The woman was full of mysteries, puzzles impossible to unravel. She was scared of her father, but he'd make certain the man couldn't harm her.

Reese stepped into the kitchenette and lit the gas

stove. What the hell if he was fifteen minutes late for a staff meeting. Would it really matter? When he was with Taki his constant sense of urgency, the need to work harder, faster, to cram every minute full of something productive, seemed to evaporate.

He'd boil water for herb tea and wake Taki when it was ready. The more he thought about it, easing Taki's life appealed to him a great deal. For that, he needed to keep her in his zip code.

In search of the space heater, Reese stepped back into her living room and glanced down at the cardboard box. As he rubbed his hands together for warmth, he wondered what she had decided to pack first. Probably angels or candles or a yoga mat. A manila file caught his eye.

Legal pleadings and documents had spilled all over a faded blue Oriental rug. He squatted before the box and picked up a letter addressed to one Kimberly Howell Spencer. He nodded, recognizing her previous name. These were documents from the past Taki hated. *Kim* was a nice name, but he liked *Taki* better.

As he thumbed through a stack of unopened envelopes from law firms in New York City and Newport, Rhode Island, Reese recognized the names of heavyweight legal talent.

Then he saw the elegant, embossed gold logo of the Spencer Trust and felt himself go cold. The Spencer Trust, an entity able to send the Dow Jones plummeting with the slightest sell-off, was frequently in the financial news. And the news wasn't always pleasant.

It had never once occurred to him she could be connected to those particular Spencers.

Her father wasn't just wealthy; he was one powerful man.

WHEN TAKI WOKE in bed alone, she thought Reese had already left. Of course he had to go to work. She'd wanted one last goodbye, one last kiss to hold in her heart forever, but maybe it was better this way. Then she heard a noise in the outer room and grabbed a robe.

She found him reading her grandmother's will, the worry line between his eyes edged deep with concentration as he examined the hated document.

A shrill whistle from the kitchen shattered the morning quiet. Reese glanced up and smiled at her.

She smiled back. "Good morning."

"Good morning."

She tightened the robe around her waist. Keenly aware of his scrutiny, she crossed the room to the kitchen.

She removed the kettle from the fire and shut off the flame. Reese entered the room behind her. He stood close, and she could smell her perfume on his shirt. She couldn't look at him, afraid of what she'd find in his eyes now that he truly understood what a monster her father was.

"You weren't kidding about your father's wealth."

Taki scanned the kitchen, looking for a way out. Reese had thoughtfully placed tea bags in two mugs ready for boiling water. He'd meant to surprise her.

"Did you think I was?" she asked.

"I don't think you made it quite clear."

"It's hard to talk about."

"What's wrong? Why won't you look at me?"

Her heart twisted when she heard the hurt in his husky voice. So it had already started. She never wanted to hurt anyone. She'd been hurt too much herself.

Raising her gaze to his, she said, "Has your opinion of me changed now that you know who my father is?"

"Why would it?" Puzzled eyes searched hers. "I don't know anything about your father. I don't remember even seeing a photograph."

"He's private."

"Like father, like daughter."

"Oh, please don't say that. Never even think that."

He held up a hand. "Sorry."

"I don't need the money," she said. "I don't want it."

"Okay. But why not just give away your inheritance? There's plenty of worthy causes to choose from."

"It's tainted money."

"A whole hell of a lot of tainted money. The Spencer Trust controls one of the largest fortunes in America."

She shook her head, knowing Reese would never understand. No one ever did. Not even Victoria.

"What did your father do to you, Taki?" He touched her face gently.

"He killed my mother," she blurted.

His expression clouded. "I thought your mother killed herself."

"Because of the way he treated her."

Reese took her hand and led her to the couch. He pulled her against him and said, "Tell me about your mother. You told me she overdosed on drugs."

Taki took a deep breath. She'd never told anyone about her mother, but she wanted to tell Reese, needed to tell her soul mate, even if he wouldn't understand.

"My father divorced her because he thought she was having an affair. She wasn't. I know she wasn't. She loved him—although I can't imagine why." Taki paused, realizing her love for Reese also made no sense. Her father was right. In some ways, she *was* like her mother.

"Anyway, my father got complete custody of me because his lawyers painted a horrible picture of Mom as a druggie to the court. I only got to see her once a month and it had to be at Dad's house."

"How do you know all this if you were nine years old?"

"When I turned twenty-one my grandmother's will stipulated that all the records be opened to me. I read everything and confronted my father. He laughed at me, told me I was just like my mom. I took off not long after that."

"Go on."

"He didn't want me. He had no use for a child. He just didn't want my mother to have me. She begged him for more visitation. She wrote him letter after letter, which he kept, probably to gloat over. I read those, too." Taki took a deep breath to gain control of her voice. "The day she took the pills, she came to the house sobbing, hysterical, begging my father to let her see me. I was on the stairs listening. My father sent her away, as usual." Taki swallowed hard. "I never saw my mother again. I wasn't even allowed to go to the funeral."

Reese hugged her close. "Oh, God, Taki. I'm so sorry."

With her cheek resting on his strong, warm chest, Taki closed her eyes. "And after her death, my father made my life hell. He couldn't stand to even look at me. I think it's because I look just like her."

"I agree he sounds like a monster."

She inhaled deeply. Time to get the last truth out in the open. "And you're just like him, Reese."

He stiffened. "No."

"All he does is work—just like you. He's even a lawyer, too."

"I am nothing like your father, Taki."

She sat up so she could see his face. She owed it to Reese to be completely honest. "Yes, you are. And that's why it will never work between us. You make fun of my beliefs, and you're always in a hurry to get to the next thing you've got scheduled."

"That's my job. I behave that way so I can put criminals in jail."

She shook her head. "We're too different."

"But it doesn't have to be that way. We can—"

"We'll tear each other apart, just like my parents. Don't you see? That's why I have to leave today," she said. "I don't want to hurt you. We've both been hurt enough already."

As the pain her words created tightened his face, she looked away. Maybe she'd been wrong about who'd been making whom miserable throughout their lifetimes together. Maybe she'd been hurting him. This had to stop. It hurt too much, and she didn't want either of them to go through more pain.

"So I'm a cruel, heartless, money-grubbing attorney, just like your father?" he demanded.

She met his gaze again and swallowed at the growing fury she saw in his beautiful eyes. "I don't think you're heartless."

"Just cruel? Oh, that makes me feel better."

"No, not cruel, either," she said. Now he was confusing her. "But we can't help who we are."

"Let me get this straight," he said, his words now hard. "You're running away so you won't get hurt."

"And so I won't hurt you."

"There's a chance of heartbreak in every romantic relationship. But you're afraid to take a leap of faith, take a chance on love?"

She looked down at her hands, which were fisted tightly. "I had a quiet, serene existence before I met you," she said.

"I have to tell you, Taki, it doesn't really sound to me as if your life was so Zen."

"But now it's nothing but turmoil." She'd never be able to explain to Reese how deeply he touched her, how much he made her feel. Her love for him created emotions as strong as what she'd felt after the loss of her mother. She couldn't go through that again. Wouldn't.

He shook his head. "I don't know who you are."

"I'm the same person I was last night."

"I have to go." He rose and stepped toward the front door.

She let him go. *It was meant to be this way, better this way.*

With his hand on the knob, he paused and turned. Glittering dark eyes narrowed as they met hers.

"What are you really afraid of, Taki?"

WITH AN ANGRY slam echoing in her ears, Taki strangled out a moan and collapsed on the sofa. How had things turned so horribly wrong? She pressed her palms against the tears that threatened to flow. Just when she'd grown close to Reese, discovered he was truly a good soul even though similar to her father, she'd pushed him away forever.

The knowledge that she'd hurt him throbbed like a deep, slashing wound. Hadn't she tried to keep away from him, though, so as not to cause him this hurt? She'd refused dinner with him, hadn't told him about Mayhugh.

But she hadn't tried hard enough. Not nearly hard enough. Her desire for him had trampled over the need to consider his feelings on this journey together. She'd selfishly wanted to spend the weekend with him, to get to know him better. Make love to him.

And they'd made such sweet, sweet love, which made the pain even worse.

She'd known how her actions would affect him, and she'd gone right ahead and done it anyway.

Because she'd allowed herself to become attached. To Reese, to the bowl, to Victoria, Miami. Yoga taught that attachment, especially to material objects, always brought misery. Just look at how miserable she was right now.

Taki turned her cheek into the couch and closed her eyes. Once again she'd ruined everything with no chance to make amends in this lifetime. She'd obviously lost her soul mate. *How long this time?* Another stab of regret caused her to catch her breath. She would miss him. Oh, how she would miss him. Her other half.

She must have loved Reese through countless lifetimes. They never managed to work things out probably because she always screwed things up.

Wiping away her tears, Taki moved to the cottage's back door and stepped outside. Dawn was her favorite time of day. All the world's beautiful creatures were just waking up and that new energy always lifted her spirits.

Raising her arms overhead, she took a deep breath of the fresh, cool air, then performed five half sun salutes to center herself. When finished, she felt no better, but gazed fondly at her herb garden. All the plants looked healthy. The temperatures weren't cool enough to bother them, nowhere near freezing. She knelt and dug her fingers into the rich soil, feeling for the moisture level. Miami was the perfect place to grow herbs in the winter.

But she had to go. To be safe, she should just throw what she could in the Jeep and abandon Miami right now.

If she didn't— Taki came to her feet, took a huge breath and exhaled slowly. Yes, they'd come for her. She'd have to deal with the lawyers, face judges and reporters, negative souls with hidden agendas.

She'd have to see her father. Talk to her father. Sign those papers he needed her to sign so he could make more dirty money.

And then what? Then what?

No longer sure why she continued to run and run and run, Taki clasped her hands in prayer position and looked heavenward.

No, she needed to look inward. She needed to find the correct path to lessen the hurt she'd caused Reese.

What would be worse? Running away or staying?

TUESDAY MORNING, SCOWLING at the time signature at the bottom right of his computer monitor, Reese sat back, considering how he'd tell his boss the bad news. He liked and respected Cynthia Lettino, the United States Attorney for the Southern District of Florida, but she was tough. Tough and smart. Cynthia expected results from her assistants.

And in fifteen minutes he had to inform her that one of the supports in the foundation of his case against Romero was in the wind. He believed— no, knew his evidence was strong without Claudia

Romero, but her testimony made the construction earthquake-proof.

Cynthia expected him for a status update at ten. How would she react? At the last status conference, his star witness had been exactly where she was supposed to be. Maybe he should have given Cynthia the news sooner, but he kept expecting Claudia to contact him, that there'd be no need to worry anyone.

Or maybe he'd been distracted by another woman, one who'd lost a bowl that sang.

Shit. He shoved back from his desk and walked to the window, staring at the view but not seeing anything. He shoved his hands in his pockets.

Damn Taki. Since he'd left her yesterday morning he'd concentrated on nothing but work, allowing no time for personal concerns. Total immersion in trial strategy kept disturbing thoughts of her at bay. He didn't want to think about her, refused to think about her. Didn't know what to think about her.

Last night he'd gotten two, maybe three hours of sleep at the most. He'd finally given up. No point lying in the dark, obsessing about where Taki had wandered off to, if he could find her. If he wanted to find her. So at 3:00 a.m. he got up, made a pot of coffee and went back to work preparing questions for the witnesses who would testify. People whose locations he could count on.

That's the way he felt now. As if it was the middle of the night and everything in his life sucked. He sighed. *Talk about negative thoughts.*

With a silent curse, he grabbed his coat and strode down the hall to Cynthia's office.

The door was open, and she sat at her huge walnut desk, speaking on the phone. She waved him in with a distracted smile. Reese sat in one of the chairs before her desk and watched a talented politician schmooze whoever was on the other end of the line.

Cynthia was in her late fifties, what his father would call a handsome woman. She was trim, had shoulder-length almost black hair, usually worn clipped neatly off her face, which made people notice her large, green eyes. Cynthia worked tirelessly for justice in this community and didn't play favorites. When her son was arrested on a minor drug charge, she hadn't intervened, had made certain he was treated just like any other offender. It had nearly killed her, but Reese respected her all the more for her actions, which meshed with his vision of equal justice for all—not more equal for the privileged few.

"So where are we on the Romero case?" she asked when she'd finished her call.

Her face remained impassive as he launched into the details of the prosecution, and remained that way until he got to Claudia's disappearance.

Cynthia stopped making notes and sat back.

"So no idea where Claudia Romero is holed up?" Cynthia asked evenly.

"The bureau is still looking for her, but so far nothing," Reese said. He had no clue what his boss was thinking.

"What about tracing her cell phone signal?"

"She left the phone in her apartment."

"Smart," Cynthia said, tapping her pen on the desk. "She probably bought a disposable."

"I still think she'll come in for the trial."

"Why?"

Reese shrugged. "Just my sense of her from our interviews. She's afraid of her ex, but definitely wants him behind bars."

"Do you think you can get a conviction without her testimony?"

"I hope so, but her journal contains specifics. Names, places, details I can corroborate that make the case a lock."

Cynthia nodded. "I read your synopsis of the journal. It's the sort of thing a jury loves."

"But without Claudia to authenticate—"

"So find her," Cynthia stated, her voice gone hard. "I'll call Bill over at the bureau and get him to authorize more agents for the search."

She reached for the phone again, and Reese stood, taking that as his dismissal.

Cynthia met his gaze while waiting for her call to connect. She narrowed her eyes. "Don't disappoint me, Reese."

EARLY WEDNESDAY MORNING Taki dressed in several layers, including a snug ski cap, and pulled on her hiking boots. She placed a notebook, her field knife and a thermos inside her favorite wicker basket, one with a comfortable handle, and exited the cottage into cool morning air. The sun hadn't quite made it over the horizon, but its light was beginning to streak the eastern sky.

She was going wild-crafting—or her version of wild-crafting, anyway—something she hadn't done since leaving California.

She hadn't heard from Reese, but she'd noticed a suspicious blue SUV hanging around the neighborhood. Yesterday the driver had raised a video camera to record her departure.

So the Trust had found her. She knew it would happen eventually and wondered if Reese had given her away.

Yoga and meditation hadn't eased her troubled thoughts so far, and that told her what terrible shape her mind was in. The trip to her psychic had given her nothing but more conflict with Reese. Working in her own garden only made her sad when she thought about abandoning her beautiful plants. Navi was involved in a two-day fast and retreat, so she couldn't consult him until tomorrow.

She needed help right now. What was left to calm a troubled spirit?

A hike through the forest to search for wild herbs or edible plants.

Relieved the Trust's investigator hadn't arrived this early, Taki drove south toward Homestead again. She'd noticed several large wooded tracts on her visit to Mayhugh. The best areas were those that were scheduled for development, and she'd seen at least one sign announcing that construction would soon begin. If she could find that location again, she'd start there. She wasn't going to steal anything from the earth, although she'd really be preserving anything she took. Today she wanted to just make note of what grew here, what bloomed in the chilly weather. Maybe she'd snip off a bit of a plant for study later, especially if she could find seeds to germinate.

Or at least try to get them to sprout. You never knew if the seeds would grow out of their natural home. Some important element might be lacking, the balance not quite right. To her, that was the joy of wild-crafting. Learning how Mother Nature worked in the wild and trying to replicate that in a garden.

She'd do no harm to the environment. What she was looking for most people considered weeds, undesirable and intrusive.

Like nettles, with their wicked-sharp prickles. She knew they grew in this area. She'd had more than one uncomfortable experience dealing with nettles, but they were worth it, made a fabulous tea. You just had to be careful. She sighed, her thoughts drifting, as always, to Reese.

How sad that she thought of him in conjunction with the pain of nettles. But he was definitely an irritant in her life. She sighed again. As she was in his.

Could they ever be together in harmony? Was that even possible?

Taki pulled off the road, her tires crunching gravel, and parked near the giant sign alerting residents that this ten-acre plot of gorgeous wilderness would soon be a shopping center. She grabbed her basket and jumped from the Jeep. There were no other vehicles in the area, but of course it was way too cold for most Miamians this early in the morning.

The temperature was already moderating, though. That's the way it was in Florida. Cold snaps never lasted more than a couple of days. She'd probably have to start peeling off layers in an hour as the sun rose higher in the sky.

She set off on a trail into the thick canopy of trees, and tire tracks made her realize it was a recreational route for motorcycles or three-wheelers. But what she wanted wouldn't grow close to a busy path, so she left the obvious trail. She moved carefully, stepping over rocks and roots, her gaze glued to the forest floor in hopes of spotting a tiny flower.

Birds chirped to life overhead, waking up to the new day. Gusts of wind rustled through the leaves, rubbing branches against each other, making a creaking sound. She breathed in the rich odor of the earth beneath her feet and allowed her body to absorb the peace of the natural world, to heal her soul.

She needed a calm mind, a mind as calm as the mirrorlike waters of a pristine mountain lake reflecting clouds and sky. With that serenity, she'd figure out how to repair the damage she'd caused Reese. That was why she'd come to the woods. With her mind and spirit calm, maybe she could decide what to do next.

Whenever she saw something interesting, she knelt, made a note and quick sketch, then moved on. She spotted wild plantain—great for insect bites—but only took a few snips, not the whole plant.

After about an hour, she pulled off her sweatshirt and tied it around her waist. Thirty minutes later she found a flat stone and sat down to rest. To think.

She opened her thermos and poured steaming mint tea into the top. What was Reese doing right now? Did he ever think about her? With a sharp stab of guilt, she knew he thought of her often, and thinking about her caused him pain.

Why hadn't she fled? She should have left Monday morning, but for the first time she didn't want to relocate.

Maybe she finally had to face the consequences, deal with the howling Spencer beast. A chill ran up both arms at the thought of dealing with her father. Her stomach churned when she pictured his face.

She wasn't ready.

Cupping her fingers around the warm cup, she took a sip of tea.

She knew why she'd stayed. She wanted to heal Reese.

So what did her soul mate want more than anything? Other than to put his Romero bad guy in jail, she didn't really know. And how could she help with his work? She couldn't. Setting her tea aside, she stretched both arms over her head, reaching for the treetops. Surely Reese needed something besides punishing criminals. Did he ever venture into the natural world for solace? He was so driven, she doubted if he ever took the time.

How could she figure out what Reese wanted when she wasn't even sure what she wanted anymore?

What are you really afraid of?

She shivered as she remembered his last words to her. He thought her afraid, a coward. She wasn't a coward. Hadn't she lived on the edge of society for years without any money, barely eking out a living? If she was afraid of anything, it was of allowing herself to be sucked back into her father's world of mindless greed.

So was she afraid of her father? Was she weak? Afraid to stand her ground?

What *was* she afraid of? Of loving Reese?

Taki came to her feet. Her mind remained in turmoil. How could she make a decision when she couldn't think straight? The peace of the natural world hadn't worked this time. Nothing worked.

She'd talk to Navi first, but maybe, just maybe, it was time to stand and fight.

AT 10:00 P.M. WEDNESDAY night Reese lay stretched out on his sofa, remote in hand, hoping a mind-numbing television show would lull him to sleep. The plan wasn't working, and for sure this old sitcom wasn't funny. He needed sleep, desperately needed sleep, but his mind wouldn't shut down. His brain kept rolling an endless loop of his last conversation with Taki.

No matter how many times he went over it and all their previous contacts, he couldn't make any sense of her. She put him in the same category as her father. What had he done to make her distrust him?

His eyes were too damn tired to focus on the

printed page, so work was no longer an option tonight. Of course the FBI hadn't found Claudia. "Like a needle in a haystack," Javi kept telling him, but he didn't want clichés.

Reese was beginning to think his witness might be dead, that Romero had found her. Just one more thing that kept him up at night.

He raised the remote to switch the channel when his cell phone rang.

He checked the display—Unavailable. After a pause—thinking of Taki, but, shit, when wasn't he thinking about Taki?—he answered.

"Is that you, Reese?" a hesitant feminine voice asked. Not Taki's.

"Claudia?" Reese demanded.

"Yes."

He sat up. "Where are you?"

"That's not important."

"The hell it isn't. Are you all right?"

"I'm fine. That's why I'm calling, to let you know I'm okay."

"Damn, Claudia, I thought Carlos had found you and—"

"We have to make this quick. Sorry, but I have to do this my way. The *Herald* says his trial is on for Monday. Is that correct?"

"Yes." Reese ran a hand through his hair. *Claudia. Thank God she's alive.*

"Will you need me?"

"No. Jury selection begins Monday. That should take a week at least. Then opening statements."

"When will you know?"

Reese got up and began to pace, thinking hard. "Now that I know you're still alive, I can finalize my witness list, decide the lineup."

"I'll call you back on Friday afternoon."

"Claudia, wait."

"No. Your phone could have a tap. I've got to disconnect in thirty seconds."

"My phone is fine. Please don't hang up. I need to—"

"Friday, at 4:00 p.m. I'll call the pay phone at the coffee shop across the street from your office. Be there."

"No, Claudia—"

The line went dead.

Resisting the urge to throw his phone across the room, Reese punched in Javi's number.

"I just heard from Claudia Romero," he told the agent. "She's still willing to testify."

"Where is she?"

"No clue. She'll get back in touch with me Friday."

"Cutting it close," Javi said. "Apparently she doesn't trust you."

"Apparently not. Anyway, call off the hounds. There's no point in looking for her anymore."

"Got it."

Stung by the thought of another woman who didn't trust him, Reese disconnected and went to his kitchen to brew some of Taki's valerian tea. Maybe Claudia was alive, but he'd still lost Taki. Where had Taki run off to this time?

No. Her name was Kim.

It didn't hurt so much when he remembered her name was Kim.

CHAPTER THIRTEEN

TAKI PAUSED IN the entryway of the ashram's circular meditation room, her gaze drawn through floor-to-ceiling arched windows to the endless turquoise ocean beyond. Sunlight streamed through the skylight in the domed white ceiling, illuminating flecks of dust on its path to create a halo on the white tile.

There were no corners to this room, nowhere that she could hide from her thoughts. The soothing quiet settled a much-needed blanket of peace over her.

Thankful she had come, she slipped off her sandals and padded barefoot into the deserted room. Removing shoes was symbolic of leaving the weight of the outside world behind, and that's exactly what she needed to do.

She'd found the refuge she sought.

Navi might come to visit her, but his aide could make no promises. Her teacher was weak from his fast and needed rest. Unsure if she even wanted to speak to him, Taki believed the tranquility of Navi's temple would help her decide.

She approached a small wooden altar where one white candle burned evenly inside its glass holder. She knelt and focused on the steady flame. The room was so still she could feel her heart beating inside her chest.

She evened the rhythm of her breath and tried to think only of joy and light, of peace and harmony and…

Instead she thought of the angry look on Reese's face when he had stomped out of her life four days ago.

She drew a long, shaky inhalation. She missed him. She wanted to see him again. She needed to undo the hurt she had caused.

She released her breath in an unhurried flow and attempted to focus her scattered thoughts. Here in this place of serenity she must decide. Should she remain in Miami or keep running? Should she allow the Trust to force her into actions she didn't want to take? Victoria insisted her father would never stop looking for her.

Over and over her thoughts tumbled, always arriving at the same conclusion. If she wanted to see Reese again, she would have to remain in Miami and deal with her father. Of course, it would serve him right if his precious billions disintegrated…dissipated like the people who had been sickened by the chemicals in the drinking water beneath their town.

Her natural inclination was to run, so maybe this time she would stay and see the journey through. Or was remaining what she had done in previous lifetimes? Maybe this was the time she should run. So what if the lawyers had found her. She could easily elude them again. She had been doing that for years.

Guru Navi's thin body loomed between Taki and the candle on which she focused, interrupting her disorganized musings. She smiled up at him, glad after all for the opportunity to speak with her teacher.

"Ah...Taki," he said, as if he'd just spotted a rare species of bird. "You honor us with your presence."

"Navi," Taki said with a slight bow.

Her teacher bowed in return and knelt so that they were eye to eye. "We haven't seen you in many days."

Taki lowered her gaze. "No."

"You return to us troubled, my child."

Glancing up, Taki examined Navi's gaunt, bearded face. One reason she trusted him was because he had always sensed when she was dispirited. "I have been unable to recover the Bowl of Tara Shanti."

Navi closed his eyes and remained silent for a moment. "But you have tried?"

"Very hard."

He opened his eyes. "Have you meditated and looked inward?"

"Until I'm almost comatose."

"I see." Navi shrugged, his thin lips curving up at her words. "The path to take is not always clear."

"Gee, thanks," she muttered. "But I already knew that."

Brown eyes twinkling, Navi smiled broadly, his small teeth appearing in the curly mass of his full gray beard. "Ah, Taki. You always want me to tell you precisely what to do, to clear the path for you. My child, you must do the work yourself."

"But I've done the work. Didn't I travel all the way to Tibet to locate the bowl as you instructed?"

He turned his palms heavenward in a questioning gesture. "Do I have the bowl?"

She sighed. "Of course not. You know it was stolen."

"Everything happens in the universe for a purpose."

"I know, but—"

"You must discover your own wisdom within."

"And the key to wisdom depends on my desire to know, how hard I'm willing to work. I remember." Navi had emphasized this lecture so often, she'd all but memorized it. "And I shouldn't get attached. But how can I not be attached to finding the bowl?"

"Actually, the bowl is the key," Navi said, stroking his beard. "But it is only a symbol and will provide the answers to all your questions."

"Then I should remain in Miami?" She leaned forward, hoping Navi would just come right out and tell her what action to take. "I should continue to search?"

"You must discover your own path to the light." Placing his hands in prayer position, he bowed again. "Look deeply into your heart, my little seeker, and search for the answer there."

"But my heart is damaged." She settled back on her heels. "My heart refuses to provide me with a solution."

"How has your heart been damaged?"

She bowed her head. "By my own actions."

The temple remained quiet for a moment before

Navi spoke again. "Is the missing bowl the sole source of your distress, my child?"

"No," Taki admitted. "I have other...worries."

Navi stared at her solemnly, waiting for her to continue.

"I have injured someone, someone I care about."

"No physical harm, I trust?"

"No. Much worse than that."

"Ah. Then his heart is also damaged?"

Wondering how Navi had guessed the party she had injured was a male, she nodded. "I think so. Yes, I know so."

"So. You must repair the damage. You must give him what he needs."

"I don't know what he needs," Taki whispered, thinking she didn't even know what she needed.

"Of course you do."

"I do?"

"Remember, my child, when one door closes, another always opens." With an enigmatic smile, Navi rose, bowed to the altar and withdrew from his temple.

Taki's gaze shifted to the endless horizon of the Atlantic Ocean before her. How was she supposed to unravel the mystery behind Navi's words? She could interpret them a thousand different ways.

Navi thinks I know what Reese needs? What does he—

The briefcase. Of course!

As she watched long green swells break into foamy white waves, she remembered Reese's missing case and the important papers it contained. Reese definitely needed—wanted that briefcase.

Everything happens for a purpose. She came to her feet and moved closer to the windows as she recalled Navi's words. She'd said as much to Reese a week or so ago. Maybe her bowl had been stolen so that she could help him find his property. She nodded, that's what she'd thought all along, but had gotten sidetracked by her desire for his body.

"Taki."

She turned and found Crystal, manager of the ashram's bookstore, eyeglasses balanced on the tip of her long nose. "Yes, Crystal?"

She bowed. "I apologize for disturbing your meditation, but there is a phone call for you in the office. They insist it is a matter of some urgency."

FRIDAY AFTERNOON, REESE stood when Joanne showed a Mr. David Winslow into his office, an appointment his boss insisted he make time for. He reached over his desk to shake the man's hand, annoyed by the interruption, but guessing Winslow to be approximately his age. The dark-headed man carried a handsome leather briefcase, was dressed in a hand-tailored black suit and appeared polished from his gray silk tie to the tips of his Italian loafers.

"What can I do for you, Mr. Winslow?" Reese asked.

Mr. Winslow handed Reese a card. "I understand you know Kimberly Spencer."

Reese tensed. He'd banished Taki from his thoughts,

but Winslow's question brought her back with a physical pang. Taki had blown town days ago and was removed from his life forever.

Just not his memory. Never his memory.

Reese glanced at the card, and the Spencer Trust logo leaped out at him. He glanced back up. David Winslow, Esq. was here on behalf of the Spencer Trust.

Winslow pulled a file from his briefcase. "Our investigators traced Ms. Spencer to an address on Miami Beach. Your car has been videoed there, remaining all night on at least one occasion."

"Is that so?" he said.

"Yes, that's so. She's going by the name of—" Winslow consulted his notes "—ah, yes, Taki. She teaches yoga at SoBe Spa, where you're a member. Your cars were broken into on February 3 and—"

"Enough." Reese held up his hand. "Very thorough."

What was this about? In the five days since he'd learned her identity, he'd used every trick he knew of to not think about her. Without much success. But the Romero trial would begin on Monday. He had no time for anything but that.

"Why are you here, Mr. Winslow?" Reese demanded.

"We want you to talk to her." He sat back. "Bring her in, so to speak."

"Bring her in?" Reese gripped his pen again. Was Taki still in Miami? "You make it sound like she's a criminal."

Winslow shrugged. "She's skittish. At the very least we need her to sign documents so we can make crucial decisions about the Trust's investments."

"Why do you need her signature?"

"On Kim's twenty-first birthday, she became an equal partner with her father per the terms of Old Lady Spencer's will. The board can't do much without Kim's approval. Opportunities are being missed."

"Taki doesn't care about those opportunities."

"What does she care about? You, Mr. Beauchamps?"

"That's none of the Trust's business." Reese stood, and the chair rolled back furiously with the abrupt motion. He stepped across the room to the window to where the aqua waters of Biscayne Bay glittered in the sun below. Thankfully, Winslow remained silent.

Hands jammed deeply in his pockets, Reese faced Winslow again. "Taki cares about her karma. When you figure out what that means, let me know."

The Spencer Trust attorney eyed him thoughtfully. "Don't you think it would be easier for her if you handled the initial negotiations? She knows we know… that she knows we…" Shaking his head, Winslow said, "This covert nonsense gets crazy after a while, but I think she's waiting for us to make the first move. Or anyway, she hasn't fled the area yet."

"Good luck," Reese muttered. Reese turned and stared at the endless expanse of water before him, his gaze traveling to Miami Beach. Why hadn't Taki left? "I don't have time to fool around with estate planning. I'm picking a jury for an important trial on Monday."

"Mr. Spencer would very much appreciate you

smoothing the way for Kim, and he can show his appreciation in a number of ways. He can also show his displeasure. I think Ms. Lettino agrees with us."

Reese sighed. His boss knew about Taki? Probably more than he did. But he knew Cynthia wouldn't cave to political pressure.

"If you want my help, I want all the information you have on Taki—Kim, before I decide. I want to see a complete report on her history."

Winslow considered his demand and nodded. "A lot is public record, anyway. You'll have the relevant files on your desk by five o'clock. I look forward to hearing from you."

When Winslow had left, Reese folded his arms and stared at the horizon before him, resenting this time suck. He didn't have time for Taki and her inheritance problems. He had a terrorist to put away for life and an excellent chance now to accomplish that goal. He glanced at his watch. Claudia would be calling in an hour.

From the gist of their conversation on Wednesday, she still intended to testify. Would she want to review her journal before her stint on the witness stand? Should he remove it from the evidence vault? No, he couldn't take that chance. With the journal to substantiate Claudia's live testimony, his case against Romero was a lock.

He'd ask Joanne to run another copy and make it available to Claudia if she'd agree to meet him. Damn, but he wished he had the copy that had been in his stolen briefcase. He'd jotted trial notes in the margins and wasn't sure if he'd recalled them all. Of course, wherever the briefcase was, most likely he'd find Taki's infamous bowl.

Memories slammed into his brain, bringing with them a need that stunned him. Taki combing her long, silky hair with graceful fingers. Taki smiling, handing him new reading glasses. Her legs wrapped around his waist.

With a groan, Reese returned to his desk. No matter what he did, he couldn't stop thinking about her. Working every waking second didn't make a difference. She still managed to creep into his thoughts and disrupt his concentration.

He ached for her with a longing that transcended anything he'd ever known. The idea that he'd never see her again was intolerable, the source of his insomnia. And now that he knew she remained close by, he had a sudden, undeniable thirst to see her.

How had his life become entangled with hers so quickly? How did a penniless orphan without car insurance transform into the wealthiest woman in the northeast? He shook his head.

A woman who considered him as cruel as her heartless father. That's what hurt. How could Taki believe they were so different that it would be disastrous to fall in love? Could he prove her wrong?

Reese lifted his gaze to South Beach. Yeah, he would comply with Winslow's request. But before he saw Taki again, he would learn all there was to know about the history of Kimberly Howell Spencer. Maybe then he could prove to her he wasn't anything like her father.

An hour later, in the Courthouse Café, Reese grabbed the phone the instant it rang, relieved that his missing witness was prompt and that she knew the location of one of the few working pay phones left in Florida.

"Hello?"

"Don't use my name."

"I won't." Reese glanced around the deserted café again. No one in sight except a counter waitress washing out a coffeepot on the opposite end of the room. The restaurant closed in thirty minutes. "I'm alone."

"Are you sure?"

"Yes, I'm sure. Are you all right?"

"So far."

Reese thought she sounded cautious, as if she didn't want to jinx her fate. "Thank God. I was afraid you'd been weighted down and dropped off a bridge somewhere."

"I'm sorry if I worried you, but it was for the best. I needed to disappear fast. Better that you didn't know anything about my plan. Believe me, I know what Carlos is capable of better than you."

"What happened? Why did you disappear?"

"I was being followed. When someone broke in and ransacked my apartment—probably looking for my journal—I went into hiding."

"So Carlos knew you kept a record of events in that journal?"

"He used to see me writing in it at night, but I started hiding it from him. When he saw my name on your witness list, I guess he made assumptions. I know his people are still searching for me."

"Where are you?"

"You don't need to know that."

"Meet me somewhere. I can arrange a safe house."

"Sorry, Reese. I quit trusting the government's ability to protect me a long time ago. I'm only relying on myself and one other person these days."

Reese leaned against the wall to watch the door. "Do you need anything?" he asked.

"No, I'm good. I prepared for this."

"But you're still willing to testify?"

"Of course. The only reason I'm hanging around is to nail his sorry butt. Just tell me the day you need me and I'll be there."

Reese raked a hand through his hair. Because of safety concerns—never mind strategy anymore—he should enter Claudia's testimony into the record immediately. She should be his first witness no matter how awkward. He'd connect the dots for the jury later with other witnesses and closing argument. No other choice.

"I'll call you Friday at the earliest," he said. "Jury selection should take most of the week, then opening statements. Maybe not until Monday."

"That's what I figured. You won't recognize me. I'll be in disguise."

"Good idea. How will I get in touch with you?"

"You won't. I'll call you Thursday and we'll go from there."

"Damn. I think you'd be safer in custody."

"Forget it, Counselor. Listen, when I testify, I'll need my diary for dates. Make sure you have it for me. You'll have to—" Claudia sucked in a quick breath. "What was that?"

"What?"

"I heard clicking on the line."

"I didn't hear anything. About the diary, do you want to review—"

"I'm outta here."

The line clicked once, then silence. "Hello?"

"If you'd like to make a call..." a machine-generated female voice rattled in his ear. Reese hung up, but left his hand on the receiver, hoping Claudia would call back.

When the phone didn't ring, he considered and quickly rejected the idea of waiting at the counter. Claudia sounded so spooked, likely he wouldn't hear from her until Thursday. Forget the idea of preparing his witness for what promised to be difficult testimony. But they'd discussed probable questions long before her disappearance. Claudia was smart. She'd do fine.

As he crossed the street to the federal building, Reese sifted through the evidence in his case, relieved he had his star witness back. No way would Romero skate now. So what if his briefcase and trial notes had been stolen? He didn't need them anymore.

The connection between Taki's bowl and the brief-case puzzled him, though. There had to be one, but he couldn't figure it out. He didn't like unanswered questions surrounding any case, and he found it too much of a coincidence that only his and Taki's vehicles were burglarized the same night. At first he'd thought Izzo had gotten greedy, but now he wasn't so sure. The thefts just didn't make sense. He had a feeling that—

Reese regarded himself with pure disgust. Surely he wasn't starting to believe in mysterious *feelings*.

He spotted the white cardboard file box on a chair the minute he entered his office. The receipt taped to the top bore the letterhead of the Spencer Trust. Reese smiled wryly, knowing he'd spend the rest of the evening reading about Kimberly Spencer and the horrible blight on her soul.

It galled him that Taki thought he'd betray her to people she considered vultures, but he was no snitch. How could she think that? His anger mushroomed. Didn't anyone trust him anymore?

No matter what happened, he would never hurt Taki. As that idea took root, he knew it was true. At some gut level harming her was impossible. He was nothing like Howard Spencer. Why didn't she understand that?

She believed she could make her own reality. He wished he knew what was real about her and what wasn't.

He doubted he'd discover the whole truth in the files before him.

SEATED ON HER sofa, leaning forward with her elbows propped on her knees, Taki stared at the phone on the coffee table and willed the silly machine to ring. Why wouldn't it ring?

"What time did Benny say Mayhugh would call?" Victoria asked.

"What time is it?" Taki replied.

"Nine-fifteen."

"Fifteen minutes ago," Taki said.

"Then he's late."

"I know, I know," Taki said, jumping to her feet.

Victoria sniffed. "No one is prompt anymore. The downfall of our society."

"I hope nothing went wrong." Taki stopped pacing and plopped down on the rug. Hoping a spinal twist would ease her anxiety, she lowered her spine to the floor one vertebra at a time, then twisted her knees first to one side and then the other.

Ring, phone, ring!

She'd been unable to sit still ever since Benny had phoned her at the ashram to tell her Mayhugh would call her tonight, that he was willing to hand over the bowl. Of course it all seemed a little strange. Suspicious. Why had Mayhugh waited so long? And why had he contacted Benny?

But all she could think about was if she found her bowl, she might find Reese's property, too. This was her chance to make it up to him. Probably her last chance. How could she pass up the opportunity?

The phone rang, and Taki lunged for it. "Hello?"

"Is that you, Ms. Taki?"

"Yes. Is this Mr. Mayhugh?"

"Yes. If you want your property, meet me in the conservatory at Fairchild Tropical Garden tomorrow morning at 9:00 a.m. sharp."

Taki thought it sounded as though he was reading from a script. "Conservatory, Fairchild, 9:00 a.m.," she repeated. "I'll be there. Will you have my bowl?"

"Everything will be made clear tomorrow."

"But what do you want in exchange?"

"You'll find out tomorrow."

"But if I don't know what to bring—"

"All will be made clear tomorrow. Do not tell anyone about our meeting."

"Oh, but, Mr. Mayhugh, there's—"

"You and I need to keep this exchange private," Mayhugh insisted, cutting her off. "Remember the disaster last time we met?"

Taki stared into the alert face of Victoria and realized she was about to tell a direct lie. But what could she do? Victoria had already heard every word of the conversation, including the time and place of the meet, and Taki didn't want Mayhugh to change his mind.

"All right," she told the fence, shrugging helplessly at Victoria. "I won't tell anyone."

Victoria rolled her eyes, and Taki bit her lip. What was one more lie? Surely the universe would forgive her if it meant she recovered Reese's property.

And of course she would tell Reese about the meeting. She learned from her mistakes and remembered all too painfully the scene with the FBI last time she'd met Mr. Mayhugh.

"Don't forget. Tomorrow morning at 9:00 a.m. sharp in the conservatory at Fairchild."

"I'll remember," Taki said, attempting to sound confident.

"No police, no FBI and no federal prosecutors. Come alone."

"Federal prosecutors?" Taki repeated.

"I understand you're real friendly with one."

"How do you know that?"

"Never mind, missy. You just show up if you want your precious bowl."

"I'll be there. I promise," Taki said, thinking her promise might not mean much now that she'd told a fib. "Wait. Don't hang up," she shouted, worried Mayhugh was about to disconnect.

"Yeah?"

"Do you know anything about a briefcase that was stolen the same night?"

"What about it?"

A prickle of awareness traced her spine at his tone. Mayhugh did know something about Reese's property! "I'd like to recover that, as well."

Mayhugh remained silent a moment. "Maybe that can be negotiated. We'll discuss it tomorrow."

"Bring the—" Taki grimaced and replaced the receiver. "He hung up on me."

Victoria crossed her arms. "How rude."

"Wow, talk about negative energy. Even his voice is weird."

"You know," Victoria said, "it seems rather odd to me that this yoga student of yours—Benny, is it?—always seems to be in the thick of things where your stolen bowl is concerned."

"He is, isn't he? I thought he was just being a sweetie to help me. Do you think he's involved?"

"Sounds like it to me."

"But that doesn't make any sense. Why would he steal my bowl?"

Victoria shrugged. "Maybe you should ask him."

"Maybe I should."

"Why can't you meet at the fence's house again?" Victoria asked.

"Mayhugh thinks the FBI has his property under surveillance."

"That's probably true. Are you going to tell Reese about this rendezvous at Fairchild Gardens?"

"Yes, although that will be complicated," Taki said. "We're not exactly communicating. I haven't talked to him in almost a week."

"I gather he knows who you are now?"

"Yes." *But does he really know me?*

"Then perhaps you shouldn't tell him about this meeting. He might try to stop you."

"No. He won't care what I do."

"Oh, I suspect he cares. Best not to let him know what's going on or you'll never improve your karma."

"Perhaps," Taki murmured, surprised that Victoria would counsel her not to inform Reese. Her landlady was usually quite down-to-earth and practical. "He thinks I've already moved and will be furious if I don't tell him about the meeting." Taki frowned, convinced she should tell him about this latest development. He couldn't prevent her from meeting Mayhugh. She wasn't doing anything illegal.

"All the more reason to keep quiet," Victoria said.

Taki sighed. "I don't know. The reason he's angry is because I didn't trust him."

"No one can trust a lawyer."

"Maybe," Taki murmured. "Anyway, I expect to hear from one of the Trust's attorneys any day."

"Probably that David Winslow. He called me again, but I put him off. Personally, I'm delighted you're staying, dear." Victoria patted Taki's arm. "It's been lonely since Bert passed on, and I enjoy having you around. You're welcome to live here as long as you'd like."

"Thanks." Taki hugged her friend, grateful for her support.

Victoria stood. "Well, it's past my bedtime. Now, don't forget I'm driving to Little Palm Island in the morning."

"I'm glad. You always have such a good time there."

"I do, don't I?"

"You deserve to be pampered after nursing Bert for so long. Have a wonderful trip."

"I will. Go alone to the meeting, dear. My instincts tell me that's the thing to do."

Taki followed her landlady to the door and stepped outside to watch her stride purposefully up the wheelchair ramp constructed for her late husband. Victoria had remained steadfast by Bert's side as he'd declined, seldom allowing a caretaker to assist her. Unfortunately, they'd had no children to help out in his last days. Victoria had shouldered all of the nursing alone.

When she had safely reached her back door, Victoria waved and disappeared inside the house.

Taki sighed, feeling a pang at the thought of growing old with Reese, enjoying year after year by his side as Victoria had with Bert. How lovely that life would be, living in harmony with her soul mate, sharing the journey together. She placed her hand on her belly. Maybe having a few kids. She'd love to have a family. A real family with people that loved each other. Then she'd never be lonely again.

Nonsense, Taki told herself, mentally mimicking Victoria's stern tone. *Impossible.* There was no hope for any chance with Reese in this lifetime. The best she could hope for was to mend the harm she'd caused by finding his briefcase. Maybe then they'd have better luck during their next meeting.

The flash of headlights turning into her driveway caused Taki to raise her hand to shield her eyes. When the glare subsided, she recognized a sleek black Jaguar, and her heart began a joyous dance inside her chest.

The trunk popped open, then the driver's door. Reese emerged wearing only a dress shirt without his usual jacket. He threw her a glance, then slammed the door—harder than necessary—and strode to the rear of the car to retrieve something.

He moved toward her front door with a white cardboard box in his arms.

She swallowed hard, wary of the determined look on his face, dreading to learn what was inside that box.

CHAPTER FOURTEEN

REESE'S EYES FEASTED on Taki. Gracefully balanced on one foot in what he now recognized as Tree pose, she stood barefoot on her top step, softly illuminated by an overhead light. Her long, slender fingers were wrapped around her throat, and her eyes appeared huge in her pale face.

He'd tried to tell himself she couldn't be as beautiful as he remembered. He shifted the heavy box in his arms. Too bad his memory paled in comparison to her reality.

No doubt she'd try to tell him she'd had a premonition he was coming and that's why she waited for him outside her front door.

Why the hell was he making this foolish unannounced visit, anyway?

He cursed himself and her tense expression. He'd hoped she'd be glad to see him. Of course it was almost 10:00 p.m. and way too late for an unexpected call. But after he'd finished digesting the information in this box, he simply could not wait to confront her.

Or maybe he just had to see her again. He wasn't sure which anymore. All he knew was some force had compelled him to come tonight.

With a hesitant smile, she lowered the foot propped against her thigh and motioned him inside. She didn't speak.

If he thought he'd suddenly become immune to her natural beauty and grace, he'd been very wrong. Taki tapped needs deep inside him that no one had ever come close to uncovering before. He ached to touch her.

He summoned his anger to curb that need.

"How are you?" she asked when she'd closed the door, her voice sounding airy, as if she couldn't catch her breath.

"I've been better."

"I'm glad to see you." She inhaled deeply. "I was going to call you, tell you I hadn't left, but I was afraid you would..." She trailed off.

"That I would what?"

"Nothing."

Her gaze fell to the box, and he sensed her curiosity.

"Kimberly Howell Spencer, this is your life." He raised the box toward her, then placed it on the rattan coffee table.

"That's not my name anymore," she blurted. "I had it legally changed."

He sat on the couch, examining her face in an attempt to sense her mood. She was nervous, uneasy.

"As a symbol of a new beginning," he murmured. "I remember."

"Yes. Because I wanted a different life." She stared at him across the room.

"Actually," he said, annoyed that she kept her distance from him, "I just reviewed a very thick file about your name and various aliases. You change your name a lot."

Her eyes widened, then fell to the box. "A file? What are you talking about?"

She nibbled on her bottom lip, and a glimpse of her white teeth made him remember the hot, sweet taste of her mouth. This might be harder than he thought.

In an attempt to refocus his thoughts, he jerked a file from the box and flipped through the pages. "By the way," he said, staring at a document, "there *is* a warrant for your arrest."

"What?" She sounded startled, defensive, as if she didn't believe him.

"An unpaid moving violation in San Francisco. Speeding twenty-five miles over the limit." He glanced up. "Why am I not surprised?"

Her jaw dropped open, then acknowledgment flashed across her face. "Oh, right. I forgot about that. My father located me, so I had to leave before my court date. Yeah, I guess it's still out there." She shook her head. "Why would you dig up an old traffic ticket?"

"Not me. The Spencer Trust, and they're very thorough. They've tracked you through the past four years."

Narrowing her eyes, Taki stepped forward and pulled a manila sleeve from the box.

Reese smiled grimly as he recognized the file she'd selected, the six months when Taki had lived in Santa

Fe and had given free yoga classes to AIDS patients, somehow disappearing overnight once the Spencer Trust had located her. Of course, by far his favorite period was when she'd taught yoga two nights a week at the federal penitentiary in San Francisco, apparently willing to put her own life in danger if it improved her karma-challenged path to enlightenment.

She leafed through several pages of the Santa Fe folder, then glanced at him over the top.

"Where did you get all this?"

"Where do you think? From the attorneys for the Spencer Trust."

"But why would…"

"I'm here on their behalf." He executed a mock salute. "At your service."

The horror that flashed across her face created a sense of satisfaction in him. She looked as if she'd been sucker punched. Yeah, well, he knew how she felt.

"I've been sent to bring you in," he said.

"Bring me…in?"

"Since you and I are—were, well, close, they thought I could make the situation easier for you."

"Because we're close?" Taki dropped the file and took a step backward, away from the box, away from him. "So you're working for the Trust now? For my father?"

"I'm doing them—and you—a favor."

Taki moistened her lips. "Have you met my father?" she asked, her voice barely a whisper.

"Haven't had the pleasure."

She nodded, looking relieved. "How can you have time for this? What about the Romero trial? What about your sense of justice?"

"It's temporary duty. My assignment is to smooth the way for you, arrange a first meeting."

"Is that the only reason you're here?"

"No."

Taki rebalanced her weight and folded her arms across her stomach, the liquid movement of her limbs making him remember the sensual way she'd rubbed her calves across his back.

When he didn't expand on his answer, she lifted her eyebrows. "Well?"

"Well, what?" he muttered. How could she still haunt his every thought, interfere with his focus?

"Why else did you come?"

"For answers." Reese leaned forward and placed one hand on the box. "I've just spent over three hours examining these files, trying to learn everything I could about you, hoping it would help me understand. It didn't work."

"You won't learn anything about me from those files."

"Not true. I've learned that because your family owns controlling interest in several tobacco companies, you blame yourself for the cancer death of anyone who smoked cigarettes. That's ridiculous, Taki, and you must know it."

"I don't blame myself...exactly. I just can't use the money." Raising her chin, she said, "Besides, that's only one component of the problem."

"Oh, yes. I know. There's also chemical factories in Central and South America polluting the environment. Clothing manufacturers in Asia that employ underage workers in dangerous conditions."

She nodded. "Then you do understand."

"Let's just say I've read your letters to the Spencer Trust's board of directors insisting they sell off certain investments."

"Which they refused to do."

"The board can't just do what you want. There are other stockholders to protect."

"I sent letters to the other stockholders, too."

"Wake up, girl. Life isn't all black-and-white. In London one of the Spencer pharmaceutical corporations has come up with promising advances in chemotherapy drugs, is doing research on diabetes. Your money is invested in plenty of worthwhile endeavors."

"I cannot believe you're defending them."

"Get over it."

She spread her arms and said, "If someone doesn't try to change the bad things in the world, the negative, nothing positive will ever happen. I wanted to do some good. My attempt failed, so I walked away. No one can force me to use dirty money."

Unable to formulate a response to her little speech, he stared at her. She refused to listen to reason.

"The Buddha gave up his worldly goods to seek enlightenment," she murmured.

"And have you found enlightenment?"

"Obviously not." She looked away. "I failed at that, too."

Reese ran a hand through his hair, searching for a way to talk sense into her. Did she really consider herself a latter-day Buddha?

"Did you tell them everything about us?" she demanded, meeting his gaze again.

"I don't think they know about our past lifetimes together."

Her mouth tightened, and he knew he'd hit a nerve. Of course he should have known logic wouldn't penetrate her cosmically tilted brain. Well, maybe she was ridiculously stubborn, but so was he.

"Do you remember telling me to open my mind to new ideas?" He wagged a finger at her. "You need to do the same."

She sucked in a quick breath. "How much are they paying you?"

"They're not, but do you have any idea of the amount of money that's been spent trying to find you?" He raised his voice as his frustration mounted.

"No clue."

Bothered that she managed to sound disinterested, even bored, he stood. "And you don't care, do you?"

"Why should I?"

"Of course. That's the whole idea, isn't it? Your grandmother's will ensures that the trustees can never stop searching for you even if your father has you declared legally dead."

"They can stop if they find a body."

"Taki. Please."

"All I want is for them to leave me alone."

"Have you even read your grandmother's will?"

Taki shifted her gaze from his.

"I think you're fully aware that they can't make financial decisions or changes without your approval. Your grandmother even placed separate counsel on retainer to institute action if your father petitions the court to proceed without you. So everything remains tangled in litigation, money is wasted on attorney fees and the estate dwindles each year."

"I thought it fitting," Taki said. "My grandmother hated attorneys."

Reese took a step toward her. "So do you."

Her face softened. "Not all of them."

"Is that supposed to make me feel better?"

Taki straightened her shoulders, defiance sparking in her blue eyes. "Take it any way you like."

"I'll tell you what else," Reese continued, his own fury rising with hers. "All this karma nonsense is just a smoke screen. You're only avoiding the Trust to punish your father."

Her usually tranquil face flushed a healthy pink. "You don't know what you're talking about."

"I disagree."

She shook her head. "I don't want to discuss this, Reese."

"Tough."

"His cruelty killed my mother. He threw her away like garbage. She killed herself because of the way he treated her."

"I admit he's hardly a prince, but she took her own life. She made her own decisions."

"You don't know anything about it," she said, her voice slow and perfectly controlled.

"I know he kept you isolated for years. You had home tutoring until you were thirteen, and then attended an exclusive private school."

He took another step forward, wondering why he couldn't stop himself, couldn't check the explosive emotion that roared stronger and hotter each second he spent with her. He should be distancing himself from Taki, not moving closer.

"Don't you know this is all really about getting back at your father?"

"I am not going to discuss my father with you," she said, taking a step backward, her tone now chillingly furious.

He took another step toward her. "I think this is more about your mother's death than your father's money."

She inhaled slowly, her favorite method to calm herself. Her breasts rose with the movement, and he longed to cup them between his hands.

"Be reasonable," he said. "Think about what you're doing."

What a farce that he should advise her to cling to reason when he'd abandoned all pretext of logical thought himself. He took one last step toward her. All he knew was that he had to touch her.

WANTING HIM, LOVING HIM, hating him, Taki's backward movement away from Reese halted when she bumped into her front door. She leaned against the solid surface with Reese right in her face. Much, much too close, his beautiful dark eyes glittered with unfathomable emotion. She didn't know what he was thinking.

He placed his forearms on either side of her head, trapping her. He breathed fury hotter than any dragon's breath, but the tension in his body told her his desire for her was stronger than his anger.

She ached for him to touch her, to crush her body into his.

"I don't like you very much right now," he gritted out, his voice low and menacing, moving hot air across her ear. "But I can't stop thinking about you."

"I'm sorry," she whispered. "I can't help who I am."

With a muffled curse, Reese pressed his body into hers, pinning her against the door. He pulled her head back and kissed her hard, as if he could transfer his anger to her with his lips.

She clutched his shoulders, the tips of her fingers digging into muscles beneath his cotton shirt, wondering if this was some sort of reprieve. Or additional torture…more lessons to learn.

What did it matter? Reese was holding her again. That was all that she wanted.

He was also sliding his hand beneath her sweater and massaging her breasts. She tensed, fearful his anger would make him rough, but she relaxed as his sensual touch brought only spine-dissolving pleasure. As she arched into his arousing strokes, she breathed his name and released the top button of his shirt.

He made a guttural sound deep in his throat. With a quick tug, he unzipped her jeans. His large hand moved flat against her belly, stroking downward toward her moistness. Then, without warning, he worked feverishly to remove her jeans and panties at the same time.

She kicked away her clothing as Reese unbuckled and dropped his slacks. When he moved his unyielding body against her, the delicious warmth of his muscled strength caused her to lose her center. Not knowing who she was anymore, she felt herself eased to the hardwood floor by arms stronger than she remembered.

Wordlessly, Taki hugged him closer. It didn't matter that he had defected to the other side. She needed him inside her or she'd die. He was her soul mate, and they needed to be one, to be complete. She'd been obsessed with the idea of loving him since he'd pulled into her driveway. Sharp, driving tension had escalated between them until there was no way to slow down or stop.

Besides, she acknowledged as he entered her and began a delicious, urgent rhythm, she didn't want to slow down...and she never wanted to stop. She wanted to keep him in her, on top of her, around her forever.

"Forever," she whispered, unsure if she spoke the word aloud.

As long as she was able, Taki watched passion move across the angles of Reese's face until she lost herself, felt herself become part of him.

TAKI LAY CONTENT beneath Reese for long moments until their breath merged and evened into a steady rhythm.

Finally, Reese raised his face. "Taki, I—" Troubled eyes searched hers. "Are you okay?"

Feeling as if a storm had just broken, she smoothed his worry line, wondering what would happen next. "Fine." A giggle threatened to erupt. "Way better than fine."

He released a breath and glanced around them, astonishment and chagrin washing over his features. Why was the fragile skin beneath his eyes so dark? And why were those gorgeous eyes so bloodshot?

"I don't believe this," he muttered, rolling off her and leaning back on both forearms.

"You haven't been sleeping nights, have you?" she asked after a moment.

"Sleeping?" He looked heavenward. "She's asking how I'm sleeping." With a shake of his head, he refocused on her. "No. I've been working late. How kind of you to notice."

"You mustn't forget about balance in your life, Reese."

"Of course." He gave a short laugh. "Balance. Unfortunately, I haven't had much…balance lately." She held her breath when their gazes locked, wondering what thoughts blazed behind his unreadable eyes. Did they have this much trouble understanding each other in every lifetime?

"Did you try my tea?" she asked.

"Yes."

"You haven't been to class," she murmured. "Yoga would help."

"I thought you'd left town, remember?"

"Well, I'm still here."

"And why is that? Why didn't you leave?"

"I'm not sure," she whispered. "But it has something to do with you."

"Come here." As he pulled her toward him, she allowed her gaze to sweep across his body, memorizing each muscular ridge. She loved his body, wished she could curl up next to him and stay there for the rest of her life. He settled her head on his chest and wrapped an arm around her.

"I promise I did not tell them where you were." His chest rumbled pleasantly beneath her ear as he spoke. "Please believe me."

"You didn't?"

"No. They had you under surveillance, and investigators videoed my car in front of your home. A Mr. David Winslow came to see me."

"But you agreed to work for my father, to help the Trust?"

"The idea was to make it easier for you, and that's why I agreed. That's what I want to do."

"Right, right. Smooth the way." Taki rolled away from him and rested her head on her elbow so she could see his face. How could Reese think it would be easier on her that he had gone over to the dark side? Another wrong turn away from each other.

Silence hung heavy between them, and Taki wished

that the lightning-quick passion of their lovemaking hadn't given way so easily to suspicion and doubt.

She sat up beside him. "So the plan is you'll be like a go-between? I'll talk to the Trust through you?"

"No. I'll bring Mr. Winslow here one day next week, and the two of you can talk."

"Okay, then." Why had she never considered Reese would be involved in her surrender? But the journey was as it should be. Navi said she had to do the work. Still, it hurt that Reese had become her enemy.

Reese tossed Taki her sweater and jeans and reached for his own clothing, trying to sort out his thoughts. Loving her on the floor so rashly, so thoroughly…her searing flash of desire matching his own stroke for stroke…well, total satisfaction tended to undermine a man's sense of outrage.

As he watched Taki elevate her buttocks to glide her jeans over slim hips, he decided she was the most maddening creature he had ever encountered.

She dropped the sweater over her breasts and sat cross-legged on the floor. While he buttoned his shirt, she combed her tousled hair with long, slender fingers, watching him.

"You have a beautiful body," she whispered.

Reese paused on a button and smiled at her, wanting to tell her he'd never get enough of hers. He didn't, though. Lingering confusion held rein on his thoughts. Who was she…Kim or Taki? Were they two different people?

"Listen, Taki, I want you to keep an open mind when you talk to this Winslow character. He seems like a straight shooter. Maybe he can figure a way to help you out of this process that you despise."

Remaining silent, she leaned against the door and examined her hands.

"I know you think I'm just like your father, but have I ever given you reason to mistrust me?"

She looked up, blue eyes tragic. "No."

"Then why—"

"It's as if the universe won't allow any other outcome because of how different we are."

"Come on, Taki."

"Then it's me, Reese. I told you. Somehow I always manage to screw things up between us."

"Yeah, well, I have to agree with that."

She offered a sad half smile. "Why don't I think we're talking about the same thing?"

"Words are like that sometimes," he said. "They're imperfect and don't convey what we really mean." Reese smoothed her cheek with his thumb, finding the skin soft and cool.

"In your heart, Taki, don't you think your father loves you? Maybe he just doesn't know how to say the words."

"Loves me?" She batted his hand from her face, her eyes flash-frozen into blue ice. "No way."

"Maybe you've been too busy hating your father to properly grieve for your mother. Have you considered you're running away because you're afraid you are like your mom, and you're terrified your fate could be similar to hers?"

"How could you know anything about my mom?"

"You see our lives as a repeat of your parents' tragedy, but life isn't preordained like that no matter what you think."

"What I *know* is my father drove my mother to suicide, and didn't even feel guilty about it afterward. He's a selfish brute, and he made my life hell."

Startled by the anger and resentment falling from her lips, Reese remained silent. He'd never seen Taki so agitated. Maybe he was hitting too close to home.

"Listen, Reese, you can relax," she continued, coming to her knees. "In fact, you deserve to be commended. You paved the way perfectly for the monster tonight."

"What are you babbling about now?"

She scrambled to her feet and brushed off her jeans. "Wild, mindless sex always leaves an heiress weak-kneed and unable to say no to the lawyers. Hasn't that been your experience, too?"

"Stop it, Taki." He stood beside her and placed his hands on her shoulders, wanting to shake sense into her.

"You stop telling me about my father. You never even met him. How can you pretend to understand what went on in our lives?"

"Then why don't you tell me about it."

"What difference would it make? Can you change anything that happened?"

"You are irrational on the subject of your father. Don't you see that?"

"Yeah? Well, you think I'm irrational about a lot of things."

"You're pushing me away because you're afraid, but I am nothing like your father."

She jerked open the door in an unsubtle invitation to leave. "You'd better go report in about your success this evening. I'm sure they're anxiously awaiting word."

"Taki, your father—"

"I refuse to discuss my father or my mother with you. Please go."

Reese stepped outside and she slammed the door behind him.

In his car, he sat for a moment and tried to unravel how during his brief, explosive time with Taki their emotions had gotten completely turned around. He'd arrived at her cottage furious with her, while she was appropriately repentant. But by the time he'd left, she spat pure venom at him while he wished he knew how to make things right between them again.

When he'd made the smallest attempt to heal the rift between her and her father, she had gone absolutely ballistic. Yeah, the man was a first-class jerk and should never have been awarded sole custody of a young girl. But money equals power, especially in their legal system. He'd seen it happen before. If what Taki had told him were true—and he had no reason to doubt her—the man didn't deserve his very special daughter. But she was only hurting herself by constantly running away. Why couldn't she see that? Reese understood it would be hard to forgive the man, but Taki needed to reconnect with her father so she could regain control of her life.

What had made her go off so crazy on him?

And even stranger was how he had again experienced an uncanny sense of coming home, of being where he belonged while he'd made love to her. At least this time he could explain the bewildering feeling of familiarity by the fact that they had made love before.

Well, he'd done what Winslow had asked. He could set up a meeting with Taki—Kim—whenever he wanted.

But it was time for him to face the painful facts. Any chance of understanding or compromise with Taki was impossible.

Her reality *was* different from his.

CHAPTER FIFTEEN

THE NEXT MORNING Taki stepped into the oxygen-rich atmosphere of Fairchild Tropical Botanic Gardens's conservatory and moved quickly away from the door to duck behind the leaf of a huge tree fern. She sucked in a deep breath as she realized she was completely alone. There wasn't even a volunteer hovering by the front door.

Overgrown with towering palms and flowering tropical plants, this garden created its own natural temple, a richly fragrant sanctuary where a weary soul could take respite from everyday cares and search for renewal. Closing her eyes, she invited healing *prana,* the energy of life, to flow through her body. She listened to the gentle trickle of a waterfall, hoping it would quiet her edgy thoughts.

But her mind wasn't anywhere near quiet today.

Regretting that she couldn't allow time for Mother Nature to work her soothing magic, she opened her eyes to survey her surroundings with a critical eye.

She'd deliberately arrived an hour earlier than Mayhugh had instructed. She wanted to scope things out, see if there was any danger, maybe identify an escape route. And if the location seemed safe, the extra time would calm her, help her overcome a bad case of jitters.

Something about her conversation with Mayhugh bugged her. Something didn't seem right, so she'd called Reese's FBI agent Javi to let him know about the meet. Yeah, Javi would likely notify Reese, but she couldn't help that.

Certainly this should qualify as doing the work. Navi would be very pleased. Lately, she'd felt nothing but pain and harmful emotion, constantly thinking about her mom, and it was all because of Reese. She'd never been this miserable before he'd forced her to start examining her life, her motives.

Until the moment he'd uttered his nonsense about how her father really loved her last night, she'd intended to tell him all about this meeting.

Reese thought she was irrational? Yeah, right. A renewed surge of outrage shot through her. Maybe Reese was her soul mate, but he didn't know what he was talking about. He read some moldy files created by lawyers and thought he had all the answers. He thought her beliefs were a smoke screen? How insulting.

He wanted her to trust him and had the nerve to be furious because she didn't do everything he said. But how could she trust him when he'd gone to work for her enemy? His defense of her father had finally pounded home the concept that matters between them were hopeless. He would never experience the universe the way she did.

She took another deep inhalation and straightened her shoulders, forcing her thoughts away from her rising temper. Navi had taught her to use moments of anger to breathe deeply, close her eyes and reconnect with her spirit. She needed to remember why she was here.

Reese wasn't the only one who could smooth a path. If she found his briefcase and returned it, their chances were bound to improve in the next life. Present-day experience is created by past actions. She believed that. She truly did. So what she accomplished this morning would positively affect her future with Reese.

Sooner or later, in one lifetime or another, they would remember hard-learned lessons and put them to good use.

But when?

She loved Reese with a fierce passion that made her breathless every time she saw him. But that same passion made her fury at him burn too hot to control. Made her react and say things she didn't mean. How could she stay grounded, remain in the present moment when her anger rose up too fast, took control of her mind so completely that she couldn't even think? That behavior wasn't who she was. Not really. Or was it?

They were no good for each other.

She ran a finger along the smooth spine of a palm frond. She might be furious with Reese, but she couldn't deny the strength of her feelings for him, feelings of belonging, completeness and what she recognized as pure, perfect love.

Well, maybe not perfect, but the kind of love her parents had shared before it all got ruined with her father's jealousy, hateful accusations and lawyers' intervention.

When you loved someone that strongly, did it always turn out bad? Did half of the couple become obsessive about the other like her father had about her mother? Reese believed in happy endings. He'd told her so on the trip to Cassadaga. Victoria and Bert had lasted a lifetime together. A long, happy lifetime of marital bliss. Why couldn't she and Reese have that?

She longed to help him, to make things better for him. Even if it had nothing to do with their future lives together—which he didn't believe in any way—she wanted to find the briefcase to apologize for the mean things she'd said to him.

She had to remember that's why she'd come.

Drawn by a sweet, heady fragrance, Taki moved into the orchidarium where she admired healthy plants adorned with dazzling blooms of deep purple, lavender, yellow and white. Beyond the trellised wall that displayed the flowers, she saw row after row of wire benches where the garden staff nurtured seedlings to maturity. They did excellent work at this botanical garden, gathering and conserving rare plants.

She tried the screen door leading to the nursery. When it opened easily, the tension in her center loosened its grip a bit. She could make a quick getaway through this gate if things soured when Mayhugh arrived. Hopefully Javi or another FBI agent would arrive by then.

Hearing the main door open, she whirled, her heart pounding so hard it scared her. A young woman entered the conservatory pushing an infant in a stroller, accompanied by a rambunctious little boy. With a gentle admonition to her restless son, the mother made her way toward the waterfall in the back.

Not Mayhugh. But at least now there was someone else nearby, although that knowledge didn't ease her nerves. A woman with two young children would be of no help. Who knew Fairchild would be deserted this early in the morning? Had everyone slept in? She'd expected the conservatory to be crowded, like the restaurant had been. Where was the FBI?

She was vulnerable here. Anything could happen.

A sharp noise behind her caused her to turn back to the blooming orchids. Mayhugh already? She fingered the pepper spray in her pocket and sucked in a breath.

No. Only a staff member dressed in a khaki uniform who disappeared behind another door.

Taki heaved a sigh and placed her palm over her queasy belly. This was all wrong.

She shouldn't be here. Not alone. Of course she was anxious—she had good reason to be worried.

Hadn't she arrived early to scope out possible danger? Well, this location absolutely was not safe. She needed to get out of here before Mayhugh arrived. She needed to rethink this whole idea.

Taki exited the way she'd entered, scanning constantly for any sign of the fence or Javi. She made it outside and hurried out of sight of the conservatory without seeing anyone. With a quick decision, she stepped onto a path marked Tropical Rainforest.

A quickly moving stream followed the trail, its tumble over limestone rocks creating a soothing sound. The dense tree canopy overhead blocked out almost any sight of a pale blue sky peeking through thick limbs. Lower tree branches and trunks featured more blooming orchids and colorful bromeliads. The air hung dense with humidity.

She sat on a wooden bench in an open area next to a gentle cascade and allowed her pulse rate to slow.

What was wrong with her? She'd allowed her anger with Reese to make her stubborn, to behave foolishly. But she wasn't stupid. She'd lived on her own for years without getting herself into any trouble.

She needed to calm down and figure out what it was about her conversation with Mayhugh that bothered her.

From the very beginning, all the communications, including the notes, only said she'd receive information about the bowl. They never actually said they'd give her the bowl. What did that mean? Was it a scam? No, they'd sent her a photo with a dated newspaper. They had her property. Whoever "they" were. And why were the notes made differently? That seemed strange.

What really didn't make sense was Mayhugh's refusal to tell her what he wanted in exchange for the bowl. He'd said, *All will be revealed tomorrow.* She didn't believe for a minute he would hand it over because he was a really nice guy.

Why would she even consider meeting a man, a known criminal even, in a deserted garden? She should have confirmed everything with Javi. No wonder Reese had been so angry when she'd gone to Mayhugh's home. Why hadn't she seen this before?

The longer she remained in the peace of the rainforest, the more she understood her bowl was gone. She'd never see it again. She'd gotten attached, and attachment brought misery. And the bowl had only been a symbol, anyway.

Or maybe it was an illusion. Yes, like in the sutras where you see a stick on the ground and think it's a snake. Your mind can play tricks on you. Her mind had been playing tricks on her.

But not anymore.

She looked up to judge the time by the sun's angle. How long had she been sitting here hiding from Mayhugh? She wanted to wait until she was certain he had given up and left. As added security, she'd parked next door at Matheson Hammock, although she doubted Mayhugh would recognize her Jeep.

For the first time in her life she wished she owned a cell phone. But she'd find a phone somewhere and call Reese and Javi. They needed to know why she'd aborted the meeting. She'd tell them to question Benny again, although the FBI had already spoken to him once. Oh, but she hoped he wasn't involved.

And then she'd wait for that man from the Trust to call.

When certain enough time had passed that May-hugh would consider her a no-show, Taki exited the rainforest area.

Trudging back to her Jeep, she decided to call the Trust herself. Today. Why wait any longer? Better to just get the surrender over with, move on with the next phase of her life. Reese would give her the number.

As she neared the Jeep, she dug for her keys in the bag draped over her shoulder. When she raised her head, she was startled by the appearance of a familiar face emerging from the vehicle parked next to hers. A car she didn't recognize.

"Hector?" she asked, amazed to see SoBe Spa's popular personal trainer, his powerful physique completely out of sync with the tranquil natural environment. She frowned. Had Hector been using steroids? Something else she hadn't considered before.

"Hey, Taki."

"What are you doing here, Hector?"

"I followed you from your home," he said with his usual carefree grin.

When he raised his muscled arm toward her, a spurt of alarm caused Taki to take a step back. What was Hector...

"Thanks for making me rich," he said.

Before Taki could react to his nonsensical statement, she heard a strange zapping noise, and a jolt of electricity shot through her.

Intense pain paralyzed her, stiffening her limbs. Unable to move, she collapsed to the ground.

REESE PAUSED READING and glanced at the clock by his bed: 5:00 a.m. He removed his glasses and rubbed the bridge of his nose which had lately become irritated. How could Taki's gift make the print so clear when everything about her was so muddled? Like this information he was trying to digest. He picked up where he'd left off in the text.

"Even soul mates follow a rocky path to pure harmony. This is because a soul mate relationship is more intense than a normal relationship, in both negative and positive ways. However, true soul mates learn to love each other's flaws, so they find it easier to move beyond the bad moments and resolve their conflicts."

He shut the book, examined its cover and shook his head. Facts suited him much better than vague theories that couldn't be proven.

Last night he'd slept only fitfully, waking long before dawn. His normal pattern these days. Unable to stomach further research on Carlos Romero, he'd sifted through the reading list Taki had sent to the Spencer Trust's offices when she'd gone on the lam. Winslow had forwarded several of the texts. Around 4:00 a.m. he'd selected one on reincarnation.

Maybe if he understood Taki's offbeat thinking, he could find a flaw in her logic and a way to convince her to face her problems. She believed they were soul mates, and he was trying to understand exactly what that meant.

Could they really have known each other through countless lifetimes, failing on each go-around to learn the mysterious lessons referenced in the text? His natural inclination was to immediately dismiss that far-fetched possibility, but he had to admit since he'd known Taki he'd experienced some novel reactions. Besides, for some unfathomable reason, the theory rather pleased him.

Meeting up with Taki in life after life would have its rewards.

Growing annoyed with his thoughts, he tossed the book aside and headed for the kitchen to brew coffee. The most important trial of his career began in less than three hours, an event that would shape his political future. A future of public service that he'd worked toward since being elected senior class president at Princeton. He couldn't let a beautiful yogini distract him with impossible-to-prove theories on reincarnation.

How had Taki managed to warp his perspective? The whole concept of meeting a soul mate in countless lifetimes was preposterous. Completely out of his frame of reference. Certainly could never be proven.

And where the hell was she? She'd called Javi about a new meet with Mayhugh, but hadn't showed. Reese shook his head. She probably received one of her mysterious "feelings." He'd been trying to reach her since yesterday afternoon to nail down a time for her and Winslow to meet. Winslow was impatient. His client was in a hurry.

Forty-five minutes later, the phone rang as Reese

knotted his tie. "Reese Beauchamps," he answered, cradling the receiver between his neck and shoulder, wondering who would call this early.

"This is David Winslow, Mr. Beauchamps. Have you reached Kim yet?"

"No."

"I'm sorry to hear that."

Reese took a sip of lukewarm coffee, his thoughts now redirected to Taki rather than questions for potential jurors. Whenever he conjured her beautiful face, that image acted like a computer virus invading his brain, taking over and short-circuiting all normal thought processes.

"I haven't confirmed a time yet. I've been trying to reach her for several days."

"I thought you said you…"

"I don't have a time yet."

"But you left a message?"

"You must not be aware that voice mail creates bad karma."

"What?"

"Never mind. Besides, I think I got that concept wrong, anyway."

Winslow laughed, which irritated Reese. "Nothing about Kim surprises me. It's a wonder she turned out as normal as she did."

"Because her father kept her isolated. I read the files." Files which had revealed that after her mother's death, Taki wasn't allowed to socialize except on rare occasions. When she hit sixteen and got her driver's license, she cut loose, taking the quirky notions of her mother to a whole new plateau, finally rejecting everything about her father's way of life, including the money. Especially the money.

"Why don't you call Kim now?" Winslow suggested in a tone that told Reese he regretted revealing anything about his employer. "I doubt if she's an early riser."

"You want me to wake her?"

"How else will you catch her in? Tell her I'll juggle my schedule to suit hers."

"All right. I'll let you know as soon as I have a date and time for you."

"Thanks." After a pause, Winslow asked, "Will you be joining us?"

Reese also hesitated. This was one meeting he definitely wanted to attend, but would his presence make Taki even more uncomfortable? "Only if she wants me there. Will her father be flying in?"

"No."

"No? But surely after all this time—"

"Mr. Spencer has no interest in seeing his daughter. I look forward to hearing from you."

Reese stared at the receiver when Winslow disconnected. He had no interest in seeing his daughter after four years? Damn, the man was ice cold. Even so, for her own good, Taki needed to bridge this huge gap between her and her father. She deserved a beautiful life, but couldn't create one while constantly on the run.

Not giving himself time to think, Reese dialed

Taki's number. He let the phone ring twelve times, but no one answered.

Could she have changed her mind? Had she run away again? As he replaced the phone, he considered the evidence. She'd stood up the FBI at Fairchild. What had that been about? The message he'd left at the Paradise Way Ashram hadn't been returned. After several phone calls, he'd discovered nobody at SoBe Spa had seen or spoken to her since her Thursday night class. No one at her house at 6:00 a.m. Mayhugh didn't show at Fairchild, and Javi had been unable to reach the fence.

Would Taki blow town without telling her soul mate? Maybe she'd spit fire at him on Friday night, but he believed she'd tell him before leaving. So where was she? Perhaps she was staying at the ashram and didn't receive his message for some cosmic reason. He'd try to reach someone there again later today on a break from court.

He grabbed his glasses from the nightstand and placed them in his briefcase. Today of all days he needed to see clearly. He looked forward to sealing the fate of Carlos Romero. Of course, Taki believed that karma would eventually punish the terrorist, but he preferred to do the punishing in the here and now. Reese wondered briefly if even Romero had a soul mate…then snapped the briefcase shut.

Had Taki altered the way he looked at life the same way she had altered the way he looked at the printed word?

And where the hell was she?

TAKI DRIFTED TO awareness wondering why her head hurt so very, very much. And her back. And her arm, her wrists. Every part of her body ached. Beneath her was a cold, hard, unforgiving surface.

She sat up, and the world tilted, taking her with it.

Fighting waves of nausea, she lay back down and pressed her cheek against a damp concrete floor. A floor that smelled like mold. Where was—

A horrifying rush of memory flooded her.

Hector. He must have…oh, God, he'd surprised her with a Taser, then tied her up and shoved her into the backseat of that car parked next to her Jeep. And then while she couldn't move, he'd injected something in her arm that had knocked her out.

But why? And where was she now? How long ago had that happened?

She rolled on her back and opened her eyes. Total darkness surrounded her. She blinked. Was it day or night? No way to tell. She moved her hands and realized with relief that she wasn't restrained any longer, but her wrists stung, the skin raw. When she lifted an arm in front of her face to try and see her hand, the throbbing inside her skull pounded like the drums at the equinox festival. Everything blurred. She couldn't even focus overhead, couldn't find a ceiling.

Why would Hector do this? She thought they were friends. And what was that he'd said about how he was going to be rich?

It hurt too much to think, to move, so she lay still, her breath shallow and slow, until oblivion moved over her again like a dark mist.

REESE ENTERED THE courtroom reserved for Romero's trial and placed his briefcase on the prosecution counsel table, the sound echoing in the cavernous room. Except for personnel testing the audio system, the room remained empty. But soon this huge chamber would be buzzing with attorneys, guards, observers and of course a swarm of eager journalists.

The interest generated by this trial was enormous, increasing the pressure on him for a conviction.

On the first day of a big trial, he liked to arrive early, to think about the process before getting swept up in the intricate and sometimes tedious minutia of the system. To outsiders the American method of justice seemed cumbersome, slow. But he believed in the jury system. He believed any accused citizen, even one as obviously guilty as Carlos Romero, was entitled to be judged by a jury of his peers. Everyone deserved a fair trial.

Maybe occasionally the jury got it wrong, but not often. No system was perfect, but in his mind an impartial jury was the surest way to true justice.

And that's what today was all about. He needed to select an impartial group of men and women to weigh the evidence he'd bring forth to convict Romero. Jury selection might take time, but the process was a vital component of the system.

Reese snapped open his briefcase and withdrew his notepad. He sat and began reviewing the questions he intended to ask.

"Good morning, Reese."

Reese looked up from his work to find the first-year attorney assigned as his second chair, as well as scores of other people, had arrived. The room was no longer quiet. "Good morning, Max."

"It's already a zoo out there," Max said as he took a seat at counsel table.

Reese's cell phone rang. He answered, reminding himself that he needed to mute the ring tone when the judge entered the courtroom. "Yeah, Javi?"

"I've got Izzo in custody. Lucky thing, too. An agent spotted him filling up at a gas station in Liberty City."

Finally. Reese sat back, thinking this was an auspicious start to the trial. Maybe a good omen. "Well, better late than never. Have you questioned him?"

"Not yet. He's asked for counsel. I assume you're already in Judge Robinson's courtroom."

"We're just about to start. I'll be turning off my phone."

"We have to wait until his lawyer arrives, but check with me on a recess. I'll let you know if we learn anything."

Reese looked up as the bailiff entered. "Have you heard from Taki?"

"Not a word. And Mayhugh is still off the radar, too."

"Thanks. I'll call you later."

"All rise," the bailiff announced.

Reese put his phone on vibrate and rose, briefly wondering whether Izzo had Taki's all-important bowl. The briefcase no longer mattered, but by this afternoon they'd get some answers to the mystery behind the theft. Izzo might even provide new evidence against Romero.

Judge Sylvia Robinson swept into the courtroom, her black robe trailing behind her.

"Good morning, Counsel," she stated. "Let's start with the defense's motion to exclude."

The morning sped by. The judge efficiently dealt with preliminaries and called in the first panel of potential jurors. By noon they'd made good progress on narrowing down the pool.

"Any more questions of Mrs. Sigler, Mr. Beauchamps?" the judge asked.

Reese smiled at a kindly white-haired lady with five grandchildren he'd just questioned. One of her sons had recently been the victim of a violent mugging.

"Do you believe you can render an impartial decision in this case?" Reese asked.

"Of course, young man. I've always judged everyone fairly."

"Thank you, ma'am. No further questions, Your Honor."

"Just a moment, Counsel," Judge Robinson said, and swiveled her chair for a whispered conference with her bailiff.

Reese returned to his table and scribbled notes regarding candidate number nineteen. Mrs. Sigler was bound to be friendly to the prosecution. He'd definitely accept her, but Romero's attorneys might not. No matter what they claimed, crime victims tended to hold grudges against defendants.

Jury selection had proceeded a lot swifter than he'd anticipated. Romero's defense team had surprisingly few preliminary motions that were easily disposed of this morning. Opening statements might well begin Wednesday. He could possibly use Claudia on Friday.

He glanced at Carlos Romero, wondering how a man facing life in prison could look so smug. Sitting between two well-dressed, fat-cat lawyers, Romero issued a hearty laugh. When he spoke, he gestured with contemptuous self-assurance, often stroking his dark goatee. The man's arrogant demeanor rankled Reese.

Naturally, he expected Romero's counsel to behave as if their case was a slam dunk, that charges should never have been lodged against their wholly innocent client. But usually defendants put on a concerned affect for the jury. Not this guy. His ego was as obvious as his expensive suit.

Reese tapped his pen on his legal pad. Did they know something he didn't?

He dismissed the notion, his own confidence returning. First day jitters, that's all. The truth was, he'd finally caught a break and now knew something that Romero's team didn't.

He had Claudia to testify against her ex, and Javi had finally caught up with Izzo. Wishing he could watch the agent interrogate the bum, Reese smiled at prospective juror number twenty, a young Hispanic female. *One thing at a time. Stay in the present moment. Selecting a jury is important work.*

Judge Robinson swiveled back to face her courtroom. "All right, Counsel. Let's continue. Next juror, please."

CURLED IN A fetal position on the damp floor, Taki stared at the tiny sliver of light that entered her prison. It looked as if the light filtered in from underneath a door at the top of a short flight of stairs. She squinted—yes, there was light around all four sides. She raised her head cautiously, afraid the ferocious pounding inside her skull would overpower her again.

Only a dull ache persisted, so she sat up and waited for her eyes to adjust to the dark.

She reached back to rub a tender lump on the back of her skull. She must have banged her head when she fell. Or maybe the headache resulted from whatever Hector had drugged her with.

Had he robbed her? If so, Hector would be very disappointed by what he found—but no. She patted her body and discovered her purse still draped over her neck and shoulder. Theft wasn't the answer.

She sniffed the stale, moldy air. She'd never heard of a basement in South Florida, but this damp place sure smelled like the ones she remembered up north. She shivered as the thought of darkness-loving rats skittered across her mind.

She scooted backward across the floor until her shoulders rested against a solid wall. She felt its clamminess with her hand. Where was she? More important, why?

She hated the dark and the feeling of being closed in. She'd always feared being confined, especially as a child when her dad had locked her in her room.

What evil thing had she done in a past life to cause this torture? How long had she been here? Well, she couldn't remain here. She had to get out of this horrible dark box.

This coffin.

She hugged her knees to her chest and fought the panic that threatened to overtake her.

Blocking her right nostril with her thumb, she inhaled through the left, held the breath to a slow count of five, and then exhaled to the count of ten. She alternated nostrils five or six times and gradually the terror subsided. If she wanted to escape, she had to keep herself centered. She wouldn't find any path to take if she let herself go nuts.

When calmer, Taki considered her predicament. So had Hector stolen her bowl? As she thought back to the night of the theft, she wondered if that was possible. She'd seen him soon afterward in the parking lot, but he could have hidden the stolen merchandise and circled back to throw the police off track. But why?

She always came back to the same thing. Why would anyone steal her bowl? It had no real value except to her. And why would Hector take Reese's briefcase, for that matter? Was Hector involved with Reese's bad guys?

Hector said he'd followed her to Fairchild. Okay. Obviously to abduct her. So maybe he'd been hired because of his brawny build to do the dirty work. But by whom?

Or maybe he was one of those crazies that stole women and locked them away for decades. Was that what was going to happen to her? Maybe this had nothing to do with her bowl or even Reese's property. Was Hector going to keep her here and rape her? She took another deep breath, pushing away the horror of being held prisoner for years. She refused to even consider that possibility.

She rubbed the bump on her head again, wishing she could drink some of her willow tea for the pain. Actually, she wished she had anything to drink, as the thought of a beverage made her realize how dry her throat was. She swallowed, trying to create some saliva in her mouth.

Her head hurt too badly for logic. She'd figure out what was going on after she escaped.

And she *would* escape.

Now that her vision had better adjusted to the lack of light, she examined her surroundings. Maybe they'd left her some water somewhere.

No water, but there were stairs, five of them, leading to the door. The only way out. The room was a cube and the walls solid concrete. Like some sort of a bunker. She decided it was probably fifteen feet square. There was a toilet to her right, but no furniture.

She levered herself to her feet by slowly feeling the wall behind her. Blood pounded through her pulses, magnifying the ache in her head a hundred times. She slid back to the floor and waited for the pain to ease.

She wouldn't give up. She absolutely refused to give in to weakness. Wasn't that what her father always said, that she was weak like her mother? And had goofy ideas. She wasn't weak, and she wasn't goofy. She needed to find out if that door was locked. For all she knew, she could walk right out of this dungeon.

Moving slowly, she rose again. Keeping her hand on the wall, she took a small step forward. Staying at the edge of the room, probably another five strides would bring her to the small staircase. She could manage that.

But the door swung open, blinding her with brilliant, painful light. She squeezed her eyes shut and turned her head, placing her back against the cool wall.

Maybe now she'd learn what was happening to her. And why.

CHAPTER SIXTEEN

TAKI SQUINTED AT the figure silhouetted in the door frame. From the round shape of the body, this could be Mayhugh. But she couldn't tell for sure. Holding her breath, she waited to see what he'd do.

"Are you awake?" an unfamiliar voice growled. Could be Mayhugh.

"Who are you?" Taki asked, her own voice surprising her with its hollow croak.

The form bent down and placed something on the top step with a soft thud. "Brought you a cola and a burger."

"Wait. Don't go." Taki tried to shout, but that effort sent the drums in her head crescendoing into a thunderous roar. "What do you want?"

The door slammed shut, taking away the intrusive light. The harsh sound of a deadbolt slamming into place echoed inside her prison—again totally dark.

And there was no longer any need to check the door.

She swallowed, but her throat remained dry as the sauna at SoBe Spa. With knees now too shaky to support her weight, she slid to the floor and blinked back tears. Why didn't he at least tell her what was going on, why they were keeping her in this miserable place?

She heaved a breath. At least they'd brought her something to drink. Hunger had been the least of her worries, but she was thirsty and should retrieve the sustenance in case something else in here claimed it first.

She felt her way up the stairs and found a warm paper bag and icy cup. She eased back down and collapsed against the wall to wait for the pressure inside her skull to diminish. Closing her eyes, she breathed in the smell of greasy fast food and gagged.

Of course they'd brought her a burger. Her tormenters probably thought they were offering ambrosia, but her stomach churned at the thought of eating meat again. No matter. She would ignore the beef and eat the bread. There might even be some lettuce or tomato.

Maybe her kidnappers were Reese's bad guys after all. He'd said they were vicious, and this behavior certainly qualified. At least in her opinion. Maybe they hadn't beat her, but not telling someone why something happened was the cruelest thing of all. The sort of practice her father had loved to indulge in.

I am not required to explain why, Kimberly, her father would say in his stern voice when punishing her or refusing a request. *Let's just say it's for your own good, so you don't turn out like your mother.*

Taki sipped the cola, refusing to dwell on the chemicals and sugars inside the liquid. She didn't have an option. She needed to maintain her strength if she wanted to escape. She rolled the cool waxy container across her neck and began to feel a little better.

What time was it?

She'd rejected the idea of being focused on time because how could you rejoice in the present moment if you were always worried about the future? Life was a journey to be enjoyed along the way.

Only she wasn't enjoying herself very much right now, and she'd give anything to know how long she'd been locked away in this hovel. She didn't even know what day it was, how long she'd been unconscious. She'd never had any use for a watch before, but right now really wished she had one.

She'd been taken prisoner on Saturday. Was this Sunday? Depending on the drug Hector gave her, it could be Monday. When she woke up, it sure felt as if she'd been out a long time. Like in a coma. Rubbing the bump on her head, she again wondered how she'd gotten it. Did she have a concussion? Is that why her head ached?

Probably no one had even missed her yet. The ashram had come to expect only sporadic visits, and she wasn't due to teach there until Wednesday. Surely it wasn't Wednesday. Victoria planned to spend three days on Little Palm Island at her favorite getaway. The students in her Monday night class at SoBe Spa would wonder why she didn't show and probably complain to management, but Lourdes certainly wouldn't notify the police. Probably no one would worry until the Thursday night class.

She shivered. That would mean being locked away for six days.

Reese might try to call her to set up the meeting with the Trust. Oh, how she'd love to talk to him. Her spirits lifted just thinking about him. He would know precisely what to do in this situation. If only she had a cell phone.

She shook her head. Suddenly she coveted all the technology she had rejected, but could see how in a crisis electronics had their uses. Of course a cell phone would also tell her the date and the time. Reese always had a cell phone clipped to his belt. What had he said the night of the theft? Right—his whole life was inside his phone. He bought a new one the next day.

She'd thought that was ridiculous. Now she wasn't so sure.

If she got out of this prison—no, *when* she did, maybe she'd start taking advantage of modern technology. Kind of nice to have for emergencies.

But of course Hector would have taken her cell phone if she had one.

She sighed. Even if she had a phone, she couldn't tell Reese where she was. She didn't *know* where she was. But maybe they could trace the connection. The FBI likely knew how to do that. More technology.

Thinking about Reese made her feel better, comforted her somehow. She hugged her knees to her chest. What was he doing right now? Was he in court? In his office? Was he aware that she was missing? Probably not. Even if he'd tried to call her, why would he be alarmed when there wasn't any answer?

But maybe—maybe if she cleared her thoughts and meditated she could focus on contacting him. He might tune in. In her new book, the author talked about how a psychic connection could exist between soul mates. Maybe he *could* trace the call. She almost laughed. Just, well, a different type of a call.

She arranged her legs in lotus position and elongated her spine so that energy could travel freely. No flickering flame to focus on, but she'd make do with the light around the door. Breathing in an even, controlled rhythm, she cleared her mind by murmuring over and over the calming mantra that Navi had given her.

"Let all beings be happy and free. Let all beings be happy and free."

Meditations were visualized journeys. She'd visualize a journey to visit Reese.

What would she say to him when she found him?

REESE STARED INTO the interrogation room at FBI headquarters where Javi was seated across from Izzo and his public defender.

Judge Robinson had adjourned at 4:45 p.m. and instructed counsel to be in her courtroom promptly at nine the next morning. Reese immediately called Javi to get an update and learned Izzo's appointed counsel had finally arrived.

Yes, the wheels of justice move slowly.

"I'm still going at him," Javi had told him. "Come on over and watch the fun."

So far the interrogation wasn't much fun.

"Briefcase? Jaguar?" Izzo issued a short, unpleasant laugh and tilted his chair, balancing on the rear legs. "I'm telling you I don't know what you're talking about, man. Do I look like the type that would work out at a ritzy spa? Gimme a break."

Eyeing Izzo's wiry frame through the one-way window, Reese agreed the hit man probably didn't pump much iron. Romero used him for his stealth and cunning, not his muscles.

Izzo's attorney, David Roemer, a man Reese didn't know and had never worked with, whispered in Izzo's ear. Izzo made a face and returned the legs of his chair to the floor with a bang, the sound echoing in the interrogation room.

Javi placed his hands on the battered table and leaned toward the suspect. "Then tell me where you were between 6:00 and 10:00 p.m. on February 3."

Izzo glared at Javi but no longer appeared quite as cocky. "I already told you, man."

"Tell me again."

"I picked up a hooker that night near Seventy-ninth Street. Peaches. She'll remember me. We had a memorable evening."

"So you say." Javi placed his hand to an earbud, obviously listening to a message. He rose and moved toward the door. "We're trying to locate this mysterious Peaches. Maybe we just did."

"Hey, that's your problem, man." Izzo raised his

voice as Javi exited the room. "I didn't steal nothing that night. No damn punch bowl, nothing."

Through the window Reese watched Izzo pound a fist on the table while his attorney again tried to calm him. Roemer was likely counseling his client to cooperate. Funny thing, though. Javi hadn't been able to poke holes in Izzo's story after hours of questioning. The scumbag just might be telling the truth.

Reese turned when the door opened. Javi and Mark Scott, another special agent, entered the observation room.

"We found Peaches," Scott said. "She confirms that Izzo was with her."

"All night?" Reese asked.

"Late enough."

Javi leaned against the wall and folded his arms. "I believe him, Reese. Izzo knows nada about the theft at the spa. Someone else lifted your briefcase."

Javi and Scott exchanged glances. "A third car reported items missing the night of the theft," Javi said, "but the insurance company denied the claim, citing fraud."

Scott checked his notes. "Apparently one Hector Morales is a real solid citizen who regularly files questionable claims against his auto policy."

"Does this Hector work at the spa?" Reese asked.

"Personal trainer."

Reese nodded. "I know who he is."

"He waited until the next morning to report a radio missing," Scott said. "The receipt he provided turned out to be bogus."

"Okay," Reese said. "I agree he sounds shady. But why would he break into my vehicle? Does he have any connection to Romero?"

"None that we can find." Scott shrugged. "Maybe he wanted to substantiate his phony claim, make it look like one theft of many."

"Or maybe he really wanted a new radio," Javi added. "We're checking out him and other employees of the spa now."

Reese nodded. "You can reach me on my cell. Let me know what you find out."

"Do you think Taki is acquainted with this Hector?" Javi asked.

You mean Kim? Reese wanted to say.

"Taki knows him," he told Javi. "Hector even spoke to her the night of the theft."

"I'd like to interview her and see what she knows," Javi said. "You never know what we might learn."

"Good," Reese said on his way out the door. "Let me know when you find her."

"You still haven't talked to her?" Javi asked.

"No."

On his drive to the federal building, Reese's worry about Taki resurfaced. Where was she? And what exactly was the relationship between Taki and Hector? The personal trainer had been damned friendly the night of the theft, but flippant about her loss when she'd obviously been upset. He'd probably decided after the fact to take advantage of the situation and make his own phony claim.

Did Taki know her coworker liked to dabble in insurance fraud?

In his office, Reese dropped his briefcase and collapsed in his huge leather chair. What a day. And the week only promised to get worse as the Romero trial proceeded.

With the office switchboard now closed to incoming calls, no one could reach him except through his cell. He placed the phone on his desk. Javi might need to contact him with good news. There could always be a break in the case. Hell, maybe the agent would manage to contact Taki.

Reese picked up the neatly stacked pile of messages left by his secretary. He flipped through them. Nothing from Taki, so they could all damn well wait.

Worry niggled at him again. Where was she? Maybe her landlady would know.

Mrs. Van Buren answered on the first ring.

"Mrs. Van Buren, this is Reese Beauchamps."

"Oh. Yes, Reese."

An uneasy feeling settled in his gut when he heard her high, breathless voice. She didn't sound happy to hear from him.

"I hope you remember me. I met you with Taki in her cottage a week or so ago."

"I know who you are," she said firmly. "What can I do for you?"

"I'm hoping you can tell me where Taki is. I haven't been able to reach her."

"Oh, dear. Well, I was away all weekend. I just returned home a short time ago."

"The thing is I'm getting worried," he said. If Mrs. Van Buren had been out of town, she wouldn't know if Taki had bolted.

"I'm sure she's fine," Victoria said.

"I think it's possible she left Miami. Could you check to see if her clothes and other personal effects are gone?" *Like maybe the angels over her bed.*

Mrs. Van Buren didn't answer for a moment, then sighed. "I suppose I could let myself in."

"Thank you. Please call me back. I'll give you my cell number."

Reese held on to the receiver after Mrs. Van Buren disconnected, trying to figure out what about their conversation seemed off. He tapped the receiver against his chin.

He was being ridiculous. The landlady had obviously been expecting to receive a call from someone else, that's all. And it shouldn't surprise him if Taki had disappeared. He'd seen tangible proof of how the woman jumped from city to city. Hell, she'd even told him she was leaving. Stress and lack of sleep were making him jumpy.

He replaced the receiver. Would she inform him of a decision to bolt? Friday night she'd been angry enough to never speak to him again.

He left his hand on the phone while the foreboding rose again. Taki would never leave without telling him goodbye. No way. No matter how mad she got.

And just how the hell did he know that? He didn't. Of course he didn't.

He shook his head. When Victoria Van Buren

called him back, he'd find out if Taki had moved. He just had to be patient, wait fifteen minutes, maybe a half hour. An hour tops.

He loosened his tie and leaned back in his chair. Eyeing the sofa on the opposite side of the room, he decided to rest his eyes until he heard from Mrs. Van Buren. In fact, he'd spend the night in the office. He always kept an emergency change of clothing for court and could take a morning shower in the fourth-floor locker room.

He couldn't sleep at home, anyway. Maybe that couch would work better.

He collapsed onto the plush cushions and closed his eyes. Just a few moments of rest. That's all he needed.

Gasping for air, Reese jolted awake, aware only of an overpowering impression of Taki—of her feeling closed in and frightened. As the comforting reality of his office sofa beneath him registered, her presence faded. Feeling claustrophobic himself, he swung his feet to the floor and sat up. Worry about her had obviously caused a nightmare, but he had no specific memory of any dream.

Morning light filtered into his office, and he moved to the window to watch the sun rise over Miami Beach. With an endless horizon spread out before him, how could he feel shut in?

Reese grabbed his cell phone when its ring tone sounded in the quiet room. Damn. Almost 7:00 a.m. He needed to get moving.

"Where are you?" Agent Rivas asked bluntly.

"In my office," Reese said, his head clearing. What bug was up Javi's ass?

Reese checked his phone for a missed call or a voice mail. Victoria Van Buren had never called him back. Why was that?

"There's no easy way to say this, Reese, but Taki's Jeep was pulled out of a canal yesterday afternoon."

Reese felt himself go ice-cold. He squeezed his phone hard. "What?"

"I put an APB out on her vehicle and just got an email. I'm on my way to the impound lot now."

"I'll meet you there," Reese said.

WHEN TAKI AWOKE, it seemed as if she stood on top of the world—or a mountain, anyway—with the sun warming her face.

But the reality of her damp dungeon terminated that precious feeling of freedom. Bitter disappointment was followed by an exhilarating rush of memory.

She'd dreamed about Reese. It felt so real—as if she could reach out and touch him.

She sat up and leaned against the wall trying to hold on to the images rapidly fleeing her head. But of course that's the way dreams were. You could never remember the details. But she'd had the sense that he'd been working, maybe even in his office. Well, naturally she'd dream about that. Reese practically lived to work, and wasn't the most important trial of his career about to begin?

Or had it already begun?

She frowned, again confused about time. Well, if she ever saw Reese again, she'd tell him what she thought about him working all the time.

Most likely her vision had been a dream. Even so, it'd been a nice one. She had tried to communicate that she needed help, to show him her location. But of course she'd failed in that particular task since she didn't know where she was.

Taki stood and stretched her arms overhead, her fingertips grazing the gritty top of the small prison. Time to salute the sun—even if she couldn't see it— and center herself. She needed to remain open because she intended to try to contact Reese again and again. Why not? If she kept sending out a psychic signal, maybe he could use it as a beacon and home in on her.

While she moved through her yoga positions, Taki again cautioned herself that the vision might have been an ordinary dream. She'd fallen asleep while visualizing a journey to Reese, so it was logical that she would think of him in her sleep.

No matter. It'd been a comfort to be with him again. She enjoyed the comforting sensation that he would rather die than harm her, that she could trust him…that she should trust him. And maybe he was right about her motivations. Did she fear ending up like her mom? Was it possible she hadn't properly mourned her death? She used meditation and yoga to avoid even thinking about her mother.

Taki froze midstretch and placed her knees on the

floor, her thoughts paralyzed by the force of the star-tling idea that gripped her.

She needed to trust Reese. If she truly trusted him, totally and completely with her whole heart, would her soul mate come for her? Was that the lesson she needed to learn?

The thought stunned her with its power and clarity.

Oh, she ached to believe in him. She truly did.

But Reese wanted her to stop running. If she did, if she let her father back into her life, she'd have to forgive him. In order to do that, she'd have to trust Reese that this was the right thing for her. Could she do it? Could she let go of all the bitterness and for-get the past?

If pardoning her father meant release from this hell hole, surely she could do it.

But maybe not. She found herself turning away from the idea, wondering if maybe she'd clung to the pain and resentment for so long that she couldn't let it go.

REESE SHOVED ASIDE soaked vegetation from the bum-per of the wrecked Jeep and read a faded message: Free Tibet.

A cold wind swept across the impound lot, and he shivered. Was Taki at the bottom of a murky canal? Had she lost control of the Jeep and swerved in? He closed his eyes against the chilling thought that she might be dead.

Javi approached, and Reese moved to meet him.

"It's her Jeep," Reese said. "No question."

"I know." Javi's face was grim. "Listen...I'm sorry, man."

"Did they find a body?" Reese asked, his voice sounding hollow even to himself.

"The county scuba team searched, but came up empty. The good news is that the Jeep was pushed in, not driven. Probably whoever junked the vehicle just wanted to hide it."

Relief swept through him. There was a chance that she was still alive. Now all he wanted to do was find her.

"Any idea yet how long the Jeep had been under water?" Reese asked.

"Not more than a few days, but the lab will tell us for sure. The local fisherman who made the report said it wasn't in the canal last weekend."

Reese nodded. The Jeep had been parked in front of Taki's cottage Friday night and this was Tuesday morning. Three days. She could have been in trouble for three days.

"When did you last see her?" Javi asked.

"Friday night. I haven't been able to reach her since then. Have you questioned Hector?"

"Can't find him. We've posted an APB and someone's watching his apartment." Javi hesitated, then said, "No one has seen him since Friday, either."

"This is crazy." Reese ran a hand through his hair, trying to cut through the shock of Taki's disappearance so he could focus on the facts. What was going on? Had someone at the spa discovered her real identity?

"I want you to requestion a SoBe Spa member by the name of Benny," Reese said. "He attends Taki's yoga classes and delivered the first note about her bowl."

"I'll try," Javi said, jotting notes. "The thing is my supervisor is squawking about the time my team is spending on this case. He doesn't see any connection to a federal crime now that we've determined Izzo didn't break into your vehicle."

"Come on, Javi."

The agent shrugged. "In my boss's mind, this is now a missing person case. A problem for the local authorities."

"Maybe not." Reese folded his arms and stared at the Jeep. "There's something you don't know."

"What?" Javi asked.

"Taki's not who you think she is."

"What do you mean?"

"Her real name is Kim Spencer, and she's the heir to an immense fortune."

"No shit?" Javi's tone dripped shock, and Reese knew it wasn't easy to surprise the seasoned agent.

"Yeah. And I'm talking about a serious amount of money. I'm wondering if someone found out who she is and..."

Javi narrowed his eyes. "You think she's been kidnapped?"

"It's a possibility."

"But no ransom note?"

"Not yet anyway."

After a moment Javi nodded. "Okay. You owe me big-time, but I'll get a warrant to search her home. Maybe we'll find a lead there."

Reese sighed in relief. He couldn't search for Taki alone. He needed the FBI's assistance. "Thanks, man."

"By the way, aren't you supposed to be in court?"

Reese glanced at his watch and groaned. "I'm already late."

Javi whistled. "If I know Judge Robinson, she'll make you pay for that."

OUT OF BREATH, Reese entered Judge Robinson's hushed courtroom at nine forty-five. Every eye in the room focused on him as he proceeded up the aisle.

"Thank you for joining us, Mr. Beauchamps."

Reese winced at the frosty sarcasm in Judge Robinson's voice. Joanna had made a phone call to the judge's chambers, but who knew if she had even received the message.

"My apologies to the Court," Reese said in his most respectful tone. "I was unavoidably detained."

The judge leveled her gaze on him. "You not only kept me waiting, but several hundred prospective jurors."

Reese placed his briefcase on counsel table, refusing to glance at Romero and his team of lawyers. "I'm sorry, Your Honor."

But he wasn't. He'd had no choice but to confirm the vehicle removed from the canal had indeed been

Taki's. Hell, he'd gladly suffer through a tongue-lashing all day if it would undo the painful truth that she was in trouble. Big trouble. He jammed a hand in his pocket and tightened his fist.

What had happened to her? How soon would the FBI lab have answers from the Jeep? Would Javi find out anything from Taki's home? Would he learn anything from Benny?

Or would Javi's boss reassign him?

"You can make your explanations to me later, Mr. Beauchamps."

"Yes, Your Honor."

"Bring in the first panel of jurors," the judge instructed her bailiff.

Off the hook for now, Reese sat at the prosecution table and nodded at his white-faced assistant. Poor Max. The first-year attorney looked damned relieved that his lead prosecutor had appeared. Reese trusted Judge Robinson would remain unbiased even if she was thoroughly pissed off. Of course she didn't know or care that a precious light in the world might have been extinguished.

Reese grabbed his pen and slashed lines on a legal pad to create the outline that he utilized in making juror decisions and refocused his thoughts. He needed to concentrate on the business of selecting a good jury, one that would put a bottom-feeder like Romero away for life.

A group of seven men and five women entered the jury box and sat down, their curious gazes examining the high-ceilinged courtroom. Reese tried to smile at them, but he couldn't. He didn't want to be here.

"All right," Judge Robinson said. "Let's proceed, Counsel."

He wanted to be searching for Taki.

CHAPTER SEVENTEEN

TAKI FELT CAREFULLY around the gritty floor of her prison, searching for something to help her. A rock, a nail, anything. Surely she could find something in this miserable hole she could use to loosen the hinges on the door.

Maybe it was a foolish plan, but it was a plan nonetheless, and she felt better for having thought of something to do to get out of this prison.

She couldn't sit around and do nothing hoping Reese would find her. She needed to trust him, yes. And she would. She did. She now believed he was right about her father.

Every time she thought of her father and tried to soften her heart toward him, she could hardly breathe. She remembered being locked in her room as punishment for breaking one of his rules. Rules put in place, he insisted, so she didn't end up a cheater like her mother.

Her mom. Taki closed her eyes and allowed herself to absorb more pain. Indirectly, she was the cause of her mother's death since losing custody was what pushed her mom over the edge. Taki now realized she'd used yoga as a crutch to keep from feeling the hurt too deeply. She'd kept her heart locked up inside a block of ice, hiding not only from her father but from the pain of her mother's suicide.

Meeting Reese, falling in love with him, had initiated the big thaw. Her soul mate had shown her what path to take. She needed to trust Reese. She needed to stop running. Yes, she'd have to let her father back in her life, even work on forgiving him, and that was her path to enlightenment. It wouldn't be easy, but she could do it with Reese's help.

But to take those important steps—of course Navi would call it "doing the work"—she'd have to first find her own way out of this dungeon and get back to the warmth and light of the sun.

She crawled to the only section of the room she hadn't yet searched, the area under the stairs. She'd saved this space for last because none of the scant light penetrated and the dark still frightened her. With a deep breath, she patted along the floor, hoping for any sort of tool, and her hand brushed against a smooth, cool object. Maybe metal.

With a surge of excitement, Taki flicked her finger against its side, and a full, musical tone filled the room.

Her bowl.

She hugged the sacred object to her chest and offered a silent thank-you to the universe for returning the bowl to her. Maybe it was just a symbol, but its presence buoyed her spirit.

With renewed hope she continued her search and soon encountered a hard rectangular object. Could this be Reese's briefcase? She felt for a handle and found one, then moved into the center of the room for more light.

When she opened the briefcase, she experienced a flash of pure joy. Reese's cellular phone! She punched buttons searching for an on switch. No lights came on. No sounds. Nothing happened at all.

Disappointed, she realized its battery was dead and tossed the device aside to continue her quest for a tool. None of these treasures would matter if she didn't make her way to freedom.

Next she found a bound legal-size folder with photocopied pages of a neat feminine scrawl. This had to be the copy of the journal Reese had wanted for his trial. The large margins contained notes in a different handwriting. Probably Reese's. She gave the file a quick kiss. Her karma-mending path-smoother.

Now she just needed to find something sharp to pry the hinges off that door.

WHEN JUDGE ROBINSON adjourned court at 5:00 p.m., Reese drove straight toward Taki's cottage. Stuck at a light, he loosened his tie and cursed rush hour traffic on the route to Miami Beach. Today had been the worst day of his career—hell, the worst day of his life. It had taken every shred of hard-won discipline to remain in that stifling, overheated courtroom and ask meaningless questions of strangers.

Now he had twelve hours to concentrate on finding Taki.

But he was on his own.

On the lunch recess he learned the FBI had processed Taki's home but found nothing that would lead them to her location. Still no sign of Hector. Agents dispatched to interview Benny hadn't hooked up with him by the time the noon recess ended. Ditto with Bruce Mayhugh.

And that was all the help he'd get from the FBI. Javi's boss put an end to further man hours until if and when someone received a ransom note. At least Javi had turned over his file to the Miami-Dade police, but to them Taki was just another missing person in a county full of lost people.

Reese punched in Winslow's number. He needed to know Taki was in trouble. He'd been unable to reach the man on the recess but left a voice mail.

Winslow answered after one ring. "Reese, what's going on? Your message worried me."

"Taki is missing."

"She's been missing for years."

"The FBI found her Jeep at the bottom of a canal. She wasn't in it."

"What? Are you—"

"I assume by your response the family hasn't received a ransom note."

After a long silence, Winslow said, "Not that I'm aware of. Oh, my God."

Reese released a breath. No note. Maybe she hadn't been kidnapped after all. "You should notify her father."

"I'll do that immediately."

"I'd like to talk to him. He might know a motive

for a possible abduction. Maybe someone had threatened him or he'd been involved in a recent conflict leaving someone with a grudge."

But three days and no ransom demand? A kidnapping seemed unlikely, but a possibility he had to cover.

"I'll see what I can do," Winslow said, sounding doubtful. Reese shook his head. Surely Spencer would fly into Miami now that his daughter was in danger.

Reese disconnected. He wanted to speak with Victoria Van Buren. If anyone knew where Taki was, she would. He couldn't quite wrap his mind around why, but something about his conversation with the old woman last night bothered him. And why hadn't she called him back?

Mrs. Van Buren answered the door to her waterfront mansion wearing a flowing red caftan.

"Reese. What a…surprise."

Was that worry he heard in her high-pitched voice? Definitely tension. "I'd like to speak to you, Mrs. Van Buren. May I come in?"

"Certainly. And please call me Victoria." She swept her arm in a regal fashion to show him the way.

Reese followed her into a parlor, noting that the room smelled musty and was sparsely furnished.

"Any word on Taki?" she asked. "The FBI searched the carriage house today, but wouldn't tell me anything." She motioned for him to have a seat.

"I expected you to call me back last night," Reese

replied as he sat on a sofa that had probably been new when Victoria was young.

"Oh, dear. Perhaps I should have." She pursed her lips and looked away. "But the truth is I needed time to decide what Taki would want me to do. Can I offer you a drink, Reese?" she asked, moving toward a small bar in the corner.

"No, thank you."

Victoria poured herself two inches of straight Bourbon. "I couldn't reach Robin in Cassadaga until almost midnight, and after that it was much too late for telephone calls."

"You called the psychic to find out what Taki would want you to do?" Reese stared at Victoria. No wonder Taki liked her so much. They thought exactly alike.

Mrs. Van Buren nodded and took a healthy swallow of whiskey.

"Exactly what did you need spiritual advice on?"

Victoria joined him on the sofa. "Whether to tell you anything. The last time I spoke to Taki she was—well, actually quite cross with you. I'm sorry to say she wants nothing more to do with you, Reese. That's why I didn't call you back."

Reese shook his head. That explained Victoria's obvious evasiveness. But because of her misplaced loyalty, Taki's trail was at least twelve hours colder. He needed the lost time back.

"If that vintage Jeep didn't break down, Taki is likely in North Carolina by now." Victoria took another swig of liquor, then added, "She certainly won't need her Miami clothing in the mountains."

"Yesterday I might have agreed with your theory," Reese said. "But she didn't take the Jeep."

"Of course she did."

Reese took a deep breath. Javi was right. There was no easy way to say it. "Yesterday Miami-Dade police discovered Taki's Jeep submerged in six feet of water."

Victoria's wrinkled face blanched. She placed a hand over her heart. "Oh, dear heaven."

"We think her vehicle was pushed into a canal to hide it."

"Poor Taki," Victoria murmured.

"So you have no idea what might have happened to her?"

"None," Victoria said, shaking her head. "Have you checked with the ashram?"

"I'm hoping to speak to her guru later tonight. You knew Taki was Kim Spencer, didn't you?"

"Yes." Victoria averted her eyes and took another swallow of Bourbon. "She came to me for help, and I was happy to give her a place to live."

"Is it possible that anyone else could have learned her identity?"

Victoria nodded and thought for a moment. "Well, of course you know that's always possible. But Taki—Kim was very careful. I can't imagine who would make that discovery. Or how."

"All right." Reese rose. He needed to keep looking for answers. He'd found nothing here. "Thanks for your help."

Victoria placed a bony hand on his arm. "Please let me know as soon as you find her. Taki is like a daughter to me."

TAKI FLEXED HER cramped fingers and refocused on the hinges of her prison's door. More light would certainly help. She took a deep breath, reminding herself of Navi's lessons for the hundredth time since beginning this project: Patience opens the door to opportunity.

Hoping patience would open *this* particular door, she resumed gouging at paint and dirt with her makeshift screwdriver, created from a hinge off Reese's briefcase. Fortunately, the door hinges were rusted and weak, but the built-up crud didn't easily dislodge. And her improvised tool was difficult to manipulate. She had to go slowly or risk breaking the point.

She'd worked for hours and hours—she had no way to track the time, but knew it was night because light no longer filtered in around the door—and had managed to loosen the bottom two pins. Her fingertips were now raw and painful from the constant friction. The top hinge was harder to reach and the metal remained strong. Probably because less moisture reached it over the years.

Her plan was the dead bolt would hold the door in place when she finally worked the last pin loose. Then she'd pry open that side and squeeze through the opening. Shouldn't be a problem since she'd probably lost five pounds. Burgers made her queasy, and that's all they ever brought—although no one had delivered any food in a long while.

At any rate, this escape route had worked once before when she was fifteen and her father wouldn't let her go to Rob Fulton's surprise birthday party. She smiled bitterly as she recalled her father's fury when he confronted her the next day.

She'd had a much better screwdriver then, of course. And several days to work at the pins. Had her father been angrier about the damage to the door or because she had thwarted his edicts?

The sound of a key entering the door's lock froze Taki midscrape.

Surely the kidnappers weren't bringing her dinner this late. They'd never come after dark before.

Terrified of her plans being ruined, she scurried to her customary spot on the floor directly in front of the stairs, arranging herself just as the door opened.

As usual, her tormentor waited on the top step. Sometimes it was Mayhugh; tonight it was Hector. Neither one would ever answer her questions, always refused to tell her what was going on. The night sky was a black hole behind him. She squinted, and thought she could see a few stars. What time was it?

She briefly considered rushing up the stairs and tackling Hector, knocking him off balance, but knew she didn't have the strength to overcome a two hundred pound personal trainer. Plus, she was weak and he'd probably catch up to her within a hundred feet.

Better to stick with her original strategy. If it wasn't wrecked by this late dinner delivery.

He clicked on a flashlight and almost blinded her with its beam. "Hey, Taki."

She put her hands in front of her face. "Please."

Hector laughed and moved the light to the left, illuminating the toilet. "Bet you thought I forgot your supper." He shook a paper bag and then tossed it to her.

Taki ignored the food and pressed a hand against her racing heart. What if Hector noticed something weird about the door? She'd left the bottom two pins in, but...

"I have good news," he said.

"What's that?"

"We've had some real progress on your situation."

"Are you going to let me go?"

"Can't do that." He laughed softly. "Hey, I know you don't want the money, girl, but I do. Guess what? Your father is going to pay two million dollars to get his precious Kimmie back."

A dizzying wave of disbelief washed over her. *My father?* Hector knew who she was. But how?

"I always knew Taki wasn't your real name."

She swallowed hard against the old resentment. Once again the Spencer fortune had wrecked her life. Another challenge to forgiving her father.

"So you're holding me for ransom?"

"We tried to do it the easy way and ransom that stupid bowl, but your friend Reese kept getting in the way. That's when we decided to grab you instead."

"You know I don't have any money, Hector."

"Yeah, but my partner believed that you'd contact your trust fund people to get the money."

"Your partner was wrong." Her mind scrambled for answers. Who was his partner? Mayhugh? Had Benny discovered her identity? For sure Hector wasn't in charge of something as complex as this kidnapping.

"No matter. We have *you* now."

Taki nodded. *So you do, Hector. So you do.*

"And your father wants you back."

Sure he does. Just not for the reason most fathers would want a daughter's return. "When are you going to get the money?" she asked.

Hector shifted his weight. "We mighta had a little problem delivering the ransom note to the right party, but that's been handled. Just thought I'd let you know since you've been asking so many questions. Soon you'll be out of here, and I'll be driving a new red Porsche."

Taki stared at Hector. Surely he couldn't be foolish enough to believe it would all be so easy. Did he think she was an idiot? She knew most hostages never made it to freedom alive. Her father had drummed that into her from the time she was ten.

"Who told you who I was? Who is your partner?"

"Never mind about that. *Dios, chica,* I couldn't believe it when I found out how rich you are! How could you turn your back on all that money? You could live anywhere, do whatever you want."

"Money will bring you nothing but unhappiness."

Hector snickered. "Yeah, right." Still laughing, he exited and locked the door.

Taki closed her eyes and exhaled when the dead bolt turned, giving silent thanks Hector hadn't noticed anything unusual about the hinges.

She lay still for several long moments as she absorbed what he'd revealed. At least she knew the truth now. She was being held for ransom. Why hadn't she considered someone had learned who she was and went after the Spencer money? How had that happened?

What did it matter? She'd been foolish to believe she could remain hidden as Taki forever. She'd gotten attached. Another life lesson, no doubt.

Hating that her father's money would free her, Taki longed to resume managing her own escape. But right now...now she could barely move a muscle.

The terror of almost being caught in the act of unhinging the door had drained her energy. The shock of learning why she was imprisoned overwhelmed her. She understood what was happening, that this temporary weakness was the result of her fight-or-flight instinct, the body's response to danger. Adrenaline had flooded her when Hector showed up, depleting all her blood sugar, and now she had zero strength left. Trying in vain to muster some, Taki rotated her ankles.

She'd had nothing to eat but chemical-seasoned meat and sugar and that didn't help her stamina, either. Not only was she a hostage, but she was being slowly poisoned.

Her thoughts turned to her father. Would he come to Miami to coordinate the ransom drop? No. He wouldn't bother to make the trip. Most likely he'd send his private security team and insist they run the show. Her father turned everything into a show.

He'd want to control the whole scenario in his usual overbearing manner and likely drive Reese and the FBI nuts with his demands. But maybe Reese wouldn't let him.

She closed her eyes. What would it be like to see her father again? Her stomach cramped at the idea. She'd spent four years trying not to think about him and his cruelty. Now she had no choice.

Yes, she did. She had a choice. Her guru taught if you controlled your mind, you controlled everything.

Willing herself to relax to speed her body's recovery, Taki touched the journal on the floor beside her. She'd take it and the bowl when she squeezed out that door. She'd take Reese's phone, too, since it was so important to him.

What was Florida's future governor doing right now? She pictured Reese when they'd last been together, flushed from sex and confused by her anger. And what exciting lovemaking it had been. Their passion for each other had consumed them. On the floor of her cottage even. But she'd liked it the first time, too, when he'd been slow and sweet and gentle.

Making love with Reese had been something special for them both, and in her deepest soul she knew it always would be. Wishing he were with her now, she smiled and closed her eyes. Maybe she could pretend he was. Fantasy wasn't a bad thing.

TAKI'S LONG BLOND hair tickled Reese's chest as she sucked and teased first one nipple and then the other. She raised her head, her eyes twinkling with erotic mischief.

"I'm going to make you forget all about work tonight," she whispered.

Her mouth slid across his abdomen, licking and planting kisses of pure pleasure against his fevered skin. He groaned and stroked her head as she moved lower and lower…. With a rushed intake of air, Reese woke from the most intense dream he'd ever experienced. He cut the shrill alarm, surprised that he didn't have to reach over Taki's nude body. Her jasmine fragrance lingered in the air.

What was going on? Had worry over her whereabouts driven him into X-rated dreams? Two mornings in a row he had woken with Taki not just on his mind, but in it and consuming every thought.

As if she were in the room with him. As if he could just ask her where she was.

Reality settled in, and a cold wave of terror washed over him. He needed to find her, talk to her, make sure she was safe. He wanted her always safe. Meeting Taki had altered his life forever. For the better. He loved her. What if he never got the chance to tell her?

Reese rolled onto his stomach, dreading the idea of spending another day in Judge Robinson's court selecting a jury. How could he endure that monotony when Taki remained missing?

He mentally reviewed what he knew. Last night, he'd reached Guru Navi, who had no information about Taki's location. A thoroughly confused Benny Schwartz readily revealed the phone call from Mayhugh to Taki setting the meet at Fairchild for Saturday morning. Benny claimed he'd only been trying to help, that he knew Mayhugh from breakfasts at the Puerto Sagua restaurant.

Had Taki already agreed to rendezvous with the fence again when they'd… Reese groaned and closed his eyes, remembering the unbelievable passion that had exploded on the floor of her cottage. Well, at least she'd notified Javi. That was something.

He loved Taki more than he had ever loved or wanted anything in his life. Okay, so far they weren't exactly on the same wavelength. If…no, *when* he found her, he'd find a way to make it work between them. He'd show her there could be a happy ending. He'd make her happy.

When he'd called Javi to report the results of his interview with Benny, Javi agreed that Taki's disappearance had to be related to the meeting between Taki and Mayhugh. With Fairchild closed for the day, Reese couldn't interview anyone there, so he'd driven to Homestead. But Mayhugh hadn't answered his pounds on the front door.

Reese returned home well after midnight, and was due in court at 9:00 a.m. He didn't want to go. He wanted to drive to Fairchild and find out if anyone had seen her. Most likely they had surveillance cameras he could review.

When the phone rang, Reese grabbed it. "Beauchamps."

"This is Winslow. Kim's been kidnapped."

Reese stood. "You got a ransom demand?"

"Yes. Some idiot delivered the note to an office in Newport that's closed for the winter. When they didn't hear from anyone, they finally found a better address. I'll fax you a copy as soon as we hang up."

"What do they want?"

"Two million dollars."

Reese swallowed, surprised they hadn't asked for more. But still, coming up with that kind of cash... "When?"

"Today at 3:00 p.m. in the gardens at the old Deering Estate."

"Have you notified the FBI?"

"Mr. Spencer has been in touch with his contacts at Quantico, but you should reach out to the local office to expedite the process."

"I'm on it. What time will Spencer arrive?"

"Mr. Spencer is far too busy to leave New York. I'm handling the ransom."

"But she's his daughter," Reese said, controlling his voice with effort.

After a pause, Winslow said, "Frankly, I think we're lucky he's willing to put up the money. He can quit looking for her if he has a body."

Stunned by that comment, Reese hung up and stared at the phone. *Taki was right. The man is a monster.*

Reese placed a call to the home of Max Levine, his first-year assistant. Max's day was about to turn very bad.

"Hello?"

"Max, this is Reese. You have to work the Romero jury today. I won't be there."

A long, silent moment passed. "Reese, you can't do this to me, man. Judge Robinson will have me for sushi."

"Sorry, Max. I'll make it up to you."

"Reese, come on, you know better. This is no way to score points with the top guns. You need—"

"Maybe I'm tired of playing the game." Reese disconnected and punched in Javi's cell number.

"Yeah, Reese," the agent answered.

"Taki's father received a ransom demand. I'll fax it to you as soon as I get it."

Javi gave a long whistle. "Damn. That changes things. What are the particulars?"

"We've got to be at Deering Estate with the money today at three."

"Aren't you going to court?"

"No way. I'm working on an expedited warrant for Mayhugh's farm. We're paying him a visit as soon as it comes through."

CHAPTER EIGHTEEN

TAKI LISTENED TO the pin from the top hinge clatter to the concrete floor and reveled in an extraordinary sense of accomplishment. Her arms and shoulders ached from reaching and hammering and pushing, but finally she'd done it. She lowered her arms.

She was free. Or would be.

She descended the stairs and looped her bag over her neck and shoulder, patting the diary inside. She grabbed her bowl and Reese's phone, then hurried back up the stairs.

The door levered open with surprising ease, and she wedged her way through. Faint morning light showed the promise of a clear day. She took a tentative step into fresh air and luxuriated in a sense of freedom. But only for a moment.

Seeing the back of Mayhugh's stone house two hundred feet to the east, she turned west and struggled through an overgrown field toward a pine forest. So she was in Homestead. She pushed weeds aside, trying to keep low and out of sight. She stumbled with the uneven footing and hated what the days in solitary had done to her strength. She'd duck inside the woods and stay close to the tree line until out of danger. Then she would turn back toward the main road.

She'd call Reese as soon as she found a phone.

REESE BRAKED HIS Jag to a stop behind the Crown Vic driven by Javi and jumped out. They'd arrived at Mayhugh's farmhouse.

Car door after car door slammed behind him as a small army of federal agents arrived to execute the search warrant. Spurred by phone calls from D.C., the local bureau took the kidnapping of the Spencer heiress quite seriously.

"Look for an underground room," Reese told Javi as they stepped onto the front porch.

"Why underground?" Javi asked.

It's a feeling I have. Reese shook his head as he held back what he actually wanted to say. "Just a hunch."

No one responded to Javi's knock.

He shouted, "FBI. Open up." Still no response.

With guns drawn and ready, agents used force to breach the front door.

As the FBI swarmed the stone house, Reese couldn't shake the sensation that Taki was close by.

Agents yelled, "Clear!" in room after room. To all appearances, the house was empty.

He let others go through dressers and closets. He was technically an observer, but he opened every door that he found, looking for one that led down. After no luck in the house, he moved outside and began searching for doors around the perimeter.

"Reese. Out here."

Reese looked up as Javi shouted. He spotted the agent in an overgrown field behind the house with Agent Scott. As Reese approached their position, he noted that they stood next to an elevated mound in the dirt. A ventilation shaft extended out the top.

"What's this?" Reese asked.

"Looks like an old fallout shelter, probably from the early sixties," Javi reported. "Someone locked inside removed the door hinges and escaped."

The three men shoved against the door with their shoulders, splintering wood to make a larger opening into a dark underground room.

"See if you can find a light switch," Javi said as they peered into the darkness below. Scott illuminated the space with a flashlight.

Reese located a breaker switch near the door and flipped it on, then stepped through the shattered door behind Javi.

His open briefcase lay in the center of the subterranean bunker. He approached and squatted before it. Someone had destroyed the case by removing its metal hinges.

"Is that your property?" Javi asked.

"Yes," Reese said, disappointment and frustration mounting steadily, convinced Taki had been held prisoner in this room. Her presence, even her fragrance filled the small space. Had she been here last night as he'd pounded on Mayhugh's door?

Where was she now? The copy of Claudia's journal was missing, as well as his old phone. Had Taki taken the diary or had someone else?

"Man, I'd go nuts locked in here for very long," Scott said as he surveyed the small room.

Silently agreeing with Scott, Reese hated the thought of Taki locked in a room with no windows. Her spirit should always be allowed to soar free.

"But where is she now?" Javi said. "Did they catch her or did she make good an escape?"

"Maybe that's why Mayhugh isn't here," Scott suggested. "They've moved the Spencer woman to another location. They might have done that anyway if they knew we were coming with a warrant."

"We need to find Mayhugh," Reese said, his sense of dread growing, convinced that Taki remained in danger.

A shadow moved past the opening and disappeared.

"Hey," Javi shouted and darted up the steps.

Reese followed, emerging from the fallout shelter as Javi yelled, "Stop where you are. FBI." The man kept running, and Javi fired a warning shot into the air.

Hector Morales dropped a paper bag from a fast-food restaurant and raised his thickly muscled arms.

"VICTORIA! THANK GOODNESS." Taki reached inside the driver's side of Victoria's old blue Cadillac and hugged her friend. "Thank you for coming!"

"Hurry and get in, dear, before they discover you're gone."

Taki ran around to the passenger door and hopped

inside. She'd hiked along the tree line for what seemed like an hour before cutting back to a major road. Then it took forever to find a phone.

"How are you?" Victoria asked as she pulled onto Krome Avenue. "They didn't harm you, did they?"

"Other than trying to poison me with red meat, no." Taki raised her arms overhead and stretched. "Ooooh, it feels good to be free."

"Did you ever get ahold of Reese?"

"No." Taki lowered her arms. "His secretary said he's in trial this morning but would try to reach him."

"Did you call the police?"

"No. I want you to drive me straight to the closest police station."

Victoria gave her a sidelong look. "Maybe you should get cleaned up first, dear. They won't let you bathe if we go to the police station, and I believe you could use a bit of a…" Victoria raised her eyebrows "…a toilette."

"A hot shower." Taki released a soft sigh at the delicious notion of cleansing, steaming water. "That would be heaven, but we need to notify the police first. Do you have your cell phone?"

Victoria frowned. "No, but I grabbed some of your favorite mineral water on my way out. Would you like a drink?"

Taki gratefully accepted the plastic bottle Victoria handed her. Finally, something to drink besides watered-down cola. The cool water refreshed as Taki took several long swallows, then noticed an unpleasant aftertaste.

"How old is this water, Victoria?" Taki examined the label.

"Oh, not old."

Taki sniffed the interior of the car, detecting a hint of alcohol. "Have you been drinking this early, Victoria?"

"Really, Taki."

Taki squinted at Victoria, wondering why her face looked so blurred. Suddenly dizzy, Taki closed her eyes.

"I AIN'T SAYING nothing until I get a lawyer," Hector announced as he crossed his arms over his muscled chest.

Javi, Scott and Hector sat around Mayhugh's kitchen table. Reese leaned against a counter and watched. The remainder of the agents waited in the outer room or had returned to their vehicles to await the outcome of the interview.

Reese grabbed a phone off the wall, wanting to smack Hector with it. "Here. Call your counsel."

"I need a public defender. I know my rights, and you gotta appoint one for me."

"We haven't even placed you under arrest yet," Scott reminded him.

"Then I'm leaving, man." Hector stood, but Javi pushed him back into his chair.

"Where is Kim Spencer?" Javi demanded.

"Who?"

"Taki," Reese said, not believing for a minute the innocent look on Hector's face.

"Save your breath," Hector said. "I ain't talking until I get a lawyer."

"That's it," Javi said. "Time for a trip to headquarters. You have the right to remain silent."

"Taki thought you were her friend," Reese said after Javi finished reading Hector his Miranda rights and cuffed his wrists behind his back.

Hector shook his head. "Well, you know, Reese, friends ain't always what they seem to be."

Reese stared hard at Hector, the bodybuilder's words triggering a memory. Where had he heard those words before?

"IF ONLY YOU had stayed away from that pushy Reese Beauchamps," Victoria complained to Taki, "none of this would have been necessary."

"Wh…what?" Taki tried to focus on Victoria's words, but they made no sense. And why was Victoria driving so fast? When Taki tried to lift her hand to rub her eyes, she couldn't. What was wrong with her? She felt heavy, like a waterlogged cushion sinking…sinking…

"My plan was perfect," Victoria said. "I worked on it for months."

"I'm not feeling well, Victoria. I think there was something wrong with that water."

"I knew you'd finally dip into your trust fund if you needed to ransom your precious Tibetan bowl. You just needed a good enough reason."

"Ransom—my bowl?" Taki tried to concentrate on Victoria's words. What was she saying about the bowl? Taki looked in the seat for the bowl to reassure herself she'd really found it. That small movement of her head made her stomach churn.

Victoria pulled a silver flask from her purse and took a quick drink. "No one would have been harmed, and I could keep my home."

"Please pull over, Victoria. I think I'm going to be sick."

When Victoria shook her head, the motion seemed jerky, like a broken toy or one with its battery running down.

"You're not listening to me, dear, and I'm trying to explain. I've lived in that house for fifty years and can't lose it. I'm too old to move. What would my friends think if I got stuck in a wretched condo somewhere in West Broward miles away from my club?"

"Victoria…"

"I gave you free rent. I helped your mother. Someone has to pay me back."

As her landlady's ramblings finally registered, Taki tried to raise her hand again. She needed to escape. She needed to open the car door—her fingers only twitched with effort as she stared at the handle.

Victoria was not her friend. She had deliberately put something in the water. Some chemical.

Victoria was Hector's partner.

"I'm sorry about this, Taki. Really I am. But now it's you or me."

Taki closed her eyes against the horror that she could have been so wrong about Victoria. She was now at the mercy of a crazed woman. "What—what are you going to do?" she gasped.

"Did you know your mother experimented with drugs?"

Unable to speak, Taki stared at the old woman.

"Your mom was arrested for smoking marijuana in college." Victoria threw her a sidelong look. "Of course, your father was busted with her. The Spencer lawyers were able to get his case thrown out, but your mom had a criminal record."

"Victoria, please." Taki's voice was a feeble whisper.

"That broke up the happy couple for a while, but you know what they say about true love. It's also how your father got full custody of you."

"Why—" Taki swallowed hard. "Why are you telling me this?"

"You'll see soon enough." Victoria smiled mysteriously and took another swallow of whiskey.

WHERE WAS TAKI? Reese pounded his fist against the steering wheel as he followed Javi back to FBI headquarters where they would again attempt to interview Hector. Or more likely wait until his public defender arrived, which could take hours.

Had Mayhugh moved her, stashed her somewhere new, or had she escaped? Surely the kidnappers wouldn't harm her—at least not until they got the ransom money. That's the next thing he needed to do, figure how to play the ransom drop this afternoon.

Had Spencer come up with the money? He glanced at his watch. Three more hours.

But if the kidnappers knew something had gone wrong, would they cut their losses and kill her? No. He refused to believe she was dead. The way her prison appeared when they entered, she'd managed to escape.

A surge of pride at her resourcefulness was quickly squelched. What would she do once free? Who would she contact?

Would she phone him? Reese checked his phone for messages, but found the device dead. Shit. He hadn't plugged it in last night and had left it on for Victoria Van Buren. Had Taki tried to call and couldn't get through?

No, he doubted she would even have his cell number with her. And maybe she wouldn't try to reach him. She considered him the enemy now, a fact he planned to remedy when he found her.

He turned his mind from a chilling prospect he didn't want to even consider. He'd find her. He *would* see her again.

So who would she contact? Victoria? The ashram? SoBe Spa?

Deciding Victoria would be her first choice, Reese dug in the glove box, looking for his mobile charger. Instead, he found the CD of his psychic reading. He pulled it out.

Robin had thoughtfully placed her business card inside the case.

On impulse, he removed the disc and shoved it into

his car player. The psychic's voice filled the interior of the Jag while he plugged in the charger.

You must keep very careful watch over the one you love. She is in terrible danger.

I can't see the trouble, but it exists.

He'd thought the woman spoke in vague generalities a week ago, but maybe...

Stay close to the one you love. She'll lead you to what you want.

What was it he wanted?

Taki. More than anything he wanted Taki alive and well and in his arms.

Or was the fortune-teller referring to the more intangible wants in life? Reese shook his head, amazed that he was trying to analyze the incoherent ramblings of— He froze at Robin's final words.

Sometimes friends turn out to be false.

TAKI AWOKE WHEN someone began dragging her out of the front seat of a car. Disoriented, confused by what was going on, she tried to resist. When her limbs wouldn't obey her instructions, she remembered.

She was in Victoria's Caddy. Victoria had drugged her.

The old lady was surprisingly strong, and Taki found herself sitting in a dirty wheelchair.

Woozy and fighting nausea from the rough jostling, she recognized the mechanical rumbling of an automatic garage door. They were inside Victoria's garage. No one could see them from the street.

"I always knew this wheelchair would come in

handy again after Bert passed away," Victoria said, a note of pleasure causing her voice to grow more shrill.

"You mean after you killed him." Taki shook her head, struggling to stay alert against the effects of the drug.

"You have no idea how difficult it is to take care of an invalid. The expense of his medical care sucked all the money out of our accounts. I had to end his life or I would have been left with nothing. It was a kindness, really."

Taki's head jerked back as Victoria pushed the wheelchair out the back door of the garage down the ramp.

"You'll never get away with this," Taki said. "Mayhugh and Hector will talk."

"I've already taken care of Bruce Mayhugh," Victoria said. "What a ninny he was, flatly refusing to become involved in anything other than extortion. Apparently he had principles. Can you imagine? A thief with scruples."

Victoria's use of the past tense with reference to the fence chilled Taki. Queasiness churned in her stomach. How many people had Victoria murdered?

"What about Hector? I refuse to believe he'd—"

Victoria snorted. "Hector. That young man is so greedy he'll never talk."

"Don't be so sure."

"Well, if he does, I'll take care of him, too."

Taki sucked in a quick breath. Without a doubt, her landlady had lost touch with the present moment.

She'd gone way too far in creating her own reality. She might even have one of the diseases that caused old people to become confused.

Taki struggled to clear her mind. Drugged and helpless as a newborn baby, what could she do? Words were her only weapon, but her mind worked so very, very slowly.

"You can't do this, Victoria. It will—"

"Don't spout any of your nonsense about my karma, missy. It's too late for that. Soon you'll be another bored heiress who overdosed on heroin. It's an old story, you know."

Shock and disbelief now morphed into bone-deep fear. Even during those dreadful days in the bunker she'd never been this frightened.

"You're going to kill me?"

"I'll place you in bed and inject you like I did my husband. Don't worry. You won't feel a thing."

As Victoria wheeled her into the cottage's tiny kitchen, Taki created mental images that the wheelchair would get stuck between the cabinets. Anything for delay, something to give her time to formulate a plan.

But she rolled through without a bump.

"It's your own fault," Victoria said. "But ransom is out now, so I'm counting on your father to reimburse me for your room and board during the past months. Perhaps even a bonus for remaining discreet about your drug use. I know him, and he wouldn't want the publicity. I'll tell him I did my best to keep you straight."

Taki closed her eyes. Her father would be all too eager to believe anything bad about her. But she didn't want the last thing he ever heard of her to be that she was a drug addict. No, the universe wouldn't do that to her.

"You know, I could threaten to tell the media about your mother's drug use," Victoria continued. "I'm sure one or two would love to sensationalize that. They might even feature me on one of those TV talk shows. It's so low class, but I'd do it if they paid me enough."

Victoria parked the wheelchair facing the bedroom. Behind her, Taki heard Victoria walk across the floor toward the kitchen. Taki swiveled her head to watch Victoria open a cabinet to retrieve her Bourbon, but that movement caused her stomach to rebel.

Taki slowly eased her head back to quiet the nausea. The freezer opened and ice clinked into a crystal tumbler. After a long, slow pour, Victoria walked into Taki's view again, now sipping a drink.

She faced Taki, her face old and sad. "You're my last chance to keep this house."

"My father won't give you a dime," Taki said, her voice hoarse. She swallowed. Whatever Victoria had given her made speech difficult.

"Why not?"

"Because Reese will prove that you killed me."

Taki blinked. Where had that notion come from? But she knew it as sure as she knew anything. He was looking for her. He'd been right about so many things, and she just hadn't seen it. She'd told him to open his mind, and she hadn't opened her own. But maybe it wasn't too late. If she trusted him this time, truly believed that he'd come for her, he would.

Talk about last chances. She had to stall until he got here.

Victoria waved her hand. "Don't be silly, dear. I have Reese convinced I was out of town when you disappeared. He knows how fond of me you are, so he's always most respectful. The young man is actually quite besotted with you."

Warmth flooded Taki as Victoria spoke. Victoria had no idea how much those offhand words comforted her. She wanted to smile, but the effort proved too costly. She forced a deep breath, praying her lungs didn't stop working.

"He won't believe it," Taki said.

"Reese?"

Taki nodded.

"He won't believe what?"

"That I shot heroin into my body."

Eyes narrowed, Victoria took a swallow of Bourbon. "The poor dear will just discover he didn't know you quite as well as he thought," she insisted. "I'll tell him about your mother's overdose and drop a hint that drug use runs in families."

Taki stared at Victoria, knowing in her heart the old lady was deluded and would most certainly be caught. Reese would make sure she was brought to justice. That's what her soul mate did. That's why they were perfect for each other.

Sadness swept through Taki as she realized that

his justice wouldn't do her any good. She would already be dead.

"What—what happened to Mayhugh?" she asked, searching for anything to keep Victoria talking.

"An unfortunate accident off the Julia Tuttle Bridge," Victoria murmured. "Tragic. If Hector had pushed your Jeep off the same bridge like I instructed, we wouldn't be in this pickle. I made a mistake involving him. That young man is all muscle and hasn't a brain in his head."

"But why didn't you demand money right away?" Taki asked. "Why the strange note to come to Puerto Sagua just for information?"

"Another mistake. Mayhugh was supposed to meet you there and explain what you had to do, but the FBI delayed him, wanting information about some other theft."

Reese's briefcase, Taki realized. Hector had truly ruined Victoria's plan by breaking into Reese's car. "How do you even know someone like Mayhugh?"

"Remember that theft from Carroll's Jewelers last year?"

Taki shook her head.

"Well, that was me," Victoria said with a self-satisfied grin. "They never suspected one of their valued customers. Mayhugh bought the stolen diamonds."

Taki stared at her landlady. *Maybe I am naive. Reese was right about that, too.*

"I wanted to do this nicely, civilized, make it easy on you." Confusion swept across Victoria's face. "No one was supposed to get hurt."

Searching for anything to keep her talking, Taki asked, "Why were the notes made differently?"

"You have no idea how messy glue is," Victoria said with a sniff. "Plus, the stuff gave me a ghastly headache."

"Why don't you have another drink, Victoria," Taki suggested, needing time to come up with another topic.

While Victoria moved behind her, Taki closed her eyes, willing with all her fading strength for Reese to find her. She imagined his gorgeous eyes, focused her thoughts and sent her location shooting like an arrow toward him.

She had so much to tell him. If she could be so wrong about Victoria, maybe she'd been wrong about Reese being too much like her father. Maybe they did have a chance in this lifetime. Her mind was open now. All she had to do was keep her thoughts positive.

Before Victoria had finished pouring, a car door slammed out front.

"Damn," Victoria said from the kitchen. "Reese is here."

Startled, Taki opened her eyes. Had she gone unconscious again? She doubted anyone could pick up on her psychic pleas this quickly.

When Victoria grabbed the wheelchair and shoved it into the bedroom, Taki's stomach heaved in rebellion. Once inside, Victoria grabbed canvas straps from Taki's yoga bag and tied her hands and feet to the wheelchair. Victoria placed another strap between Taki's teeth and pulled it around the back of her head.

"You stay quiet, missy," Victoria hissed, cinching the knot tight.

She left the bedroom, closing the door behind her with a quiet click.

Mustering her energy, Taki pulled against the bindings on her arms without success. *No strength.*

I won't stay quiet. She shifted her weight from side to side, then front to back in an attempt to move the wheelchair, but only caused her heart to race with the futile effort.

And her nausea to swell.

If she threw up with the gag in her mouth, she might choke. Closing her eyes, she released a frustrated breath.

Reese had come. Soon he would be in the next room. Somehow, some way she had to let him know where she was. But how? The drug had all but paralyzed her. In despair, she searched the room for help. What could she do?

She stared at the angels suspended overhead. They swayed slightly from the breeze wafting through the window. If she ever needed her guardians, it was right now. This exact present moment.

Taki willed her angels to move.

If she concentrated very, very hard on the musical tinkle of the heavenly mobiles, perhaps Reese would hear it and come to investigate.

REESE PARKED IN Victoria's circular driveway, jumped from his car and hurried to her front door. A cold wind swept across the property, rubbing the branches of the oaks against each other, but he didn't feel the chill.

He knocked on Victoria's door. A gust swirled leaves across the porch as he waited, and he checked his cell phone, hoping he'd managed to charge it enough. Javi knew where he was, the thread he'd decided to follow, and the agent promised to let him know if they managed to break Hector. They made plans to meet for the trip for the ransom drop.

Reese banged harder. Still no answer. He glanced toward Taki's cottage and noticed movement behind closed curtains. Was she home? His spirits mushrooming, Reese jogged toward the cottage, but slowed when he recognized Victoria's slightly stooped shape. Most likely the old lady was going through Taki's personal effects.

What was Victoria looking for?

Reese hesitated. Were his visits to Victoria bordering on harassment? Did he have any real reason to suspect she was involved in Taki's disappearance? He resumed his steps toward the guesthouse. He couldn't stop himself. The run-down condition of the home, her evasiveness, the drinking—his instincts told him it all meant something.

His gut told him Victoria was the false friend.

She answered Taki's door after several knocks, the smell of Bourbon strong on her breath.

"Good evening, Reese," she said as if she'd rehearsed her line for an hour. She gripped her hands tightly in front of her stomach.

"Hi, Victoria. I didn't forget my promise to keep you posted on our progress finding Taki."

Victoria didn't invite him in. "I frankly expected that to be by phone."

"Well, I was in the neighborhood." Reese stepped into the doorway, intending to move the crone out of the way, if necessary. She took a hasty, unsteady step back, and he pushed inside.

He took a long, hard look around the room. Nothing looked out of place or wrong. An almost empty fifth of Black Label Bourbon sat next to a full tumbler on the dining room table.

Victoria, not Taki, drank Bourbon. Damn. Of course she wasn't here.

He moved into the tiny kitchen. Nothing.

"We found where they've been keeping her," Reese said, as he reentered the main room, hoping to catch Victoria off guard.

She inclined her head slightly, but her eyes darted around the room as if uncertain where to focus. "Taki wasn't there, I suppose," she said finally.

"No. We arrested a Hector Morales who works at the spa," Reese said. "He was visiting the location."

"Hector?" Victoria repeated, as if she knew the personal trainer. She grabbed the tumbler and took a long drink. "Has he given you any useful information?"

"Not yet," Reese replied, wondering why Victoria needed a swig of booze to ask that question. How would Victoria know Hector?

"But the FBI is expert at interrogation. We'll learn something eventually."

"I'm sure you will, dear."

"Tell me, Victoria," Reese said, glancing at Taki's closed bedroom door, instantly reminded of the night he'd spent in her bed. "Did you know about a meeting Taki had with Bruce Mayhugh at Fairchild Gardens last Saturday morning?"

"Fairchild? Delightful place. But no. Remember I drove to Little Palm Island on Saturday? I knew about the first meeting, of course."

"Oh, that's right," Reese muttered. Victoria was lying. He'd interviewed enough witnesses to know when someone hid the truth, and this old woman definitely knew more than she was saying. Just like the last time he'd talked to her.

"What are you doing in Taki's cottage, by the way?"

"Looking for clues to her disappearance, of course."

"Any luck?" Reese asked. Maybe he'd look around for a few clues himself.

"Nothing at all. Now, really, Reese, I must insist that you go. I'm quite exhausted and thought I'd take a nap."

"Right." Taking his time on the way to the door, Reese gave Taki's living room some final scrutiny. He had no logical reason to remain. Mrs. Van Buren had every right to expect him to leave.

Victoria opened the door and swept grandly with her hand for him to pass through. "Do keep me informed of your progress, Reese."

"Sure," Reese muttered, but paused on the threshold, convinced he shouldn't go. Maybe he ought to search the entire cottage.

At the sound of hundreds of tinkling bells, he turned toward Taki's bedroom. The angel mobiles. What would cause them to take such noisy flight, like wild doves suddenly frightened to wing?

WHEN THE DOOR opened behind her Taki felt warm tears slide down her cheek. Reese had come to save her. Maybe her rotten karma was finally mended. If only she could do a simple spinal twist and turn to see his face...but her body refused to move.

He knelt before her, a look of warm tenderness softening his features. She longed to caress his cheek as he reached behind her to release the gag.

"Are you all right?" he asked, his voice husky.

Taki nodded, unable to form words. Because she'd believed that he would rescue her, he had.

"Say something," he said as he loosened the bonds on her feet and hands.

"It worked," she whispered.

Reese paused and glanced up. "What?"

Their eyes met, and in that moment Taki knew he understood. He knew how special their bond was. Maybe not quite the same way she did, but he loved her. They belonged together forever.

"I love you," she said.

He brushed her cheek with the gentle caress she'd longed to give him. "I love you."

"I can't move," she whispered. "Victoria gave me some kind of drug."

At the sound of an engine turning over, Reese glanced over Taki's shoulder.

"Victoria's getting away," he said.

"I've learned running away is never a good idea," Taki said, wishing she could lean forward and touch Reese's lips. They loomed temptingly close, and she remembered their warm softness, their delightful ability to arouse her.

Reese stood, gathering her in his arms. "I'm taking you to a hospital."

"Kiss me," she whispered.

"What?"

"Kiss me first."

When his lips eagerly claimed hers, Taki knew that she was finally free of her past because she had a future.

Two Weeks Later

When Reese's sedan pulled into her driveway, Taki opened her eyes, terminating her meditation. She hadn't been too deep in meditation, anyway, or she wouldn't have heard the smooth purr of the Jaguar. She was working on forgiving her father—without much success. But she'd keep trying. Maybe someday.

Reese had phoned her two hours earlier with the happy news of Romero's conviction. Claudia and her detailed diary had convinced the jury.

Taki watched from the doorway as he crossed the yard toward her wearing a huge grin. She still lived in Victoria's cottage, giving the estate a lived-in look while Victoria was evaluated in the psychiatric ward at Jackson Hospital.

"Congratulations, Counselor," Taki said.

Reese wrapped his arms around her and squeezed. "I feel great," he said, lifting her from her feet and walking into the cottage. "We need to celebrate."

She reveled in his contagious happiness, loving the intimate contact between them. But they had a lot of intimate contact these days. Reese spent every night with her, insisting with a wicked leer that the angels gave him luck—luck he needed for the trial. How could she argue with that? Apparently the angels had been successful.

"How do you want to celebrate?" Taki asked when he placed her on her feet.

Reese loosened his tie and pulled it from around his neck. "I'll tell you later. First I'm going to change." He nodded to her jeans and bulky sweater. "Get comfortable like you."

She followed him into the bedroom while he pulled his dress shirt from his pants. He flung his coat and tie across the bed and sat, pulling off his shoes and socks.

She bit her bottom lip. Watching Reese undress never failed to excite her. Right now she especially liked watching the muscle ripple in his arms. She sat beside him on the bed.

"I know of one way to celebrate," she said.

With his forearms on his knees, Reese grinned at her. She'd never seen him look sexier with bare feet, his dress shirt open, revealing a broad, muscled chest beneath a snug white T-shirt. She lay on the bed, extending her arms over her head and arching her chest.

REESE LAY BESIDE her, his head propped on a bent arm, studying her, the depth of his love for her surprising him, as it often did. How had he made it through each day before he knew her? She had changed his life in so many ways.

"Brazen, aren't you?" he said.

"I can't help myself."

"What if I have another celebration in mind?"

A look of disappointment crossed her face. "What?"

"Let's get married tonight."

She sat up. "Married?"

"At the Twenty-four Hour Church of Guru Navi."

Taki narrowed her eyes. "Are you making fun of Navi?"

"Yes, but he doesn't mind. He's a notary in Florida, so it's legal, and he's agreed to marry us in the temple at 8:00 p.m. We have to wear some sort of white robes."

Eyes wide, she said, "You talked to Navi."

"He wanted to discuss the generous endowment that the Spencer Trust made to his charitable programs."

"Then the gifts are being made?"

Reese nodded. "Just as you requested. Even my father and I are now communicating on a whole new level."

"Oh, that's wonderful, Reese."

"I think he's impressed that I gained your cooperation. But it's going to take a long time to give away all your money, Miss Spencer."

"That's not my name."

Reese pulled her down beside him and smoothed the hair from her face. "And your name is going to change again in two hours. Besides, it doesn't matter what I call you. I want to marry the beautiful person that you are." He placed his hand over her heart. "Inside."

"What a sweet thing to say," she whispered.

"It's true. You know it."

"Yes." When her eyes clouded, he knew she'd flashed to that awful morning with Victoria, who would probably spend the rest of her life in the state psychiatric hospital. He didn't believe for a minute that the old lady was crazy, just greedy. Her actions had shown clear intent, not insanity. But Taki couldn't bear the thought of her aging friend in a prison, so Reese had done what he could for Victoria.

"I know it was cosmic vibrations that made the mobiles chime," she said.

"You're certain it wasn't a gust of wind? Your windows are always open."

She shook her head. "It wasn't the wind."

He smiled at her. If she believed their love set off good vibrations, so did he. He'd let his instincts guide him in his search for her, and they had paid off. He'd live in her reality if he had to. Taki provided the meaning he'd always searched for in his life. Giving away her share of the Spencer money would help more people and right more wrongs than twenty years of public service ever could.

"Besides," she said, "you told me how you deliberately kept your thoughts about me positive while I was missing. That probably helped keep me alive."

"Whatever works," he murmured, as he lowered his head to kiss her thoroughly.

"So I'm to be Taki Beauchamps?" she said when he pulled back, as if trying the name out for the first time.

"Has a nice ring to it, don't you think? Speaking of rings…" Reese reached for his coat, pulled a small box from an inside pocket and presented it to her.

Her hands trembled when he slid the diamond on her elegant finger. Reese smiled tenderly at the moisture in her blue eyes. If she wanted, Taki could possess the most extravagant jewels in the world, but he knew she was thrilled by this simple engagement ring.

"As a symbol of our new beginning," he said.

* * * * *

LARGER-PRINT
BOOKS!

◆HARLEQUIN *Presents*®

PASSION
GUARANTEED
SEDUCTION

GET 2 FREE LARGER-PRINT
NOVELS PLUS 2 FREE GIFTS!

YES! Please send me 2 FREE LARGER-PRINT Harlequin Presents® novels and my 2 FREE gifts (gifts are worth about $10). After receiving them, if I don't wish to receive any more books, I can return the shipping statement marked "cancel." If I don't cancel, I will receive 6 brand-new novels every month and be billed just $5.05 per book in the U.S. or $5.49 per book in Canada. That's a saving of at least 16% off the cover price! It's quite a bargain! Shipping and handling is just 50¢ per book in the U.S. and 75¢ per book in Canada.* I understand that accepting the 2 free books and gifts places me under no obligation to buy anything. I can always return a shipment and cancel at any time. Even if I never buy another book, the two free books and gifts are mine to keep forever.

176/376 HDN F43N

Name	(PLEASE PRINT)	

Address		Apt. #

City	State/Prov.	Zip/Postal Code

Signature (if under 18, a parent or guardian must sign)

Mail to the **Harlequin® Reader Service:**
IN U.S.A.: P.O. Box 1867, Buffalo, NY 14240-1867
IN CANADA: P.O. Box 609, Fort Erie, Ontario L2A 5X3

Are you a subscriber to Harlequin Presents books
and want to receive the larger-print edition?
Call 1-800-873-8635 today or visit us at www.ReaderService.com.

* Terms and prices subject to change without notice. Prices do not include applicable taxes. Sales tax applicable in N.Y. Canadian residents will be charged applicable taxes. Offer not valid in Quebec. This offer is limited to one order per household. Not valid for current subscribers to Harlequin Presents Larger-Print books. All orders subject to credit approval. Credit or debit balances in a customer's account(s) may be offset by any other outstanding balance owed by or to the customer. Please allow 4 to 6 weeks for delivery. Offer available while quantities last.

Your Privacy—The Harlequin® Reader Service is committed to protecting your privacy. Our Privacy Policy is available online at www.ReaderService.com or upon request from the Harlequin Reader Service.

We make a portion of our mailing list available to reputable third parties that offer products we believe may interest you. If you prefer that we not exchange your name with third parties, or if you wish to clarify or modify your communication preferences, please visit us at www.ReaderService.com/consumerchoice or write to us at Harlequin Reader Service Preference Service, P.O. Box 9062, Buffalo, NY 14269. Include your complete name and address.

HPLP13R